McFarlin Library
WITHDRAWN

THE SAFFRON SUMMER

by Margaret Summerton

The Saffron Summer
The Ghost Flowers
Sweetcrab
The Sand Rose
The Sunset Horn
The Red Pavilion
A Small Wilderness
The Sea House
Theft in Kind
Nightingale at Noon
Quin's Hide
Ring of Mischief
A Memory of Darkness

The Saffron Summer

MARGARET SUMMERTON

PUBLISHED FOR THE CRIME CLUB BY
DOUBLEDAY & COMPANY, INC., GARDEN CITY, NEW YORK,
1975

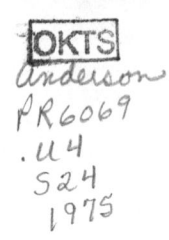

All of the characters in this book are fictitious, and any resemblance to actual persons, living or dead, is purely coincidental.

Library of Congress Cataloging in Publication Data

Summerton, Margaret.
  The saffron summer.

  I. Title.
PZ4.S955Saf [PR6069.U4]   823'.9'14
ISBN 0-385-01451-1
Library of Congress Catalog Card Number 74-9468

Copyright © 1975 by Margaret Summerton
All Rights Reserved
Printed in the United States of America
First Edition

THE SAFFRON SUMMER

1

IN THE DREAM-MISTED ZONE that divides sleep from consciousness, an old, forgotten memory was reborn to run through my head like a strip of film: black and white except for one central note of blazing colour. A squat church, scarcely bigger than a wayside chapel, over which loomed a house made huge by comparison and, separating them, an ancient graveyard, the tilting headstones whitened with a crust of snow, the mourners' dark clothes, their bowed heads sprinkled with crystal flakes. The blaze of colour was the wreaths and sheafs of brilliant spring flowers that overlaid the coffin being carried by four slow-stepping bearers towards a newly dug grave that made an oblong of blackness in the whitened earth.

The snow-muffled silence was broken only by the heavy breathing of the bearers that froze to puffs of vapour on the air, a convulsive sob from a mourner and the monotonous intoning of a man in a white surplice.

Then somewhere squeezed away from sight, a child screamed, a high-pitched, nerve-cutting sound that twisted heads either in pitying dismay or sharp rebuke. As it spiralled beyond control it was cut off by a boy who seized the child and pressed her face so hard into the soft cloth of his black coat that the screams suffocated themselves, and the words of the man in the white surplice once more became audible.

I was the child who screamed. The man they were burying in the grave cut through the crust of snow was my father. I did not know, and was never likely to discover, the name of the boy who had sought to comfort me.

When my mother and I had first come to live in Arnouvière, that buried segment of memory had frequently broken surface to haunt me, but as the years passed it had mercifully reburied itself. That it should return a week after my mother had been buried in the *cimitière* on the hill outside the town, suggested some imbalance of love in myself. It was of my mother's funeral, with the mourners to be counted on one hand, that should be poignantly alive in me, not that of my father who had been committed to the snowbound earth in another country fifteen years ago.

For a long while I watched the pale golden light fill all but the corners of the room and then I turned over and slept. When I woke the second time it was to a fast-beating awareness of a decision I had been struggling to reach and which, last evening, had resolved itself, which meant that I could look into the future with a strong beat of hope.

I debated whether, on the first day of the sale, with the windows of her dress shop placarded with *Soldes* banners, Madame Dubois would be prepared to abandon for five minutes the frenzied customers bent on snatching bargains to take note of a junior assistant's announcement that she wished to leave her service in a fortnight's time. Yet, the decision taken, that was as long as I was prepared to hold on to my patience.

To expiate that early-morning failure of loyalty—or love—before I left the house, I entered my mother's bedroom, the severity and simplicity of which was a fitting epitaph to a woman who had emerged from that snowbound churchyard apparently seeking nothing from life except a sufficiency of time to rear her child. The wardrobe held no more than half a dozen dresses, two coats, and three pairs of shoes. The Viyella dressing gown that hung on the door, stitched into its collar the name of a London store, was older than I was. The bed was varnished wood, the counterpane cotton and the toilet articles utilitarian without a single embellishment. The walls were blank except for the one immediately facing the bed. Hung on it, side by side, were two portraits in oils: one of a gaily smiling, flaxen-haired girl who had been my mother, and the other a self-portrait of my father. I stared at them so long that I nearly missed my bus. Except for blurred peepholes into the past both were strangers to me. By the time my mother was thirty her hair had been white and I had never once glimpsed that spirited smile. My father had died when I was four years old.

Racing to the end of the road, the memory of that ink-black day a year ago when I'd waited in the salon for Dr Genlis to descend the stairs, ran at my heels. He was elderly, with quiet eyes and a kind voice. To him I remained the child he had treated for earache and measles, and he addressed me as such, trying to soften and simplify his diagnosis.

"Your mother, Claudine, though still only in early middle-age, has the body and the organs of a much older woman, say one approaching seventy. What she suffers from is a disease of premature ageing. It occurs sometimes, more often in women, particularly widows, than in men. I'm afraid it is not a disease easy to arrest."

"But you can help her?" I pleaded. "There must be something you can do."

He nodded, spoke encouragingly. "Of course. Modern drugs will help her heart, stimulate her appetite. There are others that will give her a little more energy. Be sure, we will try them all." He wrote out a prescription and handed it to me.

I collected the tablets from the pharmacist. Obediently, she swallowed them. But in my heart, though I fiercely repressed its warning, I knew she was suffering from an illness no pills could cure. Day by day throughout that black year, the cruel truth inched nearer and nearer until it was beside me night and day. She had no will to live because her mission was accomplished. Her child had become an adult.

The symptoms were physical weakness, lethargy, and long periods of total abstraction, as though part of her had already abandoned this world. I left the College of Art in Paris where, for a year, I had been studying dress design, and went to work as a junior assistant in Madame Dubois's boutique. On my mother's worst days, I begged time off to get home for lunch. And for two hours morning and afternoon, Mademoiselle Greux, my mother's only friend, came to care for her.

The gift of death for which my mother had yearned claimed her in the last hours before dawn. I would never know if, during her last moments of life, she had wished for my presence by her side. That and the answers to the other questions she had either parried or ignored, made dark patches of shadow in my mind.

I had to wait until the blinds of the shop were dropped over the windows before I succeeded in claiming Madame's attention by which time she, like me and the two senior assistants, was shaking with fatigue. She heard me out without interruption while she totalled the day's takings.

When I'd finished, she looked up, her shrewd foxy eyes picking me apart, but her response less contentious than I'd feared. "I suppose it is inevitable now that your mother is dead. You are a young woman with a certain flair for fashion and a high, maybe exaggerated opinion of your talents. In any case, you have much to learn. Naturally, you seek to prove yourself. That is the privilege of youth. You intend to return to the Art College and finish your course?"

I said no. I told her where I was going in a fortnight's time, but not why. I did not intend to reveal my plan to anyone: a short span of time, probably not more than three days long—every second of which was to belong wholly to me.

My mother had kept the high gate set in the metal fence that screened the house from the road locked. Anyone seeking admittance had to pull the bell. Sometimes she answered and sometimes she ignored its summons. Since her death I had left it unlocked. Against one wall the white roses she loved too much to pick were beginning to unfurl. The limes against the other wall were in full leaf. As far as possible in an urban area my mother had hidden our home from sight. Standing with my back against the closed gate, I scrutinised with heightened sensitivity the house to which I'd come as a child of four and which I was about to abandon. It was so commonplace in design and construction you could find its counterpart on the outskirts of any country town in Europe: harsh red brick broken by four shutter-framed windows and a door, with a circular window in the attic that, three years ago, I'd claimed as a studio. A house that must once have stood at the point where the rue de Paris straggled into fields that were now transformed into landscaped gardens surrounding the new Ecole Technique, a *clinique gyneologue* and a string of smart villas.

Alerted by the clang of the gate, Gustave lumbered round the corner of the house, doffing his tartan cap, bowing low, pointing with pride to the patches of lawn which he'd mown, lumpish pink face grinning. I grinned back, and as I unlocked the front door, he went at a fast shamble to meet me at the back. I took from a shelf in the kitchen the bag of sweets, the chewing gum I put ready for him every Thursday. He stuffed them into his pocket and loped off, from the rear a man, from the front a boy, a deaf-mute, his mind that of a young child. Perhaps my mother had employed him because he could neither speak nor hear the voices of others, which to her spelt unmolested peace. The money Gustave earned by mowing lawns, trimming hedges, sweeping leaves was, by his mother's edict, paid to her once a month. If, as had happened with another client, you forgot to hand over to Gustave his gift in kind, he terminated his services forthwith.

On the draining board, still wrapped in cellophane, was a bunch of apricot roses that Mademoiselle Greux had plunged into a jug of water. The card inside the envelope was inscribed: *Abidingly Jean-Baptiste*. I smiled, guessing he'd spent an hour leafing through a dictionary to gloat over the first word. Sometimes I suspected his love for me—if love it were and not habit—had been initially inspired by the fact that I provided him with a free English teacher. Then, seeing in my mind's eye his smile that was at once tender and gay, the outward symbol of a heart that overflowed with goodness and generosity, I felt guilty at momentarily misjudging him.

I opened the refrigerator and took out the plate of cold meats and salad that Mademoiselle Greux had prepared for me. The day after my mother's funeral I had protested that she must not spend time on me—time for which she accepted no payment. A tiny, skeletal woman, with eyes that were like burnt-out coals in her shrivelled parchment-coloured face, she had silently dismissed my suggestion, underlining a fact I already knew. The service was not to me but in memory of my mother, the strange relationship that had bound them together. I'd been in my last year at the convent when a girl had whispered to me the ugly legend that hung over Mademoiselle Greux like a shroud. In 1944 she had betrayed to the Gestapo the hiding place of an English airman who had been shot down on the outskirts of the town. He had been picked up, sent to a German prison camp, and at dawn on the following morning the head of the household that had sheltered him had been publicly executed. When peace was declared six members of the Maquis, three men and three women, had shaven Mademoiselle Greux's head and dragged her through the town. I had protested to Jean-Baptiste that it had happened over a quarter of a century ago. After such an age why should she be ostracised? Who cared any more, was so eaten with vengeance as to remember?

"Ask my father," he retorted. "The man the Gestapo shot was the husband of his cousin. You talk of pages of history that were written before you were born. It is better for you not to judge."

My mother's association with Mademoiselle Greux had begun three years earlier, when she stumbled at a curb, spilled the contents of her shopping basket. Some sense, deeper and more potent than speech, must have communicated each to the other that they were both outcasts, one by her own choice, one made so by the inhumanity of memory.

I put the meat and salad on a tray, added bread, butter and a glass of wine. For two weeks now, I had eaten my supper in the attic studio, sketching between mouthfuls.

I had one foot on the top rung of the swing ladder when the doorbell rang. I put the tray on the studio floor and climbed down. When I opened the door my instant impression was of a grey man. His suit, tie, the hat he held in his hand, his thin, ashen hair, even the texture of his skin harmonised into a single colour. "Yes?" I queried.

"Claudine, may I come in?"

My Christian name on his lips both startled and offended me. His diction was dry, clipped, assured of its authority. The angles of his middle-aged face were as sharp as though every feature had been honed to a point. In a flash of fantasy my inner eye depicted him as clad in a suit of armour. "How do you know my name?"

"We share the same surname. You are Claudine Delamain. I am Conwyn Delamain. Now perhaps you would permit me to come in? We can hardly conduct a family discussion on the doorstep."

Shocked a second time, I found myself loth to allow him entry. In the end I had no alternative but to stand aside. Tall, brittle-thin, he walked at a measured pace into the narrow hall, his glance noting at leisure every inch of the surroundings in which he found himself, before he turned to me. "First, may I offer you my condolences on the death of your mother?"

The double shock was doused by a rush of anger at his assumption of the right to be where he was offering glib, meaningless sympathy. "How did you know she was dead? Who are you?"

He ignored both questions. "In the last months of her life did your mother never speak of me?"

"No. Why should she? Who are you?" Though I had as yet no evidence that he posed a threat to me, that was the message that prickled along my nerves. Too late I realised I should have shut the door in his face.

"I am your father's younger brother. That fact established, may we proceed to some room where we can talk in reasonable comfort? I have made an extremely tiring journey for the express purpose of making your acquaintance."

My instant reaction was that he was lying. This grey, bloodless creature my father's brother! If so, heredity had played a bitter joke. He had to repeat his request before, grudgingly, I opened the door of the salon. He placed his hat and gloves on a table, waited for me to seat myself. For the first time I could see the colour of his eyes that were narrow, set back in his skull. They, too, were grey, made bright as glass by some inner satisfaction at finding himself where he was.

Seated, he enquired: "Do you remember your father?"

A big man, a giant, with glittering hair and beard, at once clumsy and gentle, with pockets to pick, a rollicking laugh, dressed in shabby clothes, and with a habit, when he was painting, of forgetting my mother's and my existence. I remembered the whistle for which I must wait, sitting upright in my child's bed in the cupboard-size room, before I was allowed to leap out and dive headlong into their big bed in the next room, where they would drag themselves apart to make room for me to squeeze into the warm niche between them.

Because I could not bear to discuss my father with the arrogant juiceless stranger, I lied: "No."

"Then presumably you do not remember your grandparents?"

"No." That statement was a half-lie. There was one scene I remembered but I told myself it was so wildly improbable it could only be a fantasy woven in a child's mind.

"Your mother never spoke to you about your father's family?"

"No. Would you please tell me why you are here?"

He brooded for a second as though questioning the veracity of my answer, then shrugged the doubt away. "My dear child, as I have already told you, I am here to make your acquaintance."

"How did you know where to find me?"

"Your mother's lawyer, a Monsieur Pontoise, informed me of your mother's death. She had left instructions with him to that effect."

That Monsieur Pontoise had not forewarned me, but wished this man on me unannounced, I found unforgiveable, but that omission counted for nothing when set beside an image that was so painful that for a moment my mind clouded and my concentration failed. My mother treating secretly, furtively . . . No, I shouted to myself, I would not believe it, if for no other reason than he wished me to do so.

He looked about him, minutely observing each piece of furniture. "A modest home but comfortable. Have you lacked for anything in your childhood except, of course, the love of a father?" Without waiting for a reply, he continued: "You attended the Convent of the

Sacred Heart. For a year, until your mother became ill, you were enrolled at the College of Art in Paris. As presumably you know, your mother was without relatives, her parents having been killed in the war. The great-aunt who brought her up died during the period when she was employed as an *au pair* girl in England. Surely, at least since you became an adult, you must have questioned who provided you with a roof over your head, food, fees and pocket money, and paid for two expensive school trips abroad! Where did you imagine the money came from?"

I had never questioned its source. My mother had never enlightened me. I had only the truth. "I assumed we lived on money my father had left her."

His high-pitched laugh derided my naïveté. "Your father died a pauper, in debt to his landlord and to every shop he could hoodwink into extending him credit. I repeat, a pauper!"

I stared silently at him, trying to quell the physical nausea that rose in my stomach, not at the fact that my father had been a pauper—though I did not automatically accept as truth any word he spoke—but at the vicious note of glee in his voice. Yet surely, reason preached, he would not dare to make such accusations unless they had some basis of truth? I steadied myself, jumped back from the edge of an abyss at the bottom of which lay pain, grief, and a killing shame. Since I would never admit, even to myself, that my mother had schemed behind my back to give the Grey Man the right to invade my home, I asked myself: why was he here? There was only one answer. Either I possessed something he craved or he was bent on asserting some measure of authority over me. To suppose that he could acquire either by merit of age or a relationship that was meaningless was so ridiculous that my self-confidence came bounding back.

His eye was engaged in running along the bookshelves mounted at either side of the fireplace. "Those books." He waved a hand in the direction of matching sets of Beatrix Potter, Lewis Carroll, Dickens, Scott, Jane Austen, the Brontës, H. G. Wells, and Priestley on top of which were stacked the English paperbacks of modern authors I'd bought over the years from W. H. Smith in the rue de Rivoli. "Where did they come from?"

"From Hatchard's in Piccadilly, London. My mother bought them for me every Christmas until I was fifteen."

He crowed slyly: "Allow me to correct you. On the first Monday in December, I called at Hatchard's, ordered for you the collected works of the author I considered appropriate to your age. In return for the allowance I made your mother, I imposed only one condition: that you should be bilingual, speak English as perfectly and fluently as you spoke French. It would appear that she kept her part of the bargain. Not that I am surprised. At the end of every term your mother sent me a report of your progress at school. You were an excellent pupil. Twice she enclosed a photograph of you."

Because I could no longer control the revulsion and outrage that sprang from a base of fear, I jumped up, moved to the window, and stood with my back to him. "My mother left me F. 47,000. Obviously, it isn't my money. It belongs to you. I will ask Monsieur Pontoise to send you a cheque for the whole amount." I wheeled on him. "And in time, as little time as possible, I will repay you every franc you have spent on me."

He was bending slightly forward, a hand pressed to his diaphragm. His tight-clenched lips emitted a faint groan. The thin flesh on his face was waxy.

"Are you ill?" Dismay pierced me. Was the grey intruder about to slip from his chair and either faint or die at my feet!

With an effort he drew himself upright. "I have a duodenal ulcer. If I could have a glass of milk I can take some tablets and the pain will ease." When I did not instantly move, he fumbled in the pocket of his waistcoat, abstracted a phial and repeated: "Some milk, if it wouldn't be too much trouble."

I flew into the kitchen, poured him a tumbler of milk and put it close to his hand. As he placed one tablet on his tongue, drank, waited a moment and then repeated the process, ill or well, to me he was a thief. Not of the money my mother had left me—that was his, a debt to be paid—but of a dream I'd spun in secret for years. Now where it had been there yawned a cold emptiness that would never be filled.

He dabbed his lips with a fine handkerchief. "Thank you. If you have a plain biscuit or, failing that, a slice of bread and butter, I would be grateful."

There were no biscuits except an old box of English shortbread that I could not be sure could be described as plain, so I buttered some bread and took it to him.

He said with good manners that came from habit and not from the heart: "I must apologise for putting you to a great deal of trouble."

"I'm glad you're feeling better."

He sipped the milk until the glass was empty and nibbled his way through half the bread. When he spoke it was in a slightly more conciliatory tone. "Wouldn't it be more comfortable if you sat down? On reflection perhaps I owe you an apology. I had assumed that your mother would have, to some degree, prepared you for my arrival. Apparently she saw fit not to do so. That being so I accept that my sudden appearance may have startled you. Equally, if you are enraged and shall we say a little humiliated, which I gather you to be, shouldn't some of your anger be vented on her?"

Blame the dead! That was his refuge. His sharp-edged armour suddenly became a fake, mocked up out of tinfoil. I saw the simple grave among the miniature chapels, the ornate marble tombs reserved in perpetuity, the photographs, the porcelain flowers and marble books engraved with messages from loving relatives professing *regret éternel*. And among them the simple inscription that was to be carved on the stone that covered my mother.

> *Ici repose Mme Michelle Delamain*
> *décedée 20 Mai 1974*
> *Dans sa 40ème année*
> *Veuve de Marcus Delamain.*

Plus one last line I'd reluctantly agreed to add because Monsieur Pontoise had been mortally affronted by the baldness of the epitaph: *Priez Dieu Pour Elle,* though my mother had believed neither in God nor the existence of heaven.

"Suppose," he suggested, "we make a fresh start?"

I made one. "Why did you assume responsibility for my upbringing and education?"

"You are my brother's daughter. Your mother was penniless, without a profession except to look after other people's children. While she was doing that she could not care adequately for her own child. You would have been dragged up, deprived of an education, remained an ignoramus all your life. Do you find that alternative preferable to being indebted to me?"

The plain answer was yes, but maybe it would not have been entirely honest. I countered: "I have grandparents." Fleetingly that shining childhood fantasy lighted up in my head like a scene on a stage. "Wasn't it their duty to provide for their grandchild rather than yours?"

"My parents regarded the elopement of their elder son, his subsequent marriage to your mother as an unparalleled disaster. It was followed by a second tragedy: the suicide of the girl to whom your father had been officially engaged for a year, the daughter of a neighbour and my sister's closest friend. To your grandfather who was an honourable man it remained as little short of an act of murder on the part of his son. I'm afraid that how or where you and your mother existed was of no concern to him." He paused, drawing one hand over the other, as though to indicate a visual paragraph. "He died four years ago." He paused a second time to allow a thin-lipped, humourless smile to play on his mouth. "Happily, my mother is still alive and it would afford her immense pleasure to receive a visit from you."

Without warning a bubble of hysteria broke in my throat which I only just managed to swallow. All that elaborate preamble, the pains to emphasise my indebtedness to him, and the climax no more than an invitation to visit my grandmother, his role reduced to that of his mother's messenger boy! Doubt flickered in my head. Could it be *that* simple? Instinct warned me he wasn't a simple man, yet his expression as he waited for my answer was one of confident expectation that he would receive the right one.

"Did she send you here to ask me to visit her?"

"Not in so many words."

"Then without so many words."

He looked down, making his pale glance invisible, seemingly collecting his phrases in his head before he spoke them aloud. Anxious, again, very, a tiny pulse throbbing in his temple. "Your grandmother is eighty-five and naturally at that age is not robust. If I had informed her of my intention to visit you, and you'd refused the invitation, she would have been disappointed and distressed. It was wiser to make sure of your assent first. May I assume I have it?"

As his glance flew up to connect with mine I sensed he was balanced on a seesaw of hope and fear, something precious almost within his grasp, but still not won, nerves rubbed raw by every second's delay. I pointed to one of the four pictures signed *Marcus Delamain* that hung in the salon. A study of woodland in lemon, crimson, and bronze, in the foreground a silver waterfall. Pasted on the back was a label: MEADS CROSS. OCTOBER 1950. "That is where you live, Meads Cross?"

"Yes. Have you any memory of Saffron, that is the name of your grandmother's home?"

Only a memory in which I didn't believe. I shook my head. "And you live with her?"

"I occupy a self-contained wing of the house. My sister Louise, your aunt, lives with her."

Saffron. As I rolled the name silently on my tongue I was washed by desolation at the destruction of my dream.

He added: "It is a fine house, the gardens are famous. Both are part of your heritage."

But the dream his presence had destroyed had not been of a heritage, of being received as a guest, to be approved or disapproved, but as a non-claimant, seeing but unseen the scenes my father had painted, seeking out the church no bigger than a roadside chapel, standing beside my father's grave and perhaps, if I were lucky, discovering what scene had sparked off that wondrously enticing child's fantasy. And my dream fulfilled, to slip away, without anyone being aware that I'd made a secret journey to fill in the dark holes in my past. A fly on the wall or a spy! I hadn't cared which.

I asked in dying hope: "Is Meads Cross a large village?"

"Scarcely a village. A hamlet. A piece of rural England that has, mercifully, been left unblemished by the appalling ravages of our age. Saffron, with its three farms, covers well over two thousand acres. Our immediate neighbours own equally large estates. Before he died, my father, with immense foresight, concluded a gentleman's agreement that none of us sells land for development without consultation with and agreement from the other three. It was as though he had a vision of the unspeakable horrors the future would implant in our midst if we didn't fight tooth and nail to protect our heritage."

His heritage, presumably, as the only surviving son. I saw in my mind's eye the one small tin box of papers my mother had left—even so too large for its contents. It contained her birth certificate and mine, and her marriage licence. My parents had been married not quite a month when I was born. To my grandparents' generation, even the Grey Man's, I'd been begotten in sin. He'd taken a vicious delight in describing my father as a pauper, so no brotherly affection had bound them together. Yet he'd expended a considerable sum of money over fifteen years to keep his brother's child housed, fed, and educated, and all he asked in return was that I should visit his mother. Had he been some jolly fat uncle his altruism would have made sense. But with the Grey Man it didn't. Suspicions wreathed and multiplied, but I couldn't pin them down to any pattern.

"So," he actually coaxed, "what is your answer?"

I shook my head. "No, I'm afraid. I'd only be a painful reminder to your mother of her son's marriage to a girl of whom she disapproved, the other girl's suicide . . . Also, now I'm free to do so, I want to continue with my career."

"Fashion drawing!" An airy gesture dismissed it as nonsense. "Well, London is the current fashion centre of the world, or so I'm given to understand by the newspapers. From Meads Cross you can be in Carnaby Street, if that is your spiritual home, in two hours."

"Not only Carnaby Street."

"Well, where your fancy takes you. The big fashion houses. There are plenty of them in London. And you have your legacy . . ."

"*Your* legacy."

"Enough!" He flung the word at me in a rage that shattered his conciliatory mood. For a second before he pulled himself together he was distraught, physically shaking, the image I'd built up of him blurred, running out of shape. "Do I appear a poor man? A man so without principle that I would deprive you of money which your mother, by denying herself, saved over the years to provide you with what she would have called a *dot!* Please do not refer to it again." He forced a grimace-like smile to his lips. "Now we will make arrangements for your visit to your grandmother."

He was calm again, but the sight of him literally flying to pieces was hardly reassuring, and I hedged: "I have only your word that she wishes to see me."

"That word should be sufficient. Have you no wish to see her in the short span of time that remains to her?"

Was that the key to the undertone of haste, urgency: that she was on her deathbed? "Is my grandmother ill?"

"No, no. For her age she keeps reasonably well, but at eighty-five, every day poses a hazard."

"Does she ever talk about me?"

"Indeed she does. She met you twice as a small child. She recalls your likeness to your father."

The second time would have been as the screaming, fear-demented child at my father's funeral. The first time? Could it be there was some basis of fact in that faery scene? I doubted it, but it breathed life into a dawning quiver of speculation: Which was better, to relinquish a dream because I couldn't have it on my own terms, or accept it on his? Conscious of his pale glance hanging on me, the light of hope quickening, I was bereft of power to make a decision.

I said lightly: "I'll have to think about it."

He had to make an effort to match my tone. "And how much time do you require to do your thinking?"

"Time," I replied, deliberately making my tone vague.

He rose, picked up his fine suede gloves and hat, trying but not quite succeeding in appearing master of the situation. "I have a hired car waiting outside to drive me to Beauvais to catch a plane for Ashford. I must leave now. I suggest a week should give you ample time to arrive at a decision." He paused, pleading where I sensed he would rather have threatened. "You have all your life before you. Your grandmother is nearing the end of hers. Why begrudge her an act of kindness that would cost you little?"

He extracted from his sealskin wallet a card, handed it to me. On it was embossed:

>Conwyn Delamain,
>Saffron,
>Meads Cross, Sussex.

When he'd gone, I went upstairs, climbed the swing ladder, picked my supper off the floor and ate it while I examined the sketches pinned to the walls and to my drawing board. The front of my mind was busy discarding some as hackneyed or outdated, others as worth preserving, while the deeper level was absorbed in assessing the Grey Man who'd entered my home to lay claim to my indebtedness to him. Yet the return on his outlay, when it came, had been suspiciously modest—unless he was a doting, mother-ridden son, and my guess was that if Conwyn Delamain doted on anyone, it was himself.

Staring at Lizzy, my wire dressmaking dummy, standing guard over the sewing machine that was older than I was, I picked the scene behind me to pieces, deliberately blindfolding myself to the bits that involved my mother. For instance, surely it was his sister—I tried to recall her name, yes Louise—who, living with her mother, should have issued the invitation? Conwyn, I would be prepared to swear, was a bachelor, was she then a spinster daughter and I a solitary grandchild? Was that why he harped like a character from a nineteenth-century novel on heritages? Why hadn't I pressed him harder towards answers to which I had a right? Because very adroitly, aided by violently conflicting changes of mood, and a physical collapse he hadn't allowed himself to be pressed. So, in the end, he'd emerged the victor. And the counter he'd left behind him to win the game was so simple it made me laugh. Curiosity! In a trice the laughter died. Nothing so simple as curiosity, rather a burning, unquenchable compulsion to rip apart the thick opaque curtains that hid my beginnings. And when there were no more secrets to be uncovered, no more empty spaces to fill, I'd walk away from Saffron, live the rest of my life without a backward glance.

There was no voice to warn me I was being enticed into a trap devised and made foolproof over fifteen years by Conwyn Delamain.

2

A FORTNIGHT LATER Jean-Baptiste drove me to Beauvais Airport. After I'd checked in there was a twenty-minute wait before my flight was called. We went into the restaurant for a drink. By the time he was middle-aged Jean-Baptiste would be as stout as his father, but at twenty-six the roundness of his features, the slight thickening at the waist only hinted at the portliness to come. Despite his intelligence, never-flagging energy, his face remained as guileless, as winning as that of a sweet-tempered child's. But this evening his liquid brown eyes were clouded with melancholy.

For the hundredth time he demanded I tell him the precise length of my stay in England. I could not do so. I assumed about a week for the visit to my grandmother, though no length had been specified. That behind me, I'd be off to London, Stratford, Oxford, maybe even to Scotland. How long I stayed depended upon Lisette. The letter I'd hoped to receive from her hadn't arrived, but Mademoiselle Greux had promised to forward it to me.

To comfort him, I reminded him that I must, at the latest, be back in Arnouvière in late August, as Monsieur Pontoise had already served notice to the owners of the house that I would be vacating it in September.

Solemnly he placed his two hands over mine, expressed himself in the stilted phrases he culled from old-fashioned English novels. "I love you, Claudine. I honour you and I will continue to love and honour you as long as I live. Why don't you say we can be married? I vow I would give you the whole of the top floor of the hotel to make you the finest studio in the world, where you could sketch and paint all day long." His hands left mine, flew wide, gesturing a limitless space. "You would have everything you wished for."

But Jean-Baptiste wasn't a free man. He believed he could keep his promise, but two insurmountable obstacles stood in the way. His parents, who regarded me as a flighty foreigner who would not, they rightly surmised, be prepared to act as barmaid or waitress in the restaurant, as a totally undesirable bride for their only child.

I had gently pointed out their uncompromising disapproval of me dozens of times. Now I just shook my head.

He protested: "It is my life, not my parents'. I pick my own wife."

Not in a family business that Pierre Mouchard and his wife Anne-Marie had literally raised out of rubble of the war, built up over the years, until the Café-Restaurant Jeanne d'arc in the Place du 8 Mai, 1945, was the best in the town, noted for its wedding receptions, private dinner parties.

"You've forgotten the hotel." He rode his dream, happy as a child playing with its favourite toy. Above the restaurant there were three floors of twisting staircases, landings that led into dead ends, and a dozen or more rooms, all of them crumbling into decay. Jean-Baptiste's ambition was to transform them into luxury suites for foreign tourists. His bright vision was of coachloads of Americans, English, Swedes, and Germans rolling up to an Hôtel Jeanne d'Arc plastered with A.A., R.A.C., and Guide Michelin *recommandé* signs.

Seeing my doubt, he insisted: "It is only necessary that my father invests a small sum of capital which I will repay him with interest as soon as the tourists arrive."

But Monsieur Mouchard was not likely to part with a centime so long as I remained a fixed star on Jean-Baptiste's horizon. "Your father doesn't want a smart, modern hotel. He is content with the bar and restaurant."

"Then I will save my own money. I will do the work myself."

But in truth he had no money of his own. As son of the proprietor he took no share of the *tronc*. I doubted whether his father paid him as much as the cook, yet he still contrived to buy me roses.

Because he was by nature so buoyant, so unendingly optimistic, the reverse side of the coin was that when doubt pounced it ground deep. "Maybe," he whispered like a man doomed, "what you want to tell me is that you will not come back. You will write to Monsieur Pontoise and order him to store the furniture, your father's pictures, while you live with your grandmother. Perhaps I will never see you after today."

I tried to tease him out of his gloom. Stay permanently in the company of the Grey Man! Not likely. Anyway, there was Lisette. He knew about our plan and how impatient I was to hear that it had been finalised.

Still he refused to let go of his despondency. "Maybe your grandmother is a rich old lady and she will make you her heir."

Conwyn Delamain talking of heritages, Jean-Baptiste of heirs! I cast my eyes heavenward, laughed. "She has a son and a daughter. If she has any riches to leave they'll be her heirs."

"Perhaps she not like them. Maybe that is why she send for you."

But she hadn't sent for me. I had only my uncle's word that she wished to see me. That neither she nor my aunt had written to me suggested a lapse of courtesy or a welcome lacking in warmth.

My flight was called. At the gate into the passengers' lounge, he asked: "Why did your uncle book you on such a late flight?"

"There was a hitch at the last moment. The chauffeur who was to meet me went sick. A friend of the family, Ross Heron, is picking me up at Ashford Airport."

"A chauffeur! Your grandmother *is* rich. She will want to buy you." When I laughed, he put his hands on my shoulders, drew my lips to his. "I feel worry about you, *petite,* in case your grandmother and your uncle are not kind and loving."

"Don't worry. In that case I shan't stay. I'll just say hello and goodbye." And I wouldn't. I would have redeemed my word to the Grey Man, made him the modest return he demanded for the money he had expended on me. More important, with a little luck I would have found the answers to the questions I'd never succeeded in coaxing out of my mother.

Waiting at the passport desk, I looked back over my shoulder at Jean-Baptiste standing motionless on the far side of the door, as wrapped in despondency as though he were seeing me for the last time on earth. Over the space between us his desolation communicated itself to me, filled me with unease that, on the false spur of curiosity I had committed myself to a course of which I could not see the end.

The crowd in the customs hall was so thick I wondered if I would be able to find Ross Heron. I needn't have worried; he found me. Tall, and made to appear taller by two dumpy women, each with a clutch of children, from which he disentangled himself with unhurried grace, he was wearing a belted raincoat with a stand-up collar. The effect was slightly dramatic, giving him a vague look of a stage highwayman.

"Claudine?" he queried with a smile that came and went in a second.

As he clasped my hand, let it go, I looked up into his face and stayed looking. When, long ago, I'd believed I was destined to become a portrait painter, faces had been my passion. I'd secrete myself in alcoves, on seats in parks, behind pillars, stripping the flesh off a head to reach the bones until my eyes glazed over. His was a curiously unmodern face, one that might have been lifted out of a mediaeval frieze, set in a frame of candle-straight corn-coloured hair. The nose was Roman, the cheeks faintly hollowed, the eyes an unusual shade of bronze-green with lashes darker than the hair. On sight I knew that if it flew out of my sight that moment, it was one of the faces I'd never forget.

"I'm Ross Heron. I believe your uncle wrote to say I'd be meeting you. The chauffeur's laid up with sciatica, your uncle doesn't care for driving outside a five-mile radius of his home base, and your Aunt Louise is a little preoccupied with your arrival. So I'm a stop-gap. Let me have your case. It's bad luck you've arrived in the midst of a cloudburst, but the car is parked as near as I could get it to the door, so you shouldn't get drenched."

I asked if he would mind waiting while I changed some traveller's cheques. He told me to go ahead. I had to wait in line for them and as I moved up place by place, signed my name, his gaze never left me for a second. When I caught him in the act he showed not the faintest sign of embarrassment, as though he had a perfect right to subject me to a clinical examination. A very cool young man, I decided, with plenty of inner ballast that would never allow him to be blown off course. And that marvellous face! I was quite content for him to go on staring at me.

As he opened the door, the wind thrust the lashing rain over us in a shower. He shouted: "Can you sprint five yards, as far as that blue Mercedes?" Then he unbuttoned his raincoat, threw half of it round my shoulders, and we ran, one of each of our arms wrapped round the other. That was the beginning, when a sudden unexpected lightness of spirit akin to joy lifted my heart, washing away the pinpricks of dreads and doubts that had assailed me for days. I could, and maybe did, have laughed with sheer happiness.

As he tumbled me into the car, the heavens were riven by interlacing forks of lightning, and the crash and crack of thunder swallowed human voices. When, momentarily, they died to a rumble, he asked: "I hope you're not scared of thunderstorms. This is a brute."

"No," I said, and looked into his face.

"Sensible girl. We'll probably be clear of the worst in ten minutes."

With a torrent pouring down the windscreen faster than the wipers could clear it, the sky so darkly purple it seemed halfway to night, he concentrated on driving. A lock of hair, darkened by rain, fell over his wide brow. I looked through the streaming windscreen, and in my mind drew his profile in chalk on a block. He proved to be a good weather prophet. In exactly ten minutes we entered a sphere still dripping from the deluge but tamed of its ferocious savagery. He drove into a lay-by at the side of a field gate, and when he cut the engine there was not a sound, as though all the birds that should have been singing had been stunned into silence by the storm.

He rolled down the window at his side before he turned, gave me a leisurely appraising look. First the firmly moulded mouth smiled, and then he broke into a ringing laugh. "I must say you're the most beautiful nigger in a woodpile that I ever did see."

Still possessed and made abstracted by that fascinating composition of flesh and bone, the words sent a ripple of shock through me. In a trice the face took on a shape of mockery, that robbed it of beauty. I'd been cheated. No, I'd cheated myself. I'd done it a hundred times. Deluded myself that physical appeal was a key to character! "I don't understand. I'm not sure I want to."

"Oh, come on," he chided. "You can't deny you're Uncle Conwyn's superstar, Cinderella exploding centre stage from a puff of smoke. Or wasn't that Cinderella? Maybe it was the demon king."

I said in a voice that sounded nauseatingly prissy: "I've been invited to visit my grandmother. Could we drive on?"

"By all means. I've guaranteed to deliver you at Saffron by eight o'clock, so we've about ten minutes to spare, which should be enough." The tone of his voice sharpened. "My name meant nothing to you, did it? You've never heard it before?"

"Not until my uncle mentioned in his letter that you'd be meeting me."

"You're saying that your mother never spoke to you of the Heron children, Ross, Caro, Sue?"

I sensed he was proceeding warily, testing the ground step by step. "No. Should she have done so?" The old, now familiar ache formed in my breast, and I felt my teeth clamp together as I fiercely shut away in the lowest depth of my mind the suspicion that by treating with Conwyn Delamain my mother had somehow betrayed me. For all I knew Conwyn Delamain was a compulsive liar. Most probably was! I was proud my voice held steady. "Did you know my mother?"

"When I was a schoolboy Michelle lived with us for two years, helping my mother with my young sisters. Caro is now teaching her daughter to sing the French nursery rhymes Michelle taught her and Sue." He paused, pressed, as though either his pride was undermined or he doubted my word. "And yet she never talked about us, not even Sue who was the baby and her favourite."

I shook my head, stared down into a hedgerow where the rain had plastered a bank of white daisies flat to the earth. In the cramped quarters in some London suburb of which I did not know the name, had my mother sung French nursery rhymes to me? If so, they had been blotted from mind by time. And after my father died I knew, without the aid of memory, she'd never sung a note.

"What about your father's family? Did she talk to you about them?"

"No." The rub of grief mingled with the aftermath of shock turned my voice as hot and angry as a protesting child's. "From the little I do know of them she had good reason not to remember them."

"Perhaps." He paused, and I could feel the weight of his glance. "Well, that's one theory down the drain. You couldn't be anyone but your father's child. Your kinship to him is beyond question."

I asked idly, as though the answer was of little concern to me: "What theory would that be?"

"That with a vacuum to fill, Uncle Conwyn needed a girl so desperately that any girl, so long as she had the correct colouring, was approximately the right age, would serve his purpose."

The inference was so outrageous that it took a few seconds for it to pierce my brain. "But that's preposterous. A piece of lunacy."

"I agree." He grinned. "Now that I've seen you. But tell me how did Uncle Conwyn know where to lay his hands on you, produce you at precisely the moment when he needed you?" When I didn't immediately answer, he went on: "The obvious answer is that Michelle maintained some sort of contact with him. But somehow I find that unlikely."

That she had was no business of his, only a burn on my heart. Automatically I defended her. "She was a Frenchwoman, born and brought up in Rouen, only fifty kilometres from where we lived. When my father died, she returned to France. Where else would she go? It wouldn't be difficult to trace me through telephone and street directories."

"You could be right. Give him his due, Uncle Conwyn is both pertinacious and resourceful."

My mind backtracked to a word he'd used. "What did you mean by a vacuum?"

He hesitated a moment, answered with a dragging reluctance. "Three months ago a girl to whom your grandmother was very attached died in tragic circumstances. It hit her hard. She has only recently recovered from the shock and grief."

"Who was she?"

"Lorraine Andrews. Hermione's nurse-companion."

It was the first time I had heard my grandmother's Christian name that fell so naturally from his lips that he must use it habitually. "I'm not a nurse, and in any case I'm not likely to remain long enough to become a companion. I'm here on a brief visit."

"A brief visit," he repeated in stunned surprise. "Hermione is expecting you to remain at Saffron indefinitely."

"I'm sorry, she's mistaken."

His eyes full of bright suspicious bafflement held mine, as he said: "That was the arrangement your uncle made with you?"

"Yes. You know, I might understand you better if you explained who you are. Uncle Conwyn, Aunt Louise! Are you their nephew?"

"God forbid!" He grinned. "I'm a neighbour. I live on their doorstep, have since I was a child. Children are taught to address their parents' close friends by the courtesy titles of uncle and aunt."

"But you call my grandmother by her Christian name?"

He nodded, his gaze fixed at some point beyond the windscreen, the profile I strove to reduce to a commonplace, absorbed in some issue that touched his emotions. "Curious, I admit. I've called her Hermione since I first knew her as a small boy of five. A child's impertinence, perhaps, which she did not check. Perhaps, too, because she's unique, a queen in her own right, the beating heart of a house called Saffron." His glance turned to meet mine, and in some way I couldn't fathom, challenged me.

"You call her a queen. Is that what she is?"

"Yes. But a very old one. Vulnerable."

Prickling along my senses came an awareness that we'd arrived at the point towards which he'd been heading even while he'd waited for my plane to land. His tension communicated itself to me, as though he were in conflict not only with me but himself.

I said: "You're afraid. What are you afraid of?"

"You." His eyes held mine. I tried to ignore their—to me—unique colour, holding my breath in suspense for what was ahead. "That you'll hurt Hermione, even cheat her. It's happened to her before . . . so many times."

I tore my gaze away from his, anger rushing to a high peak. "Why should I? I didn't ask to come . . ."

"But you came," he said adamantly. "And presumably of your own free will." He paused, said less contentiously: "You see one of the hazards when you're old and rich with favours to grant to the favoured that will set them up in luxury to their dying day, is that you become a sitting target. Do you follow me?"

"Perfectly. You're accusing me of being some sort of golddigger! And warning me off. I would imagine that cheating old ladies out of their money involved a certain amount of time, a delicate line of approach. I've no time, and no inclination to inveigle myself into my grandmother's favour."

"You would appear to be an impatient young woman in a hell of a hurry!"

"That's just what I am."

"If that were so, Uncle Conwyn having produced an ace from up his sleeve, a real winner, is backing a loser. And that doesn't run true to character."

"You make a splendid knight-errant standing guard over a helpless old lady. But where I'm concerned it's a wasted effort."

"So you keep saying. How many times have you met your uncle?"

Not only was he transformed into a stranger, but now he was acting like a lawyer cross-examining a hostile witness. I answered shortly: "Once."

"And how long were you together?"

"About a couple of hours."

"A somewhat brief acquaintance. He's a versatile man, with the ability to tailor his mood and approach to suit different occasions. Not to put too fine a point on it, he's a slick operator."

"And that's presumably another warning."

"If you need it."

"Thank you. And my aunt, is she another slick operator?"

"Quite the reverse," he said severely as though my remark was in the worst possible taste. "She is her own enemy in that she takes an inverted pride in showing her worst side to strangers. On first sight you may find her off-putting and intimidating. She's had a taxing life."

"Is she married?"

One eyebrow lifted in sardonic amusement. "Dear Uncle Conwyn didn't brief you very thoroughly, did he! Yes, married and divorced a good few years ago. She has one son, Marcus, late twenties, who's married to a nice though slightly vague child, Trudy. They and their son of six months or so live in Wimbledon but I understand that Trudy and the baby are due to arrive at Saffron tomorrow, and that Marcus will be flying in from Frankfort during the weekend. He sells computers and has been out there on a sales drive." A spice of wickedness flashed into his glance. "A family gathering to welcome the fairy princess who's dropped out of the skies, sent their cosy world spinning wildly out of orbit." In the turn of a second the light died out of his eyes, and I found myself staring into a suspicion that darkened into near certainty. "Or maybe you do know all about them and whether or not there's a name missing from my list."

"Nobody briefed me, and I had no means of briefing myself. Every name you've mentioned is a strange one to me. Is there someone else?"

Pointedly, with impatience verging on anger, as though I were an enigma he couldn't be bothered to solve, he glanced through his side window. "It appears there is another thunderstorm building up behind us. We'd better be on our way."

It seemed for a while, that we should outdistance the storm, but it caught us up, overran us. Rain poured like a waterfall out of the grape-dark clouds that were ripped and shattered into segments by lightning, while thunder burst in our eardrums. We were reduced to a silent entity of two enclosed in a metal and glass box that protected us from the violence without but not the storm of doubt that raged within.

He spoke only once. "It will be quicker to cut through the back way instead of taking the main approach road. You'll miss the splendour but then it's hardly the weather for admiring the famous vistas your grandfather created. Anyway, we're about five minutes behind schedule, and as Aunt Louise is as punctual as the Greenwich time-signal, we don't want to start you off on the wrong foot, do we!"

We drove down a track so rutted that it turned into a shallow ford, with the water splashing as high as the car roof, then across two field paths before, through the moving curtain of rain, I saw the shadow outline of a house. He manoeuvred the car close to a door in a paved, lighted courtyard, leapt out, tore off his raincoat, and threw it round my shoulders. "To save you arriving looking like a mermaid!"

Before he had time to ring the bell the door was thrown open. "Ah, Greville," he said to what I took to be my first sight of an English butler—bent about the shoulders with age, impressively dignified and presumably deaf because Ross Heron raised his voice to a half shout.

"This is Miss Claudine Delamain. May I leave her in your care? Make my excuses to Mrs Delamain-Powell. Explain that my sister is due to arrive at any minute and as there's no one else at home I don't want her locked out in this storm."

"Certainly, sir."

He bent his glance that was guardedly neutral upon me. I waited for his parting words. There was only one: "Good night." The moment's joy as we'd raced to the car receded so deep into a past that it might not have happened at all.

In fast scissor-like strides he reached the Mercedes. As he opened the door he looked back at me and in the lighted courtyard, through the rain, I saw that the doubt and suspicion had been erased from his face, its place taken by a passionate concern, so that it became beautiful again. Then, as he dipped his head to get into the car, like quicksilver the memory of a boy and the adult that boy had become coalesced. Once, on a cruel winter day, he'd sought to comfort a terrified, hysterical child. The shock of recognition set the tears spurting to my eyes so that I had to exert all my willpower to prevent them escaping over my lids and sliding down my cheeks.

3

"WON'T YOU COME IN, MISS?" Greville lifted my case, and, as I stepped into a vast oak-panelled hall made sombre by crimson shaded wall lights, offered: "Shall I relieve you of Mr Heron's coat? I will see that it is returned to him." Then he helped me off with my own, draped both over a carved settle.

The room into which he led me was such a perfect replica of my preconceived idea of an English drawing room, that I had a near sense of *déjà vu*. Greville held the door open behind me, but a new burst of thunder bawling across the sky, drowned the sound of the parting hinges. To the far right, by a window, stood my uncle and a woman who could only be his sister. Her soberly clad form was stout, but her face was cut in the same thin mould as her brother's. She had his deep-sunk pale eyes, and she was clutching the edge of a brocade curtain as though she needed its support to hold her upright.

They were quarrelling, the enmity between them of such ferocity that had Greville not barred the way, I'd have retreated into the hall. As the thunder faded into a rumble, the woman's shrill voice rose above its dying reverberations.

". . . chose this moment, when Nurse Hailey is away, and I am reduced to depending on Nancy a dim-witted and untrustworthy servant; when Lorraine's brother is as good as accusing us of murder, to bring this chit into the house. A girl who has no right here, whom you've kept hidden away somewhere until the moment arrived when she'd best serve your wicked ends."

"My dear Louise, couldn't you, for once, make an effort to control your hysteria?"

His eye moving over her head caught sight of me. Greville cleared his throat, announced with a calm that could only have been acquired by witnessing a succession of such ugly scenes. "Miss Delamain, sir."

My uncle advanced towards me. No longer a grey man, but clothed in a symphony of cream and beige, suavely at ease on his home ground as he had not been on mine. "My dear Claudine, welcome to Saffron. I am sorry you have been greeted by this appalling weather, but be assured it is only a temporary lapse. May I introduce you to your Aunt Louise? Louise, my dear, this is Claudine."

She did not stir. No muscle in her taut face relaxed as she continued to grip the curtain for support. Her brother pressed her firmly towards me. With dragging reluctance she extended a hand, touched mine. "Good evening." Those were the only two words she could force through her lips.

"Perhaps," her brother suggested, his aplomb seemingly undisturbed by the hate-packed words I'd overheard, "you would show Claudine to her room? After such a wretched drive, she'll be anxious to tidy herself up." His smile of dismissal was such as one would award a well-disciplined child. Relief? Had he been scared I wouldn't turn up? "We'll be meeting a little later."

"Would you follow me?" She still spoke with an effort and remained silent as she walked ahead of me up a curving staircase opening out on a wide, crimson-carpeted landing inset with alcoves containing display cabinets of porcelain. Greville, panting audibly, followed with my suitcase.

She showed me into a room with hand-blocked linen curtains, a silken Chinese carpet in which the centrepiece was a fourposter bed hung with rose damask hand-embroidered with flowers, so exquisite that instinctively I stepped forward to admire it at a closer range.

She said in the sharp tone of one forestalling criticism: "The bed is seventeenth century, the hangings midnineteenth, but you don't have to worry, it has a modern mattress. The bathroom is through the door on your right."

I thanked her, turned to meet her glance that was steel-hard with resentment. My response was a low-powered curiosity. She didn't, oddly, intimidate me. Perhaps even then, though I did not know her, the first whispers of pity were alive in me. Had she believed that an impostor was to be foisted on her? If so, did she still adhere to that preposterous theory? Or was it merely that she believed I posed some kind of threat to her, my presence obnoxious in that it was proof that her brother, by producing me, had gained an advantage in a battle that they seemingly waged against each other?

In the self-righteous tone of a woman to whom it afforded satisfaction to speak her mind, eschew social niceties, she continued: "Though you overheard words that were not intended for your ears, it is only fair to admit that they were the truth. Your visit to Saffron is ill-timed. I don't blame you because I have, as yet, no proof that blame attaches to you; I suspect the whole ill-conceived operation was masterminded by your uncle."

So it seemed, in her eyes at least, I was the genuine article! "Why ill-timed?"

"Your grandmother has lately been seriously ill. At the moment her state of health is so precarious that any excitement, pleasant or unpleasant, poses a risk."

My voice was as cool, though not as remorseless as hers. I had less at stake. "I certainly wouldn't want to see her if it would endanger her health. I'm quite prepared to fly back to France in the morning. Is that what you wish me to do?"

Irritation repossessed her. "Certainly not. Your uncle has already informed your grandmother that you would be arriving this evening and that she will be seeing you in the morning. Disappointment might bring on another of her heart attacks. The harm that has been done can't be undone."

I said mildly: "I was invited and told that she wished to see me."

"I accept your word. I'm levelling no charges against you personally. How long have you known your uncle?"

"I met him once, when he came to see me in France a fortnight ago. He gave me no warning that he was coming. I did not even know he existed."

"That's your story. It may be true, or it may not. I choose to reserve my judgment. But whatever else you are, you are the daughter of a nursemaid who plundered this house of its most precious treasure, your father, and returned him to his home in a coffin." Her face took on a trance-like glaze as though the blood in her veins had chilled to ice. She drew a single shuddering breath to find strength to continue. "Your mother had a talent for secrecy and deception that amounted to genius. I hope you have not inherited it from her. I am telling you this so that you will understand why I cannot with a clear conscience welcome you to Saffron."

"You've made that very plain."

"I have great responsibilities. And in this house I consider it of paramount importance that one person should speak the truth. That I have done so may, in due course, give you cause to thank me."

Her spirit lightened by unburdening herself of unpalatable truths, she continued in a brisker, less fraught tone: "I should explain that at the moment we are short-staffed. My mother's nurse-companion left the day before yesterday to nurse her own mother who is critically ill. This means our living-in staff is reduced to an elderly butler and an untrained maidservant. The cook and cleaning women only come in by the day. So if you find the service inadequate, I must ask you to make allowances."

"Since I'm not used to any service at all, I'm hardly likely to do that."

She looked a little startled as though life without servants would be unsupportable, reducing one to the level of a peasant. I smiled at her because, oddly, I wanted to win one back from her. I failed. "It is time for me to attend to Mama. Did your uncle tell you that he has his own self-contained wing in this house?"

"Yes, he did."

For the second time in less than a minute she checked her watch, as though ridden by a compulsion to count each passing second. "He wishes you to have supper with him. My son, daughter-in-law, and grandson will be arriving tomorrow, and as I have not finished preparing the nursery, I must ask you to excuse me for the rest of the evening. Your uncle will come and show you to his private apartment. Breakfast is at 8:45. Good night. I hope you find everything you need."

She wheeled on her low-heeled shoes, somehow managed to leave the room without showing me her face. When she'd gone, I pulled aside the curtains that someone had drawn and gazed at an outside world that seemed to be wrapped in a shroud, so that trees and blocks of colour were pale ghosts of themselves.

I was less disturbed by her brutal honesty—I guessed she not only didn't want, but was incapable of taming it—than the false picture she cherished. Yes, cherished was the only word, of my mother. Suddenly against the sombre shadows I saw imposed her delicate face, that cool, abstracted gaze. But hadn't she displayed a talent for secrecy in the life style she'd tailored for herself? Wasn't there a taint of deception in that she had never revealed to me her line of communication with Conwyn Delamain? Little whispers of fear penetrated my mind, but I blocked my inner ear, refused to heed them.

Four doors opened out of a lobby. He ushered me into a sitting room where leaf green satin curtains were drawn across three windows and logs were burning in a pretty iron fire basket. It might have been midwinter.

As though he caught the drift of my thoughts, he said: "I am anxious for you to see Saffron at its best, not despoiled by a storm. Tomorrow morning you will wake to its full glory."

I sat down in one of two crimson damask chairs at either side of a low table that held a decanter of sherry, two glasses. Candles in scounces burned on the milk-white marble chimneypiece, and in the silver candelabra on an oval dining-table set in an alcove.

After a discreet knock Greville entered with a heated trolley. As he passed through the candlelight, I noticed one eye was milky suggesting that little, if any, sight remained in it. My uncle asked him to pour the sherry into two exquisite but very small glasses. When he had done so, he enquired with almost protective fondness: "Will that be all, sir?"

"Yes, Greville, thank you. We can manage for ourselves now. I am sure you have arranged everything perfectly."

His response, pitched in the same key as Greville's, surprised me by its gentleness, suggesting that there was a *rapport* between them. I had not envisaged my uncle as likely to win such affectionate regard. But then family retainers had played no part in my life.

As we sipped the sherry, he gave me one of his by now familiar sharply probing glances. "I hope you were not distressed by that little scene in the drawing room. Your aunt is a woman of strong emotions and sometimes, like this evening, they leap out of control. She means well, she does well, but she is overconscientious and takes her responsibilities too hard. There are worse faults."

"She didn't seem particularly pleased to see me."

"That was just her manner. She is set in her ways. Any departure from the norm is apt to disturb her. Also, she is accustomed to a large and efficient staff. Now such staff is no longer available, and we have to make shift for ourselves, your aunt finds it difficult to adapt." His thin-lipped smile was designed to placate and soothe. It was not wholly successful. He was overanxious, bent on labouring a point that it would surely have been wiser to ignore. "Family relationships are complex, woven out of the past, the present, and flavoured with anticipation of the future. All quite normal to the family involved but incomprehensible to an outsider, which you are, though I hope you will not remain one for long. Now, if you've finished your sherry, shall we eat?"

As I got up, I said: "She seems to think you deliberately kept me hidden, like an ace up your sleeve. Was it like that?"

"Dear me! You are given to overdramatisation, aren't you! When you were a child it would not have been reasonable to interrupt your education. Adolescents, in my experience, are unpredictable and barely civilised. Later, when your mother was ill, had I suggested a visit, I doubt whether you would have agreed to it. When your nursing duties came to an end, you must admit that I lost no time in contacting you. No mystery, except perhaps for the small one as to why your mother never chose to speak of our arrangement. But that, I think you will agree, was her concern."

To reach the table alongside the food set out in dishes on the heated trolley, I had to bypass a rosewood desk in one of the three windows. On it was a portable typewriter and a pile of manuscript. With a vaunting gesture of pride towards it, he announced: "That is the history of Saffron that I am compiling. I am rather more than half-way through it."

I was guilty of listening with only half an ear as, picking at his food, he discoursed on his father's genius in reclaiming a tract of derelict land, landscaping it with rare shrubs and trees, redirecting the course of a river and building a mansion for his bride. When my lapse of attention at his long-drawn-out eulogy became apparent to him, he tapped my knuckles with a spoon. "You will have your first view of Saffron in the early morning light, when all its glory will literally burst upon you. And at precisely the best time of the year. Every season brings its own beauty, but in June, when the late azaleas, lilacs, and rhododendrons overlap the early roses, the view from your grandmother's window will, I promise you, take your breath away."

I made what I hoped were adequate responses, but vistas, trees, and a river the course of which had been rearranged did not lay a finger's touch on my emotions. I saw a face, heard a voice saying: "Conwyn Delamain is a sly operator." I asked: "Does Ross Heron who met me at the airport live nearby?"

"Yes." Displeasure at the switch of subject nipped his mouth. "At the Old Rectory, outside the main gate opposite the church. His father bought it when the Ecclesiastical Commissioners put it up for sale. Now his father is dead, it belongs to his mother, Emmy Heron. Ross has a house in Chelsea but spends most of his weekends here. He has two young sisters. Caroline is married and Sue, the younger, has some sort of job on the B.B.C., or had last time I heard. Young people change their jobs as often as their clothes these days. They have no perseverance, no stamina."

"What is his job?"

"He runs the family business, a firm of goldsmiths and silversmiths in Regent Street. They have the Royal Warrant, which means they occasionally serve the Royal Family, though now he has become infected with the current trend for modern design, I doubt whether he'll keep it for long. *Outré,* hideous! English silver embellished with enamelling; it's a desecration." He gave me a quick, sly look. "I imagine he told you that your mother was Emmy Heron's *au pair?*"

"Yes, he did." I tried to set Ross Heron in a trade of which I was totally ignorant except that it was concerned with precious metals, demanded an eye for beauty and a rich creative talent, then checked myself. Maybe he did no more than sit in an office and tot up the balance sheets! I smiled, because somehow the setting didn't fit the face.

By the time we'd eaten the chicken casserole and raspberry ice cream I'd been primed on the number of visitors who were admitted to the gardens on the two afternoons a week they were open to the public, the Saffron Pottery that was on sale, specially made by a talented Rye potter, and that Conwyn Delamain was a man so totally possessed by a house and the earth beneath and around it that it amounted to a form of idolatry.

Fatigue began to steal over my limbs, numb my tongue. Without warning, I was overwhelmed by nostalgia for a commonplace house, for Jean-Baptiste, Gustave, Mademoiselle Greux, and half a dozen of my girl friends. Irrationally, since I'd never loved it, in retrospect the graceless red-brick house became a sanctuary. Yet had it been one? Or only made to appear so? In a room that was crammed with antiques, pretty bibelots, and objets d'art, exhaustion induced a strange sense that I was existing in a dream, with the eerie foreknowledge that accompanies some dreams that it would transform itself into a nightmare.

At ten o'clock precisely he escorted me to the door of my room. If I'd given him the chance, he'd have placed an avuncular kiss on my cheek. As I didn't, he wished me good night, warned me that the visit to my grandmother was timed for 10:15 next morning, and that he would collect me a few minutes earlier.

Alone, I parted the curtains that someone had redrawn while I had been out of the room because I could not bear to sleep in a room where the windows were covered. The ebbing storm still lashed trees I could not see. A night for witches and bad dreams? I grimaced at my childishness. Anyway, why should I fear either? Yet I was conscious of some emotion akin to fear just below the surface. I opened my door. Every light along the corridor had been extinguished. Not a gleam ascended the stairs. A house so still and locked in darkness at ten o'clock there might have been no one alive in it but me!

For comfort as I undressed I told myself I need not stay. No one had the power to keep me here against my will. When, lying between the rose-coloured hangings, my eyes closed, I saw the mediaeval face that in my imagination I'd drawn in chalk on a block. A man who, as a boy, had shielded me from the sight of my father being lowered into a dark hole in the snowbound earth, and for some reason I did not know had grown into a man who nurtured a savage distrust of me.

At 6:15 I was woken by a host of carolling, twittering, trumpeting birds, as though a million tiny throats were bursting. Realisation was a clap of wonder, like receiving an unexpected gift: by waking me the birds had given me two and a half hours in which I could maybe snatch back the dream my uncle had stolen from me.

I leapt out of bed and ran to the window. Before my eyes, rising eerie as a spectre from the morning mist, so it seemed to float was, not a child's extravaganza plucked out of an illustrated book of fairy stories, but a golden ruin with trees growing out of its unroofed rooms, the sunlight beginning to flash through windows that were no more than oblong spaces in the ancient walls through which the birds flew.

It was a moment of distilled joy such as I had never experienced. I knew it was carpeted with grass on which I'd danced, one of a ring of small children before an old lady enthroned in a high wicker chair, a parasol held over her head by a woman who stood motion-

37

less as a slave behind her. She had laughed as she placed a circlet of flowers on the head of each girl child, and then beat time with a hand weighted with flashing rings to music that could, surely, only have come from an old-fashioned record player. Were my parents watching? I did not know. The years had reduced all the adults present to faceless background blurs.

As I stared, ablaze with excitement, through the ground mist I saw the ruin of my dreams was on the opposite bank of a river encircling the house like a moat—and I recalled my uncle's psalm of praise to his father who had reshaped nature. As though if I wasted a second, the dream that was no longer a dream, would dissolve with the mist, I pulled on jeans, a sweater and stuffed my feet into moccasins.

All the doors lining the corridor were closed. Not a breath of sound disturbed the house. I skimmed down the stairs, through the sombre panelled hall. I had to tug hard on the bolts, use both hands to turn the key before I was free. That was the electrifying word: free. In the flagged courtyard the mist was thicker, as disorientating as stepping into a cloud, so I stood questioning which direction I should take to reach the river moat. I stumbled onto a bridge set between stone walls, ran across it and reached a gravel path. Already with the mist drifting away in swathes, I could see the ruin's splendour. L-shaped. Towering towards the sky, I counted three tiers of arches that had once been windows, with an outside staircase leading to nowhere, but where there must once have been a door. The shorter arm was lower, partly roofed, with a bell tower where swallows nested.

Nearer, I saw the lower openings were crossed by struts of timber, presumably to deny entry. Something wild and delighted broke in me as unheeding of the makeshift barriers I scrambled through and stood on the emerald turf floor—some hurt I'd never acknowledged miraculously healed. I gazed at the pearly blue sky towards which a silken-stemmed birch reached, at the honeysuckle that tumbled out of the walls, and a chalk-pink wild rose with golden stamens that, in an angle of sunlight was unfolding its petals. What had this glorious shell been? A monastery? A castle? I did not care. Only that it existed.

I leaned through a paneless window. So near, that I could have tossed a coin into it, was the silver curve of the river, on its banks black swans asleep with their necks twisted under their wings. I touched the stones with love in my fingertips, picked a sprig of honeysuckle. In this great slumbering ruin, where the roof was the sky and the birds charted their flights between the tiers of arched windows, I'd been loved and cherished and crowned with flowers.

I turned slowly, wonderingly, and saw, separated from me by half an acre of sward, a tree, its trunk and branches so black they might have been ebony, laced and threaded with minute petunia-pink blossoms, the shade so rare that I was drawn towards it, treading on a carpet of the pink droplets that the storm had stripped from its branches. Under its canopy I read the lettering on a metal plaque that was mounted on a spike hammered into the ground.

> This Judas Tree (Cercis Siliquastrum)
> was planted by Marcus and Hermione
> Delamain on 10 June 1914 to celebrate
> the first anniversary of their marriage.

There was one spot where the flowers were literally bursting from the gnarled black trunk. I picked one and held it in the palm of my hand. I wondered why it was called a Judas tree and how old my father had been before his painter's eye had delighted in it.

When I'd scrambled back through the crossed slats, I inspected the lower building: brick and timber, of a later period, I guessed Tudor, but erected on older foundations with a curve of deeply eroded stone steps leading into the darkness of what might have been a dungeon. The door to the little bell tower, through which swallows dived, was bolted. While I was exploring a miracle took place behind my back. The last scarves of mist dissolved and when I turned round my sight was astounded, rendered spellbound by the explosion of vermilion, yellow and purple, lavender and white. Huge plantings of azaleas, rhododendrons, laburnums, roses, silver and green conifers shelved up to the edge of the horizon, like a gigantic living palette—a multicoloured maze through which I had to plot my way to a tiny church overshadowed by a tall house!

I climbed up the forking gravel paths, my outer gaze absorbed by the miracle of all that fantastic colour, yet inwardly abstracted, my heart set firm on a single objective. A wider track let me into a tunnel that had been carved out of dense, overlapping shrubs that smudged out the sunlight, its exit guarded by a giant beech tree, its roots exploding from the earth as high as my head. On the far side there were notices limiting cars to a speed of ten miles an hour, and an arrow pointing to a car park.

The living rainbow of colour was behind me now. The lane twisted first through wild thickets and then, separated from me by a ditch, grazing land on which cattle made legless by the ground mist raised their heads to gaze curiously at me.

Farther on I passed a prefabricated cedarwood shop, its shelves stacked with yellow pottery—guide books and racks of postcards. And there, at the end of the drive, beyond the double iron gate was the toy-size church enclosed in its graveyard that my child's mind had photographed and preserved for fifteen years. Only the snow was missing. Facing it, separated by the road, was the house memory had enlarged. It was in reality comparatively modest in size, built of blocks of smooth golden-grey stone, with narrow mullioned windows, made to seem more imposing by two tall chimneys sprouting from the russet-tiled roof that reached higher into the sky than the church tower. A severe-looking house, that had an air of dignity and quietude, inside which Ross Heron and his sister were asleep.

The tall grass round the crosses and squares and oblongs of the gravestones was roughly scythed leaving brown ridges of dead grass. The only sound as I searched for my father's grave was of sheep bleating. I found it midway between the lych-gate and the church porch, the encroaching grass and weeds neatly trimmed back to reveal the double-sized black onyx slab and headstone. Unlike my mother he did not lie alone. His father, who had christened his son with his own names Marcus Charles, had been buried with him. I felt the dampness on my cheeks without being aware that tears had overrun my eyelids. But the tears, the stifling pain in my breast were, paradoxically, not for the man I'd adored, but for the woman who, after his death, hindsight told me, had no more use for her life than to bring up her child. In the cool, many-faceted morning light I saw, as though it were three-dimensional, Love with its passion and torments, its pitiful vulnerability and dependence for existence upon another human being. I searched my conscience. I had not been an unloving daughter, but had I been a blind one? Or deliberately made blind? Poised on a knife-edge of doubt, suspicion and guilt overlapped leaving me without a clear-cut answer.

I walked slowly up the path and when I reached the church porch I looked back. I was standing on the stones where my four-year-old self had screamed in terror, and a boy out of the crowd who now lay sleeping in the house that overshadowed me, had pressed me to his heart. I wondered why one of the adults who crowded into the snow-bound churchyard had not comforted me. Because the presence of my mother and her child was unseemly? Pariahs who, Aunt Louise swore, had destroyed a precious life. And hate breeding hate, so that my mother had never let the name of my father's home, that of any member of his family pass her lips. Yet accepted what amounted to a pension from her brother-in-law.

Like shock waves, the reverberations of the past flowed through me. I could no longer wholly subdue an ugly suspicion that I was where I was because my mother had willed it. To act as a proxy for her after her life was ended? That was to malign the dead. Then, in the mistaken belief that, when she had left me, I would find solace, support from my father's family? No. She knew me too well—and presumably them—to have been capable of such a misjudgment, and the pact she had made with Conwyn Delamain went back too many years. But gazing down the path at my father's grave, a terrorising sense persisted that I *had* been manipulated . . . But to what end? An instrument of vengeance? The idea was at once so spine chilling and so ludicrous, that I had no difficulty in thrusting it out of sight.

I took a side path that looked like a short cut to the main gates, and found myself in a newly laid-out cemetery, with only a dozen or so graves arranged in neat symmetry against a wall. The one nearest to the path bore such a starkly simple inscription that it caught and held my eye.

Lorraine Mary Andrews
1948–1974

The girl who, according to Ross Heron, had left a vacuum that I'd been summoned to fill. But for one long-spun-out moment all she symbolised for me was the desolation that runs on the heels of death, leaving you screaming questions into the wind that would never be answered.

Time was slipping by, and I had used up nearly all my precious ration. I ran through the tunnel, picked out what seemed to be the most direct route through the meandering paths, and when I breasted a hill, came upon my first clear view of my grandmother's house where, from a distance, the moat seemed to lick the walls.

Impressive in size but unremarkable except for one handsome feature: a great semicircle of pillars that supported a first-floor balcony looking directly into the water-lily-starred moat. I counted three sets of floor-to-ceiling windows opening on to it, behind which my grandmother was presumably either asleep or waking before the day was old enough for her to exult in what my uncle had described as a view that would rob me of breath. Or maybe she was too old, or too dim-sighted to enjoy it.

My glance moved over the water meadows where the black swans still slept, and was hanging on the towering golden shell, when I heard the sound of a heavy, slow-moving vehicle. By being where I was, I was guilty of no offence. But what to me constituted a private pilgrimage was so deeply impregnated with secrecy, that my instinctive reaction was to seek out the nearest hiding place. It was behind the trunk and beneath the down-sweeping boughs of a cedar tree. From its shelter I watched the scarlet tractor draw to a halt in the flagged space in front of the bell tower.

The driver climbed out, disappeared down the worn steps into the dungeon-like opening and returned bearing in his arms a heavy crate. As he manoeuvred it into the tractor his face was turned towards me. I suffered an explosion of shock, and with it a sense that I was dreaming and had never left the rose-curtained fourposter. I dug my nails into my clenched palms until I felt pain. I drew into my nostrils the scent of the sprig of honeysuckle I had tucked into my sweater. Physical pain and scent played no part in dreams.

When the crate was loaded into the tractor, instead of climbing into it the driver turned and with total concentration stared at the cedar. I pressed myself against its trunk. My jeans were a washed-out blue, my sweater a faded grey-green. Both merged into the spreading arms of the cedar. All I had to fear was my hair, a gilt-red flag that was the precise shade of his own.

For maybe half a minute the man I knew gazed at the spot where I was hiding. Then he took a couple of paces forward, stopped dead, changed his mind and climbed back into the tractor. When he'd reversed, he gave one final backward look at the cedar tree before he drove away. He couldn't have seen me, but some sense had told him I was there. So why hadn't I run to meet him? The simplest explanation was that shock had locked my muscles, slowed up my reactions, but that wasn't the whole answer.

When the sound of the engine faded, in the becalmed silence I wondered if I had been guilty of creating a phantom man out of the air, or seeing a mirage. But the number of the tractor had printed itself in my head. And hallucinations do not include any fact as precise as figures. So who was the man whose face I knew as well as my own?

Praying that in moccasins that clung like wet skins to my feet, sweater and jeans that were sodden and dripping, I could reach my room without being spotted by Aunt Louise, I tiptoed up the stairs, taking two at a time to minimise the marks I made on the carpet.

I was within two doors of my room when a girl came hurrying from the opposite direction, thin, pale-skinned with a thick mop of coarse black hair that fell to her shoulders. I guessed she was Nancy the girl Aunt Louise had called half-witted and since, unlike her mistress, she wasn't likely to scold me for returning to the house as wet as a half-drowned cat, I smiled, said good morning.

She stopped dead, mumbled: "Morning, miss," while a glance from eyes that were as black as her hair literally ate me up. As I reached for the doorknob she began to hurry. Something fluttered from her hand, spread itself on the crimson carpet, and she had to turn back to retrieve it. It was an English five-pound note. As she picked it up, I saw that her eyelids were as swollen and discoloured as though she had wept the night away.

4

BEFORE I MET MY GRANDMOTHER I dug deep into my memory to attach a face and a form to the central figure in that long-ago faery scene, but it remained permanently buried, yielding no more than a beringed hand reaching out to garland my head with a wreath of flowers.

For the occasion I picked out my favourite summer dress: lavender cotton with white insertion let into the bodice. Madame Dubois restricted her staff to one presale bargain, and the lavender dress had been my choice.

I was ready by ten and at one minute past my uncle knocked at the door. I expected the would-be avuncular figure of the evening before, intent on impressing me with the unique splendour of his home, reassuring me of my welcome. But during the night he'd reverted in mood and manner to the Grey Man who'd come uninvited to my home to exert an authority over me he did not possess. There was the same ashy tone to his skin, the suggestion of a nervous system that had leapt out of control. Inwardly I groaned.

Without even wishing me good morning, he launched into what was obviously a carefully prepared speech. His voice was as stilted as though he were reading from notes. "After careful reflection I've decided, in view of a comment of your aunt's you overheard last night, that you should be informed as to what, or rather to whom, she was referring. For two years your grandmother had a devoted nurse-companion, Lorraine Andrews. Three months ago she died." After he spoke that most final of all words, though his lips moved, no sound left them, and it needed a visible effort of will for him to make his voice function again. "Lorraine was an orphan, her sole relative an older brother. He is employed as a mineral prospector in Australia. On the day of her death, I sent a cable to his headquarters in Perth, but he was upcountry and his employers were unable, or failed, to contact him. He only learned of Lorraine's death ten days ago. It was naturally a severe shock. I accept that. What is not acceptable, indeed is intolerable, is his callous determination to reopen the enquiry conducted by the police into the circumstances of her death."

I remembered Aunt Louise hanging onto the curtains for dear life, her cold fury that Lorraine's brother was practically accusing them of murder, and wanted, surely had a right to know "what circumstances." The question was on my lips when grief wrenched his face out of shape and anguish distorted his voice. "Lorraine is dead. She can't be brought to life by Bernard Andrews dredging up the past."

Instead of asking my question I said: "I'm sorry. What is it that you want me to do?"

"Mama must on no account hear a whisper that Andrews is in the locality engaged on an investigation that is both heartless and irresponsible. She made a deposition to the police, which was presented to the coroner. So far as she is concerned that is the end of it. Now it is conceivable that Andrews, who is both uncouth and ill mannered, may approach you. What I'm asking from you, if he makes any attempt to cross-question you, is that you inform him that you only arrived at Saffron yesterday, never met Lorraine, and have not been informed of the circumstances of her death. Have I your promise?"

"Of course. I couldn't give him any other answer. I know nothing about her, except what I overheard Aunt Louise say."

"Which was a gross exaggeration of the facts. The unhappy affair has preyed on her nerves. There was no vestige of foundation for her remarks. You will dismiss them from your mind. Do you understand?"

I was a long way from understanding. What I was beginning to grasp was that deliberate mystification for its own sake, a relish of secrecy were built into his nature. Slowly, I nodded obedience.

"One further point. On the table by your grandmother's chair, there is a photograph of Lorraine. She may well show it to you. Please lead her away from the subject as gently but as firmly as you can. It only serves to make her relive a harrowing experience that prostrated her for weeks."

I promised to do my best.

Some of the tautness eased out of his body and his smile of relief was as commending as it was possible for him to contrive, though it was still little more than a grimace.

Aunt Louise's voice bade us enter. I found myself standing on the threshold of a room literally ablaze with light. It was clothed over-all in yellow, a shade that was neither butter nor lemon, but pure and deep and gleaming. Saffron! Colour was all my eyes absorbed before they were claimed by the figure rising from a yellow velvet chair, a King Charles spaniel that had been dozing across her feet, rising with her, his plumed tail waving. I had imagined, as far as I'd visualised my grandmother at all, as old, enfeebled, and immobilised by invalidism. The woman who rose, admittedly with an effort, pressing her palms hard on the chair arms, was wand-slender, straight-backed, her head crowned with floss-soft silver curls, her face a marvel of delicate bone structure, not dressed in the drab, indeterminate garments of the elderly, but in a classic Chanel suit of a shade of sapphire that matched her eyes. Oh yes, frail, but endowed with rare grace, a grace I sensed at the first sight of her came not only from beauty of form, but from some deep well of inner strength, a natural autocracy.

For a long moment she regarded me with piercing concentration across the space that separated us, and then without uttering a syllable, she held out her arms for me to run into them.

Twice she whispered my name before she eased me away, commanded in a voice with a bell-like pitch: "Let me look at you."

And so, for maybe half a minute we stood gazing at one another. In close-up the magnolia skin was etched all-over with hairline wrinkles, in repose the pale rose mouth lost a fraction of its firmness, but she still retained an entrancing beauty. In that half minute my grandmother laid a spell of enchantment on me from which I had scant hope of escape. Or was it that I, who had been starved of emotional love, when it was bountifully offered, grabbed it without questioning its veracity?

A button nose pressed damply against my ankle. I looked down into lustrous brown eyes, a cinnamon and white domed head.

"Don't be so forward, Carlo. It's rude to press your attention where it isn't wanted." She explained: "He's only nine months old, a mere baby, with manners that leave a great deal to be desired."

I stooped, stroked the silken head. He quivered with joy and licked my hand.

"You like dogs?"

"Yes, very much." As a child the gift I'd craved above all others and never received was a puppy. There wasn't a dog in Arnouvière I didn't know by sight, and most of them by name.

Behind me I heard my uncle's step, but a shadow on my left reacted more swiftly. "Mama, dear, please sit down and relax." Aunt Louise eased her back into the yellow chair. Uncle Conwyn, calm restored—how distractingly he vaulted in and out of nerve-ridden panics—placed a kiss on his mother's brow. "What did I promise you?"

"For once, no more than you've given me."

Greville entered with a laden silver tray so enormous I marvelled the old man didn't buckle at the knees. Uncle Conwyn cleared a space on a table covered with books and newspapers and once again I was conscious of some link of affection—or dependence—between them. Maybe Greville had dangled Uncle Conwyn on his knee as a baby!

Aunt Louise during the fussy process of handing round the coffee and biscuits, seated herself next to me and in a formal manner invited me to admire the rioting swathes of colour that formed a magnificent backcloth to the three long windows that opened on to the semicircular balcony I had seen in the distance that morning, bearing not the slightest resemblance to the coldly incensed woman of the evening before.

Her brother chattered in murmurs to his mother. Such replies as she made were abstracted, her sapphire eyes between their crumpled lids never far from my face, except when she lifted the lid of a silver cigarette box with the letter H inset in delphinium blue enamel that I studied with an intentness I derided in myself. As he lit the cigarette, Uncle Conwyn enquired: "What happened to the holder I gave you that filters out the tar?"

"Unfortunately it also filters out the taste."

As soon as the coffee cups were empty, she sat up straighter in her chair, the beringed hand making a gesture of dismissal to two courtiers who had outstayed their allotted audience. "Now will both of you be good enough to leave Claudine and me alone?" Her eyes that were almost as densely blue as my father's passed from one to the other with deliberate mockery. "You are forever preaching Dr

Knox's gospel to me: no more than one visitor at a time. Well, today I propose to obey him."

Aunt Louise countered: "Dr Knox also advises a time limit for each visitor, one hour."

"But Claudine is not a visitor; she is a member of the family."

"Even so, Davinia is bringing Michael to have tea with you this afternoon. It is his half-term, and you specially asked to see him while he was home. And then Trudy and the baby will be arriving."

"My dear Louise, you are becoming quite an expert in vetoes."

"Mama, dear," Conwyn interjected. "We are only anxious that you should not overexcite yourself, which you well know tires your heart."

Her smile was charming, but there was an imperious ring to her voice. "How many million times have I heard those words! They are probably the last I shall hear on this earth. Now away with you. Claudine and I propose to engage in nothing more exciting than getting to know each other."

To my amazement, like a couple of obedient children, they went.

She bent a little towards me as though to get me into clearer focus. "Do you know that when I last saw you, you were only four years old?"

Delight that her memory confirmed mine flooded through me. "I remember. With some other children I danced round you in a circle and you put crowns of wild flowers on our heads. Until this morning when I saw the ruins of the Abbey on the other side of the river, with the birds flying through the window arches, I believed it was all a dream!"

Her smile was so rich with love that it half intoxicated me. "Your father brought you from London to see me. Emmy Heron had arranged to bring Sue and Caroline and two other children who were visiting them to tea. Because it was so hot, we had it in the great hall of the Abbey and you all danced for me." Suddenly the joy on her face snuffed itself out, and she spoke in a brisk rush of words to banish a memory she did not choose to recall. "My husband was in London for the day. When he returned your father took you home."

If, as I suspected, I'd been intended as a peace offering, I'd failed in my mission.

She put her hand on my wrist and enclosed it in a grip that was surprisingly strong. "But this time no one is taking you away from me."

Her smile wrapped me in love that warmed me down to my bones.

Luxuriating in it, I could not bring myself to despoil her pleasure—or my own—by protesting that I was with her for no more than a little while. Instead I got up and took from a table near the door the gift I'd bought when, totally without any knowledge of her, I'd fallen back on the hackneyed: twelve of the finest lawn handkerchiefs I could buy in the rue de la Paix, interwoven with a shadow pattern of roses. Her ringed fingers untied the silk cord and she gave a cry of delight as the wrapping fell away. "They are exquisite. Why, they even smell of Paris. And it is so long since I have been there, nearly ten years, on my last trip abroad with your grandfather." She kissed my cheek. "And now, my darling, I have a gift for you to mark the day when you've come back to me. But first you must close your eyes, and put your hands over them. It is a surprise, so no peeping."

I promised and sat in an uneasy, mystified darkness as I heard her, with an effort, rise from her chair. Her slow steps, though deadened by the thick carpet were sufficiently audible for me to chart their direction, backwards into the room, away from the great band of floor to ceiling windows. There followed rustlings and the prolonged squeak of a key being turned in a lock, shuffling noises and the crackle of paper, with an occasional whimper from Carlo. Second by second I was becoming more terrified that she might stumble. When, at last, she subsided into her chair, I listened with mounting anxiety to the unevenness of her breathing, as though she was having to wrest it painfully from the bottom of her lungs. I had come to the end of my endurance when she announced: "Now you may look."

A many-faceted pyramid of flashing brilliance struck my eyes, and I blinked in bewilderment until I realised what she was doing: placing a tiara on my head! When she'd settled it to her satisfaction, she handed me a silver mirror. "There! A real crown this time, not one made of buttercups and daisies."

I had a sense of some foundation that I'd believed firm, slithering from under me. The sight of myself with a high peak of diamonds protruding from my hair reduced all that had passed between us since I'd seen her rising from the yellow chair to the baseless fabric of a dream.

She gave a drily amused laugh. "You're still such a child that your thoughts write themselves across your face. Ah, you're saying to yourself, here I am alone with a crazed, miserly old woman pawing over her jewels and making a pretty fool of herself!"

The truth struck so near the bone that I was horror-struck. "No.

No. But I've never seen a tiara, let alone worn one. Coming out of nowhere to sit on my head, it startled me."

"So it appears. Let me set your mind at rest. Money is the plaything of witless chancellors the world over. There was a time, not more than half a century ago, when a German pushed a wheelbarrow filled with marks to the bakers to buy a loaf of bread, and by the time he arrived, he had to race home for another. But one small diamond would have provided him with food for a year." She lifted the tiara from my head, held it out in the palms of her hands. "If to you I appear to hoard my jewels, it is because they will appreciate in value for my heirs." Her smile both teased and admonished. "Do you still regard me as a senile old woman playing with her toys?"

"I've had my knuckles rapped, and I deserved it. Not that I thought that, or anything near it." I looked in disbelief at the white-blue blaze of fire. "My excuse is that, except in jewellers' windows, I've never been within touching distance of a small mountain of diamonds."

"You must accustom yourself to them," she said with a spurt of tartness. She reached for a second box on the table beside her. "Come, let us try the other one." She popped it on my head. "Do you prefer that one?" She slanted her head sideways, narrowed her eyes. "I think on the whole, it suits you better."

Despite her mini-lecture, which admittedly made economic sense, it still remained a bizarre game to me. Scared that I was about to be presented with a tiara there and then, I protested: "You can't give away something that is worth a fortune?"

"Nonsense," she said crisply. "I can give it away to whosoever I choose. Come, let me see you in both of them again."

Obediently I sat as motionless as a wax dummy while she placed each in turn on my head, considered the effect. "The diamonds in this one are finer cut. It shall be yours when I am dead. Trudy shall have the other."

To my relief she wrapped each of them in their covering of chamois leather, placed them in their kid boxes, and then picked up a smaller leather box, that I hadn't noticed, snapped open the catch, and lifted out of its velvet nest an amethyst as big as a pigeon's egg, encircled in tiny diamonds, suspended from a thin gold chain. In a gesture that in her was neither absurd nor theatrical, she raised it to her lips, kissed it as though it were a holy relic and slipped it over my head. "It was my husband's gift to me the day your father was born. Now it is yours because you are my darling son's child, and after so many long years of waiting, you have come home to me."

Even as the protests formed on my tongue, my heart was moved by a wave of emotion. I'd loved my mother; she had loved me. Of that I had to be sure or the crust supporting my world would cave in under my feet and I'd be entombed in blackness—but it had been a love devoid of the enrichment of the outward play of emotion. But this was a special gift of love, a link between the flawed past and this moment.

"There," she said commandingly, watching me as I held it in the palm of my hand. "We are both happy, and that is how it should be. It is what my darling boy wanted all those long years ago."

I thanked her, my voice none too steady. She lifted the amethyst over my head, fitted it back in the velvet nest. "Slip it in your pocket, and then you can put the tiaras back in the safe before your aunt returns, or I may lose my breath, which sends her into one of her tiresome panics."

The safe formed the only incongruous note in a room that was furnished with antiques, a variety of small tables adorned by tiny ivories, jade or crystal scent bottles, pieces of Sèvres and Dresden. An upright oblong painted a hideous pea-green, presumably bolted to the floor, and so jammed with deed boxes, bundles of documents and an assortment of jewel cases that I had difficulty in packing the tiaras in. When I finally closed the door, I looked round for the key. It wasn't there. "Do you want me to lock it?"

"No. I will do that later."

When I reached her chair, she was holding a silver photograph frame on her knee. She handed it to me. "That is Lorraine. She was my nurse-companion and friend for nearly two years."

A dark-haired girl with a broad forehead and pointed chin, eyes slightly narrowed, maybe against the sun, maybe not. It was a face that without natural beauty conveyed attraction and liveliness and somewhere, maybe in the line of the mouth, or the directness of her glance, strength of character.

Before I had finished examining it, she took it from me, spoke in a low, grieving voice, not to me but to the photograph. "When I wake before dawn, I forget she is dead, and stretch out my hand to ring her bell. She'd come running, not grumbling at being woken as most nurses do, but shining with gladness. She'd make tea, and we'd drink it together and talk, or she would read to me until I fell asleep." With a hand that wasn't quite steady she replaced it on the table, setting it at precisely the angle where she could see it best. She stared at it, while old age, like a spectre laid hold of her face, robbing it of vitality, so that she became a grieving shadow of the woman who'd poured love on me, rapped my knuckles and read me a lecture.

Her whisper was barely audible as she communed with the photograph of a dead girl. "The black nights are those when I lie awake and believe she died because I loved her."

Shock struck me, a disabling helplessness, coupled with a wild clamour to coax her out of the cataclysm of grief in which she was locked. I took her chilled hands and pressed them between mine to warm them, and knowing nothing of the images that haunted her, heard myself fall back on a personal article of faith. "People don't die from being loved, only from not being loved. Then you're not quite alive; you only exist on the fringes of other people's lives." And the words out, I was ashamed of their inadequacy. When she gave no sign of hearing, I bent forward, kissed her cheek.

Slowly, over seconds that passed so leadenly I could have counted them, a semblance of life returned to the mask-like face. Slower still, recognition returned to her eyes, and she heaved a sigh that seemed to come from the depth of her being. In silence she gazed at me with such intensity that I had a sense of her drawing strength from me. When, at last she spoke, her voice had a vestige of its old spirit. "To distress a child with talk of grief and death is unforgiveable." She made a gesture of dismissal. "Only cowards look back into time, indulge in self-pity and grief." The old loving smile curved her lips. "You and I, my darling, are going to look to the future."

She examined every inch of my face. "Your father's child could never have been plain, but you are prettier than I dared to hope. My dearest wish, maybe my last, only God knows, is to live long enough to see you grow into a beautiful young woman. Oh, my precious child, I have such plans for you."

Once more my courage wasn't equal to explaining my visit was not designed to last for the duration of her life. Yet that is what I should have steeled myself to do.

After a perfunctory tap on the door, Aunt Louise entered, paused on the threshold and gave a cluck of dismay. "Mama, you're exhausted! You must rest at once otherwise you won't be fit to come downstairs for lunch." She performed half a dozen actions simultaneously: stuffing another cushion behind her mother's back, a footstool beneath her feet, confiscating the cigarette box and ash tray, taking her pulse.

"For pity's sake, spare me your hysterical concern, Louise. I'm perfectly well, and there is no question of my not going downstairs for Claudine's first lunch at Saffron."

Despite her protestations, she looked so alarmingly frail, that I felt not only anxiety but a stab of guilt. As though she sensed it, she gave me a flicker of a smile. "Don't look so frightened, child. I'm not dying. Nor do I intend to die for a while yet. You and I have too many things to accomplish together."

"Come," Aunt Louise ordered, slipping a lead on Carlo, "your grandmother must be left undisturbed until lunchtime."

I went ahead of her down the staircase, my hand on the jewel case. It was a present from my grandmother who had a perfect right to give it to me. Even so, under a compulsion that I couldn't in the short space of time my aunt's footsteps trailed mine, wholly rationalise, I withdrew the box from my pocket, handed it to her.

"Grandmother gave it to me. I thought perhaps you should know." I was ignorant of the mechanics of jewelry insurance, but presumably when any piece changed ownership the insurance company required to be notified.

She handed Carlo to Greville, who was waiting in the hall, before she lifted the clip, gazed at the amethyst with, as far as I could judge, no reaction whatsoever. When, eventually, she raised her pale gaze to mine, it was to exclaim: "So she is able to open the safe! Where did she find the key? She swore to me that she had mislaid it."

"I don't know. She asked me to close my eyes while she opened the safe." So that little charade had not been conceived to astound me at the sight of myself crowned in diamonds but to ensure I didn't learn where she hid the key!

Aunt Louise gave me a look of flat disbelief. "But when she locked the safe; you must have seen where she put the key."

"She didn't lock it when I was in the room. I never saw the key to the safe."

She raged to herself. "She hides it under floor boards, in the hems of curtains, the most preposterous places. And all the time there is a fortune accessible to any petty thief or burglar! I've warned her time and again that her jewelry should be lodged in a bank vault. What else did she give you?"

"Nothing."

The air in the gloomy hall was becoming oppressive in my lungs. Longing to short-circuit the inquisition, I moved towards the door. She stepped ahead of me, barred my way, and held out the ivory case.

"Take it. It is yours. But it is only fair to warn you that on occasions Mama's memory is fickle. A promise she makes one hour is swept out of her mind the next." She literally forced the box into my hand. "Accept it on the strict understanding that if she forgets she has given it to you, is distressed by its disappearance and imagines it has been stolen, you return it."

"What you're saying is that I may borrow it!"

"You hold it in trust," she corrected. Subtly her expression changed. Bitterness remained, but the anger had either burnt itself out or been suppressed. Her tone was deceptively reasonable. "You are very young, and it would be unfair to expect a mere girl to understand the burdens the old have to bear; one above all others: the threat of death that never leaves them, night or day." The whole of her concentration was deployed on laying down a principle she expected me to accept without question. "It clouds their judgment, makes them ripe for exploitation and . . ."

It was the calm, almost unconcerned way in which she tossed the ugly word at me that sparked off a rage I was powerless to control. "I want nothing from my grandmother, nothing at all, for the simplest of all reasons, there is nothing she has that I want."

"That's childish talk, worse, the talk of a child who has lost its temper." She regarded me with a cool appraisal in which I could detect criticism but no malice. "It is your good fortune that you closely resemble your father, who was Mama's favourite child. You've entered her life when old age and ill health deprive her of many pleasures and diversions, for which to some extent you have the power to compensate her. That makes you wittingly or unwittingly, dangerous."

I said with cold fury: "Neither wittingly nor unwittingly am I the slightest danger to her."

"Well, you'll have to prove that. I hope for her sake, you're right."

I tried to bypass her, but her arm restrained me. "Did she give you money and ask you to buy her cigarettes?"

"No."

"She will. She bribes Nancy to do so, on the sly, so that I am never able to find them on her person." I remembered the fluttering five-pound note. "If she asks you, you must refuse. Dr Knox rations her to five a day. Even those, to someone of her age with a serious heart condition, are poison. So please remember if you give her any, which she'll hide in some secret place she's never used before, you're putting the little of her life that remains at risk."

5

ONCE OUTSIDE, anger singing in my ears, I began to run. I had sprinted halfway across the bridge when a low whistle halted me. There was no one behind me, no one in sight ahead. I ran on. It came a second time, followed by: "Hi! Down here."

Moored under the arch nearest to the bank was a punt, in it a girl peering upwards, and on a pink woolly rug beside her a sleeping naked baby. I walked back, hung over the bridge.

"I'm Trudy. Cooling off after a fiendishly hot drive. If you want a formal introduction: Gertrude Powell-Delamain. I thought we might say hello."

She was a short, plump girl, in a size too small sky-blue bikini, with light, streaked hair falling to her waist. She had round cheeks, large cinnamon brown eyes, and a pudgy blob of a nose. She gave the sleeping baby a gentle poke in his middle. "And this, if you haven't already guessed, is the latest member of the dynasty: Marcus IV. That is, if you're not aiming to put his little nose out of joint."

"Why should I?"

She gave a hoot of laughter. "That's what's called the sixty-four dollar question!" She cocked her head sideways, surveyed all of me she could see above the bridge. "Well, you appear to be the genuine article, not some girl Uncle Con picked up to play the part. So that one bit of suspected foul play sunk without trace. How did the big scene go?" Suddenly she grinned and I grinned back.

After the blasts of love, suspicion, and resentment to which I'd been subjected, Trudy on that first meeting was as refreshing as a waft of cool, life-giving air. "I'll tell you when I've got my breath back."

"Like that, was it! You know, I rather hoped you'd come swanning across the bridge wearing a tiara!"

I laughed and the sound was strange in my ears, as though it was one I hadn't heard for a hundred years. "She's leaving us one each."

"A tiara, just what I need! They're all the rage in Wimbledon. When he was born"—she gave the baby a second poke in the stomach

—"she presented me with a triple row of matched pearls. Very lush, but so valuable that Marcus sprinted to the bank with them before I could lose them in the supermarket. By the way, did you know she sometimes wants her presents back?"

"Aunt Louise explained." I took the jewel case out of my pocket, dangled the amethyst over the side of the bridge. "Borrowed treasure!"

"You could always pawn it, so long as you didn't lose the pawn ticket." Her tilted glance became shrewder. "You hared across the courtyard like a bat in hell. Who upset you? No, let me guess. My Ma-in-law."

"Does she always assume that everyone is out to exploit her mother?"

"More or less. And you can't blame her, a good few have tried it on. She suffers from an outsize anxiety neurosis plus permanent nervous exhaustion, especially now, when with Hailey away, she's directly in the line of fire. Don't let her get you down. It was a year before she forgave her precious ewe-lamb for marrying a girl out of a typing pool. But when Marco arrived, I was formally received into the family. Mother of the heir! I can't help feeling sorry for her. What a life! Walking a tightrope spun out of an old lady's whims! You see Ma-in-law is hell bent on Marcus becoming lord and master of Saffron, and after he's dead Marco! Signed and sealed, trusts and covenants." She giggled. "By the time Marco is twenty-one, it'll probably be state-owned, with him showing the trippers round and grateful for their tips." She squinted at me through a pair of false eyelashes, one of which had become detached at the corner, on the turn of a second becoming shrewder, even outrightly calculating. "But maybe you're hooked on it. Do you see yourself as queen bee of Saffron, complete with accommodating husband who'll have to tack Delamain onto whatever surname he was born with?"

I swallowed my indignation. "Do I look the type?"

"I wouldn't know. Everyone round here puts on a great big act to fool an old lady because they want to figure in the Will. So why not you!" Her cynical burst of laughter was without malice. "Will-making happens to be her hobby. One of her motivations for living I guess you'd call it." She shook her head. "It must be hell to be old and rich, playing a version of Russian roulette to discover who is genuinely fond of you and who is fooling you to get a bigger slice of the cake when you're dead." Suddenly her gamin grin flashed. "I don't need to be told how she reacted to you, folded you to her bosom with rapture, but how did you react to her?"

"Mostly by surprise. I expected her to look much older."

She laughed until her plump shoulders shook. "Like a latter-day Queen Victoria, in a bonnet and shawl! That's where money pays off. It buys the top hairdresser, beautician, masseuse, all masters of their trades, and hideously expensive. It's damned hard work keeping glamorous at eighty-five, but give her full marks, she never lets up. But then she's a very downy old bird, up to all the tricks in the book, with charm she turns on like a tap provided you toe the line, *her* line. My guess is that she's got you well and truly hooked. Well . . ." She stopped, changed her mind about what she'd been going to say, suggested: "Hadn't you better put that bauble away before you drop it in the river, just in case she asks for it back?"

As I put it in my pocket, the baby woke with a yell. She picked him up. "That's enough, honey bun." She hugged him then sat him upright on her knee, stroking the moist dark quiff of hair. "His mistake was not to be born with blue eyes and a halo of ginger curls! Poor sweetie, he can't help being the image of his dad, when his dad is the image of his. Crazy, when you work it out, a fortune hanging on pigmentation or whatever you call it." Her glance fastened on my hair. "You did all right for yourself, didn't you?"

"You don't have a choice, do you?"

The baby nuzzled his head into her neck. She kissed the quiff. "He could have green hair or purple for all I care."

Shyly he twisted round, coyly poked a chubby starfish hand in my direction. I laughed. "Or a combination of the two. He's a gorgeous baby."

"Except when he screams blue murder at 2 A.M. Anyway, if he yells tonight, his fond papa can walk him round. For which I've you to thank. Summoned posthaste across Europe four days earlier than he was due back to support his mum in a family crisis! By the way, where did Uncle Con find you?"

"In France. Arnouvière."

"With the aid of a battalion of private eyes?"

"No." I hesitated, then tired of putting up smokescreens, admitted: "It seems he kept in touch with my mother by letter and when she died her solicitor contacted him."

"Which makes me right. That was my guess. The old creep has been keeping you under wraps, all ready to produce like a white rabbit out of a hat when the appropriate occasion arose. Congratulations!"

"Why? I didn't know he existed until he walked into the house one day, announced who he was. My mother had never mentioned him to me." I looked across the river at the ruin that was not a dream and added: "Or any of this."

"But when Uncle Con said please walk into my parlour, my pretty niece, and see what God will send you, you trotted after him!"

"I was curious. Who wouldn't be?" It was the nearest I could bring myself to confessing the dreamlike fantasies, the gaps in my past I had a compulsion to fill.

"I bet you were! And now he's got you safe in his clutches, what now?"

"He hasn't. I could walk out, catch a plane to France this afternoon."

"Ah, but you won't, will you," she said with unexpected spirit. "At least I hope not. Marcus losing some of his commission, in the doghouse with his boss for bolting back four days early, and then finding his rival flown! Grandmother as like as not staging a heart attack, and Uncle Con back in a psychiatric clinic. What an anticlimax! I think that having dangled your toes in the water, you should have the guts to swim to the deep end."

I repeated the two words that had shaken me. "Psychiatric clinic!"

"Three visits, the last only a couple of months back. A girl who was Grandmother's nurse got herself drowned. Uncle Con was crazy about her."

I saw that dry, juiceless figure and felt a squirm of revulsion. "But he's old. He must be over fifty!"

"What's it matter how old he is if he doesn't feel it! And when he was in love with Lorraine, he looked younger. She even managed to persuade him to eat proper meals, and on her days off they went on merry little jaunts in her car."

"Are you saying she was in love with him?"

She shrugged. "I wouldn't care to commit myself on that one. But he certainly convinced himself that she was. He was obviously working up to an honourable proposal of marriage, and she'd certainly have had a lot going for her if she'd married him and produced an heir. For one thing, I doubt if you'd be standing where you are now! You'd have become redundant so to speak."

I felt nauseated, and obviously looked it. She giggled. "You needn't look so shocked. My dad was forty-five when he married

Mum, getting on for fifty before they produced me. Confirmed bachelors do recant, you know. Golly, the time! With his lordship to feed I'll have to rush to get through before the gong goes for lunch. That's what Greville actually does in this day and age, bangs a gong, and heaven help you if you're not within sight of the dining-room door when it sounds off." She pinned a nappy round the baby's middle, threw a towel over her shoulders, poled the boat to a point where the bank was split in two by a flight of steps, topped off by two stone lions. When she'd humped the baby over her shoulder, she turned, called: "Coming, or had you in mind a grand tour of the ancestral acres!"

"I'll come with you." I hurried over the bridge, along the stone-paved walk that separated the house from the lily-starred moat. In the bright sunlight a dark image formed itself inside my head: the girl whose picture my grandmother kept close to her side, floating Ophelia-like among the waxen flowers, heard myself ask: "Where was she drowned?"

"They fished her out from the weeds by the Abbey wall."

"How did it happen?"

"Either she tripped, jumped, or was pushed. Accident, suicide, or murder. Take your choice. At the time the betting was on murder, though in the end the police couldn't whip up sufficient evidence to prove it."

Her callousness shocked me. "You sound as if you didn't care."

"Do I?" she said in the same voice. "Then, you see, this isn't my home. I visit it on an average of four times a year because it's important to Marcus that I do. He comes down oftener for his mum's sake. I suppose I spoke to Lorraine half a dozen times. We were never buddies. She was a bit too bright and bossy for me. Grandmama's pet with a power complex. She certainly wasn't the accident-prone type, too much on the ball. Nor suicidal, but then I've never known a suicide. Have you?"

"No." I thought of my mother's death, that had been a kind of passive suicide—in that she had exercised an option to live or die, and the familiar guilt and grief chilled me. "And murder! Why would anyone have wanted to murder her?"

She shrugged. "Why does anyone want to kick another human being off the face of the earth? Because they pose some kind of threat, I suppose. It's one of the risks you run, if you set your sights on a prize that someone else covets." She gave another of her giggles. "Let that be a warning to you, and watch your step." She turned and walked ahead of me to the french windows of the drawing room. Looking at her with the baby's arms forming a stranglehold round her neck, all thought of death seeped out of me, as I was possessed by a passion of concern for the living. Should I chance it? Even if she only paid four visits to Saffron a year, she could have met him, know his name. Hope bursting within me, I touched her elbow. "Have I got any other relations, even distant ones, living here or nearby?"

She turned her head in slow motion, her expression dead-pan. "Relations?" she queried as though the meaning of the word was unknown to her.

"Yes. Cousins, second cousins . . . anyone."

She reverted to her throw-away, don't-care voice. "I wouldn't know. Ask Uncle Con. He's the expert on the Delamain family tree." She opened one of the windows leading into the drawing room. "Lunch is at one, the only meal of the day Grandmother eats with us. One minute late, and you're in the doghouse. That's why I've got to fly to get Marco fed, bedded-down, and myself decently clothed. See you!"

When, just before one, I went downstairs, I found Uncle Conwyn already stationed at the foot, his hand resting on the carved newel post. His mouth opened, but whatever remark he'd been about to make, was lost as Greville thumped a brass gong, the reverberations of which sounded in the air after he'd ceased to beat it.

On cue the tall, elegant figure began to descend the stairs. My uncle's upward tilted smile softening the sharply honed edges of his features was so fond that it became faintly credible—though no less nauseating—to conceive of him in love with a girl at least half his age. My grandmother, head erect, hand never leaving the banister, proceeded slowly, but still with regal grace, down the stairs. Aunt Louise followed behind, arms stretched out to snatch her mother to safety at the first hint of a stumble.

When she reached the hall, Grandmother held out her hand, tucked it into my arm. "I hope, dear child, you have a good appetite. Mrs Harper is an excellent cook, except on her off-days, and I ordered her to serve a simple but typical English meal: roast beef and Yorkshire pudding, with our own strawberries and cream."

I told her I'd heard of Yorkshire pudding but never tasted it. In that case, she pronounced, I was in for a treat.

The dining room in which I'd eaten a solitary breakfast, was now flooded with sunlight that washed over the rosewood table and brass inlaid chairs, drawing out their glowing depths of colour. Grandmother sat at the head, motioning me to the chair on her left. Uncle Conwyn took the seat next to me. By Aunt Louise opposite there was a vacant place.

"And where," Grandmother demanded, "is Trudy?"

"Here!" Trudy scrubbed, with the mane of streaked hair as damp as though she'd just emerged from a shower, wearing a tight magenta pink dress, half ran, half skipped to her place. "Sorry I'm late. Or nearly late. Marco played me up, spit out all his apricot soufflé."

As Greville moved forward to serve her, Grandmother chided: "I have never been able to understand why you didn't accept my offer of providing him with a trained Nanny."

Trudy, spearing a piece of sole in sauce, answered: "Because she'd know my son better than I do, and that would give me an inferiority complex for life."

Aunt Louise spoke quickly to cut short what sounded like an old grievance. "Did you leave Marco asleep?"

"No. You'd think to look at him the human race had never heard the word. But Nancy took over for me."

"I don't wholly approve of Nancy being left in sole charge of Marco. She has no experience with babies and . . ."

"And you, Louise," Grandmother interposed, "are absurdly prejudiced against Nancy. So far as you are concerned, she can't do a single thing right."

Aunt Louise held her ground. "She is untrustworthy and overemotional."

Grandmother answered with an air of sweet omnipotence: "She has gentle hands, is never in a hurry, and she does not knit." She turned to me. "Nurses are addicted to knitting, forever counting stitches aloud when you need some small service. What's more they display each piece to be admired as it is completed, and then a second time when the garment is sewn together. I find it all excessively tedious. So you've been warned, if you knit shapeless garments, keep them out of my sight."

"I wouldn't know how to begin."

"Good!" Her look wrapped me in fondness. She turned a sharper one on Trudy. "Is Nancy prepared to look after Marco while you drive to Heathrow to meet Marcus?"

Aunt Louise answered for her. "I will take charge of Marco until Trudy and Marcus arrive back."

This sparked off a flurry of questions and answers concerning the arrival of the afternoon visitors, Marco's airing, and the probable hour of Trudy's return, during which my uncle spoke in an aside to me: "I see you are an early riser. Did you enjoy your before-breakfast exploration of the Abbey and the gardens?"

"Yes. Very much." I watched Greville turn the dish of potatoes he was offering him so that the smallest were to his hand, and to which he helped himself to one. Tending his master like a delicate child, perhaps because he ate so little and his appetite required to be tempted. "That makes you an early riser too."

"A poor sleeper." Something in his tone made me look directly into his pale, practically colourless eyes. They told me nothing, but the thin smile suggested it afforded him immense satisfaction to hold me in suspense. I did not believe, unless he had used binoculars, that he had seen me hiding under the camouflage of the cedar tree. But I could not be absolutely certain.

In ready-made sentences he set out to inform me on the Abbey's history. It was a Cistercian foundation, built in the latter half of the twelfth century, one of the most renowned in the southeast until it was destroyed in the dissolution of the monasteries. Later it had been partially restored and a small Tudor extension erected on the west side. Both had fallen into decay, been half buried in a wasteland when his father, before his marriage, had set himself to the task of reclaiming them. There was a booklet containing an outline history of the Abbey and Saffron, of which he would present me with a copy after lunch.

"I had," he continued, when I thanked him, "been looking forward to the pleasure of escorting you round the gardens. Unfortunately, Mrs Thorpe, who is in charge of the gift shop telephoned me an hour ago. Her husband was admitted to a hospital intensive care ward this morning suffering from a coronary thrombosis, and naturally she wishes to be with him. That means I must stand-in for her. However, the shop does not open until two-thirty when the first visitors are admitted, so if you will be ready at two, I will draw you a sketch-map of the routes that will lead you to the most rewarding viewpoints at this season of the year."

Grandmother tapped my wrist. "And at six o'clock we will drink a glass of champagne together." She assumed a mock expression of docility. "At seven-thirty I am served my invalid's supper, am permitted to smoke my last cigarette of the day, after which I am tucked into bed and dosed with sleeping pills."

"Mama, dear," Uncle Conwyn chided: "What is the point of hav-

61

ing an excellent doctor, a highly skilled consultant physician, if you don't follow their advice?"

"A measure of satisfaction in exercising the remnant of independence that remains to me. A passive bundle of flesh and bones, is that what you'd like to reduce me to?"

Momentarily colour flared into her daughter's cheeks, but for once she was not intimidated. "You know very well it is not. All I ask is a promise that you do not smoke after you've taken your sleeping pills."

The back seats of the small estate car were heaped with pottery, roughly packed in newspaper, and a pile of slim guide books adorned with a pencil sketch of the Abbey shell on the front cover, one of which he presented to me.

Though he drove with exaggerated caution, I calculated it would take him no more than ten minutes to reach the cedarwood shop, which left me with no time to waste on a delicate line of approach. "Have I any other relatives besides you, Aunt Louise, and cousin Marcus?"

He took his eyes momentarily from the road, causing the car to jerk. "What makes you ask? Are you planning on drawing up a family tree?"

"No. I'm just curious. Have I?"

"Your grandfather had one brother who predeceased him. He had one child, a daughter who married a farmer. They emigrated to Canada soon after the First World War. We never kept in touch, and I wouldn't have the remotest idea whether they are dead or alive, or in what part of the world their children, if any, are living. Does that satisfy you?"

I ignored the question. "While I was in the gardens before breakfast I saw a man." I resorted to the adjective I used to describe my own hair. "With ginger-blond hair, tall, about thirty. He was driving a tractor, loading on to it a crate he carried up from the underground cellar underneath the bell tower. I wondered who he was."

He said, with an assumption of airiness: "My dear child, he could have been anyone employed on the estate. With three farms, ten acres of garden, there are over forty employees on the payroll. And you expect me to identify a man merely by the description of his hair." He forced a chuckle. "Blond what?"

"Ginger. Exactly the same colour as mine."

There was a pause in which I could literally feel the tension build up in him. "Did you speak to him?"

"No."

"Why not, since he apparently aroused your curiosity."

"There wasn't time. Even among forty employees there can't be many who are the living image of my father. He might have been my father."

He scoffed. "You are indulging in a childish flight of fancy. Your father, let me remind you, died when you were four years old."

"I remember him as clearly as if he'd died yesterday. Why not tell me the man's name? Why make a mystery of it?"

"There's no mystery." He drew in his breath, said pettishly: "You could possibly, though I doubt it, be referring to Adam Terson."

"Who is he?"

"He is the estate manager."

Painfully my certainty drained away. A paid employee! The threads I'd woven in my mind refused to cohere into any credible pattern. In the silence he turned his head, and the glance that swept across my face was so uneasy that I could feel, rather than see, the fear behind it. I remembered the gilt-haired man standing in front of the little bell tower, drawn towards me by a sense more powerful than sight, and then, for some reason, resisting the impulse to walk up the slope towards me. No, I had not deceived myself.

He braked with a jerk in a small lay-by behind the cedarwood shop. Out of the car, there followed a fussy business of unlocking, which involved two keys. He waved me ahead of him. "We've ten minutes before the first visitors arrive. First, you must see the specially designed Saffron pottery."

It consisted of ash trays, mugs, bowls, and vases all glazed a dusky yellow, inscribed in a running black script Saffron. I'd done potting for a year at the convent, long enough to form a judgment. It was pretty mediocre. But my uncle regarded each piece as an object of beauty. He presented me with an ash tray, and then busied himself behind the counter unlocking the till, tipping in a leather bag of small change. By some quirk of nature, he appeared singularly at home in his role as make-believe shopkeeper, his jittery nerves, soothed, his arrogant poses abandoned.

With the ash tray tucked into my shoulder bag, I asked: "Could you tell me where I can find a post office? I want to buy some postcards and stamps."

He indicated a revolving rack. "You can't do better than buy your postcards here. And the post office is closed on Saturday afternoon, but this evening I will supply you with stamps."

We were interrupted by the arrival of the first customers, two middle-aged women who had come to collect mugs they'd ordered to be labelled Jonathan and Deborah. While he was bent searching for them under the counter, I made my escape before he had time to remember he hadn't presented me with the sketch-map he promised.

I skirted the church, cut diagonally across the stream of approaching coaches and cars, onto a road. Except that a red mini was parked outside the front door the stone house with the tall russet chimneys looked as blind-eyed and empty as it had done in the early morning light.

I found a signpost pointing a white finger towards Meads Cross. I followed it, walking between hedgerows that billowed with white plumed flowers that scented my hands when I touched them. In about a mile I reached a crossroads flanked by open fields. Lining the heart of the cross were three shops, a garage, and a public house called The Cock Pheasant. Painted over the doorway of the largest shop was the name of its proprietor: ALICE TERSON, LICENCED TO SELL TOBACCO.

6

I STARED AT IT SO LONG that a woman waiting to enter the shop touched my arm. "Excuse me, dear." I stood aside, hope and fear producing a mental chaos, so that it was a little while before I could line up probability against improbability, strike a balance. In English villages, as in French, there would be several branches of one family with the same surname. Alice Terson could be a distant cousin, maybe even no relative at all. Alternatively, Uncle Conwyn could have fobbed me off with the name of a man who bore no more than a passing resemblance to the one I'd hidden from under the cedar tree.

A bell above the door pinged as I opened it. One woman was being served at a grocery counter, two others were chatting as they waited their turn. Three pairs of eyes focused on me, two with the natural curiosity merited by a stranger, murmuring good afternoon. The third just stared, and to the woman behind the counter I appeared to be invisible.

The post office section was on the far side of the shop in a caged-off, padlocked area. To the left was a rack of postcards. As I chose three, I became conscious of the weight of silence, as though my entry had rendered shopkeeper and customers dumb. I looked up suddenly and met head-on the gaze of the woman behind the counter. Dark eyes that from a distance were slits of jet, in a thin, almost emaciated face, with pale lips folded in a dead-straight line, and hair, part brown, part grey, dragged ferociously back from her forehead and confined in a net. It was a face at once haunting and intimidating. The lost artist in me classified it as part shrew, part martyr.

When two of the customers had left and the third was being handed her change, I went towards the counter, and was standing by it when, as she snapped her purse, an old man walking with a stick entered and stood waiting a pace behind me.

The jet, bitter eyes bypassed me. "Yes, Tom?"

"Quarter of tea and ten Woodbines, Alice."

It was natural enough to serve an elderly customer ahead of a young one; it was not that I resented, only her pleasure—no, that is too mild a word—her malice in exerting the miniscule power she possessed over me. When the old man left, no other customers entered, and the woman I now knew was Alice Terson, held out her hand, counted the postcards, slid them into an envelope, snapped: "Nine pence."

The one pence change left on the counter for me to pick up, she swung about, mounted a stepladder and began to rearrange some tins on a high shelf, her narrow back, in a shrunken out-of-shape purple cardigan a silent shout of outright rejection. She changed the order of two pyramids of fruit. Now, instead of being in tidy blocks, the tins of peaches and apricots were mixed up. It was a meaningless exercise except that it provided her with an excuse not to look at me. As I closed the door behind me, I knew as clearly as if I could see inside her head, that was what she had not been able to bring herself to endure.

The effect on me as I walked along the lanes palpitating with heat that drew the scent out of the flowering hedgerows and the high grass swaying in the fields, was of emotional exhaustion, a wild, incoherent desire to pull down the shutters and for a little while be safe. But safe from what?

I climbed over a gate and lay down on a bank where there was no sound about me but the hum of bees that tumbled in and out of the golden hearts of wild roses, alone, mercifully released from the pressures of eyes that hated, loved, or distrusted me. I fell asleep. My dream was so peaceful that when I woke, I kept my eyes sealed to preserve every fragment. We had been walking through a wood, freckled by sunlight that filtered through the leaves, the path so narrow we were bound close together, the light weight of his hand on mine a life-giving force that filled me with contentment. We did not speak, but every few yards, he bent his gilt head and smiled the smile that I remembered.

I opened my eyes, looked up through the sprays of honeysuckle at the azure sky and recognised the dream for what it was: childish wish fulfilment, a pillow of comfort conjured up by my subconscious. I jerked upright, and in a moment of dizziness, pushed my head between my knees, shivering in the heat.

As I came within sight of the Old Rectory, Ross Heron was locking the boot of the red mini, at the wheel of which sat a girl. Of their own accord my feet slowed, came to a stop. Their voices, though not their words reached me, intermingled with careless bursts of laughter. Then, with a wave of her hand the girl started to reverse. As he stood back, I was directly in his line of vision. I turned away, but not quickly enough. He shouted my name. The girl stopped the car with a squeal of tyres, jumped out, and came racing towards me. She was small, skinny-thin, with waist-length ash-blond hair, her mouth made to seem wider than it was by her small pointed face. She threw her arms round me, tilted her head up to kiss my cheek. "Claudine! Wonderful! Super! I was longing to see you."

A voice above her head murmured: "My sister Sue."

"Who else!" Her glance skimmed my face. "Ross, Claudine looks beat. I don't wonder in this heat. Go and brew up a pot of tea and we'll have it on the terrace where it's cool. If you hunt around you're sure to find one of Marty's cakes. She'd never take off for the weekend without leaving her darling boy with a good cook-up."

"Five minutes ago you hadn't time to wait for tea."

"Five minutes ago Claudine wasn't here. Get cracking."

"Yes, ma'am."

She slotted her arm through mine, and led me round the house to a terrace that overlooked a lawn and flower borders brimming over with lupins, delphiniums, and great blowsy red poppies. At the bottom was a paddock, its boundary line a low hedge, over which a pony hung its head and neighed for attention.

She tugged a cushioned swing-seat deeper into the shade. "Put your feet up and don't take any notice of Silas. He's putting on his usual act of being starved of food and affection. Actually, he's the worst spoilt pony in the county." Her slightly pixie-like, triangular face, dominated by wide grey eyes glowed with excitement. "My sister Caro, she's two years older than I am, swears she remembers you, but she's a bit given to flights of fancy, plus an elder-sister syndrome of being one up on her sibling. She says it was at some party Aunt Hermione laid on in the Abbey. Did she dream it up?"

"No. It happened, when I was four years old. I remember it, other children being there, but not clearly enough to separate one from the other."

"And your mother, I'll never forget her, never, never! How wonderful she was with us. We all adored her . . . those marvellous games she invented! Endless fun! We used to play Mummy up, nearly drive her crazy, but never Michelle." Sadness strained her face. "I can't bear to think she is dead, that you've lost her. She must have been a super mother . . ."

The two images of the same woman, mine and hers, refused to merge into one. Once again guilt burst out of its shallow grave, threatened to overwhelm me.

She bent, horror-stricken, across the space that divided us. "Oh, I've been so clumsy. I didn't think fast enough. Forgive me. The last thing in the world I wanted was to upset you. Oh, dear! You poor darling. I'll go and hurry Ross with that tea. I'm sorry . . . really I am." In passing she lightly ran her hand over my hair.

When they came back together, I smiled reassurance into her anxious face, and she gave a quick little sigh of relief. Pouring the tea, she said: "We're to have a wedding in the family. Mummy's getting married again." When her brother rose with that lazy grace I remembered to take the cups from her, she angled her head, deliberately looked behind her into the garden to screen her face. "Daddy died two years ago. So it's a good idea, really. We're all three delighted, aren't we, Ross?"

He spoke with a deep gentleness that was new to me. "Indeed we are."

"It's just," she hedged, "that she rather sprang it on us. He's been a friend of the family forever, a retired Army colonel, a bachelor. It never occurred to us to visualise him as husband material."

"Sue," he said in a voice that sought to comfort, "it'll work out. You'll see."

"But he's so regimented and Mummy's so fluid, so gorgeously disorganised. I know in my bones he'll try to discipline her out of her natural state of semi-chaos." She glowered at him. "Besides which you're going to make it worse, moving out of your basement workshop, she'll hate not having either you or Tony down there. Why do you have to make even more unsettlement right at this moment?"

"You know we've been negotiating for the Lambeth lease for six months. Now it's signed, and the builders have finished, the urgent need is to become operational with four designers working under the same roof. Simpler for all concerned, and financially more viable." His smile glowed, with a richness that could only come from the heart. "Arthur loves her. I suspect he always has. Take a look at him looking at her when he thinks no one is watching and see if you don't agree with me. He may try his hand at regimenting you, but I doubt if he'll do more than coax her, if that."

"Um!" She sounded unconvinced. "I can see him running his beady little eyes over my shoes, ordering me to go and shine them up, which is my least favourite job." She stuck out her feet. "Susan"—she aped a voice I'd never heard—"they'd benefit by a little polish and elbow grease."

"You old stick-in-the-mud. You hate change. You always have."

She grinned philosophically. "Okay, I'm a self-centred grisler. But I bet he won't allow Marty to bring me breakfast in bed when I'm home."

He turned to me. "Sue is all for her creature comforts. Caro is the spartan."

"And which are you?"

Sue answered for him. "Neither spartan nor sybarite, a mixture of the two, and a cherisher of his private life! Yes, that's true, Ross. We never meet your girl friends until you've dated them for six months, and by then the chances are the affair's dying on its feet. Serve you right if Arthur produces a succession of eligible young women, all daughters of high-ranking Army officers. Which reminds me, how is Harriet?"

"Fine. I'm taking her out to dinner tonight."

"Fine!" she mimicked. "You could do worse, and also a lot better. Take a good hard look at her thin nose. Ugh!"

He tilted his head back and laughed, giving me a new perspective of his face, and when it turned towards me, the laughter lingered on his mouth, but his eyes remained alert, watchful, still undecided, as he said lightly: "So much for your introduction to the domestic life of a typical English family!"

"I'm loving it." They held up mirrors to each other, throwing me reflections of themselves that I'd have missed if I'd been alone with either of them. Perhaps, I thought with no means of knowing, that was the magic exerted by a family, they revealed one another in the round. "When does your mother come home?"

"She's in the Cotswolds looking after Caro's two children while she and her husband are on holiday. She's due back on Monday. You'll probably be seeing her."

"I'd like to very much." Emmy Heron had not only loved my mother, entrusted her children to her, but she had known her long before my father had died, while she was still on the far side of the great divide that had cleft her life in two.

When, after half an hour, Sue decided she must be on her way to her flat in Pimlico, I remained where I was, so that when he'd waved her off, he'd have to come back to me. Waiting for him, I collected the cups and piled them on a tray.

"That's very helpful," he said at my shoulder and I thought how silently he moved for a tall man, "even though I'm not quite so inept domestically as Sue would have you believe. She has a habit of visiting her own shortcomings on others."

He directed me through a porch hung with climbing white roses that led into a long high room with shadow-green walls, a darker shade of carpet, and sofas and chairs covered in terracotta linen and heaped with cushions. While he carried the tray through to the kitchen I prowled forward. It was a room in which natural beauty of form had been emphasised rather than embellished, making it extraordinarily restful. Here and there luminous notes of silver attracted the eye. On the pine chimneypiece was a dolphin, so charming that Ross caught me fondling it in my hand as he came through the door.

Guiltily I put it back. "He looks so bursting with joy, like all dolphins should look, that I couldn't help touching him."

"He's the work of Tony Sturgeon, one of our most brilliant designers."

I said clumsily: "I don't know anything about silvercraft, but I'd like to!"

"Would you?" His voice held a query of doubt as though he were deciding whether or not I was being a polite guest. "At the moment, after generations of sticking to the traditional designs, it's in a transitional period, as we test new metals and processes. I inherited the family business from my father, who inherited it from his. My grandfather made every piece he sold. My father had no creative talent, but immense business acumen, and was a near-genius at recognising gifted craftsmen."

"And you?"

"I'd like to believe a combination of both, but I could be deluding myself."

As I turned from the mantelshelf, I saw wedged into a cushion at the back of a chair, a Siamese cat. "Merlin," he said, "sulking for his mistress."

Hearing its name, the cat arched its back, and with one finger I stroked the chocolate hair between his tufted ears. He began to purr deep in his throat.

"He's a woman-cat! It's going to take him quite awhile to adjust to a man permanently around the house."

Was he making polite conversation while waiting for me to go, impatience not showing, but most likely there? I couldn't decide but I remembered he had a dinner-date with a girl called Harriet. Still my finger did not move from the purring cat's silken head. I felt a shiver that was both hope and dread, and spoke quickly before my will faltered. "Can you tell me where Adam Terson lives? Is it in the village?"

A cloud, veiling the sun through the window behind him, put him momentarily in shadow, so that the expression on his face was masked. I stared hypnotically at the cat, counting the seconds of silence, afraid that he would either be evasive or plead ignorance. When the cloud moved and I felt the sun on my own face, I looked up at his, to discover that the wariness, the indecision that had marked it, had vanished. In its place was a deep, pondering concern. "Did you know before you left France that you would find him here?"

"No. But it was he you meant, wasn't it, when you spoke of a missing name?"

"Yes." He waited, using silence as a weapon, or as a measurer of truth, until I could not bear its weight another second, and was driven to pleading. "Please . . . Please . . ."

Suddenly a quirk of a smile touched one corner of his mouth. "Anyone would tell you, so why not me! In the Estate House. It's on the road that follows the river, to your right, out of the courtyard. The name is on the gate."

"Thank you." I hesitated, and then asked: "Is Mrs Terson who keeps the shop in the village a relation?"

"His mother."

He waited for me to ask the next question, and when it would not leave my throat, he volunteered the answer. "His father died when Adam was six."

"His father!" It was a shout of denial. "His father died fifteen years ago."

"Ah," he said with a wry note of satisfaction: "So you have seen him!"

I nodded.

"And talked to him?"

"No, but I will . . ." I stopped, silenced by the sudden sharpening of his look.

"Yes, you will," he said slowly, "and while you're talking to him bear in mind that one of the reasons you were brought here, or came of your own free will, was to wreck his life."

"I don't understand. If that's meant to be a warning, it's wasted. I wouldn't allow it to happen. I'm not here to wreck anyone's life, let alone his."

"No!" He sounded sceptical. "How well do you remember your father?"

"Very well." I gathered my breath. "I remember his funeral. You were there, and when I screamed . . ."

Bitterness touched his face, behind its sadness. "No child of four should have been subjected to such an ordeal. It was inhuman."

"Then why was I? Why did my mother take me?"

"She was insensible with grief. Mother was laid up with pleurisy and couldn't be there to comfort and support her, neither could Father, who was abroad. I was sent as a stand-in. And a damned poor job I made of it."

That he hadn't, I couldn't find words to explain, and I doubt whether he would have welcomed them if I had. I thought with a sense of chill and dislocation how strange it was that we should be standing a couple of feet apart, remembering an identical scene with emotions that had no single note in common.

I lifted my finger from the cat's head, and when he dabbed me with his paw to reclaim my attention, I ignored him, longing to shake myself free of the doubts and innuendoes that clung to me like ghost wraiths from the past.

From the far end of the room the telephone pealed. As he lifted the receiver, he called urgently over his shoulder: "Claudine, wait. Please wait . . . Don't go."

But I didn't wait.

Cars and coaches were pouring through the gates, plus a stream of visitors on foot. I dived in among them, hiding myself in case the telephone call was brief, and he hurried after me. I remembered the inflexion of love with which he spoke his mother's name, the affection in his voice as he'd tried to calm his sister's anxiety. I told myself that the hollow feeling of rejection was a maudlin self-pity, to be dismissed on the instant.

By the time I reached the tunnel the cars, coaches, and pedestrians had drained away. It was cool, shadowy, and empty until I reached the giant beech that guarded its exit. Standing beside it was a thick-set man, with light, almost lemon-coloured, short-cropped hair. The shoulders beneath the open-necked white shirt were powerful, and his stance, feet apart, suggested pugnacity bordering on belligerence. As I passed him I glanced swiftly at his face, noted the chalk-blue eyes fixed on me, then away again, and found my feet hurrying. He could, I reasoned, be anyone: a visitor, an employee whose duty it was to ensure no one was left in the gardens after they were closed to the public, but even so, as the path ahead of me curved, hid me from his sight, I began to run.

7

A BOTTLE OF CHAMPAGNE in an ice bucket and two crystal glasses were set on a low table by Grandmother's side. "Ah, there you are, darling. Let me see how clever you are at opening the champagne. Do it out on the balcony and then if the cork flies, it won't do any damage."

She looked faintly surprised when the cork flew nowhere but into my hand. "Of course," she said with no pleasure, "you were brought up in France. I keep forgetting."

To efface from memory every cankering reminder of my mother? In that she had not once alluded to her, it seemed a reasonable assumption. As she set down her glass, she ran a musing eye over my white jersey dress. "That is a pretty little dress." There was a faint undertone of disparagement in the compliment, before she added in rippling excitement: "Oh, what fun it will be to buy you a whole new wardrobe of clothes!" She narrowed her eyes as though conjuring up a vision of me parading mannequin-fashion in a succession of *grandes ensembles*. Since I was choosy about my clothes and doubtful whether our tastes would coincide, I remained deaf to that first soft knell of warning. Love, pure and unqualified, acts as a soporific on the critical areas of the mind. In any case, the lower strata of mine, as she chatted about my visit to the Herons, asked me which parts of the gardens I had explored, was fixed on the lodestar of the house on the river bank, and breaking in, like a faraway echo was the voice that was now as memorable as the face, commanding me to wait, a command that I had disobeyed, out of fear that it would trample a dream to death, so deny it substance forever.

After a tap on the door, the dark-haired girl with eyelids swollen by a night's weeping I'd seen in the corridor that morning, entered. Grandmother held out her hand, and she placed a packet of cigarettes on her palm. "I was afraid you had forgotten. Claudine, this is Nancy who runs the errands I can no longer run for myself. Nancy, this is my granddaughter."

"How do you do, miss." Her split-second glance revealed a nervy unease. "Shall I undo the packet for you, madam?"

"If you would, Nancy, and take the evidence away with you, there's a good girl."

Nancy tore off the cellophane, removed the overlap of gold foil, wadded them into a small ball which she kept in her hand. Grandmother took four cigarettes, placed three in the initialled silver box, lit the remaining one and put the packet in a pocket in her dress. An exercise in deception that would surely deceive no one, certainly not Aunt Louise.

"I've taken Carlo for his run, and now he's with Mrs Harper. I'll bring him up for his supper at seven, shall I?"

"Yes, please, Nancy. Make sure the liver is warm. Otherwise he won't eat it."

When Nancy had closed the door, she said: "As you may have gathered your aunt is a fanatical anti-smoker, but I have smoked for sixty years, and refuse to be bullied into giving it up. Contrary to the doctrine preached by my son and daughter, it helps to keep me alive, provides brain stimulus if not body food. So to save wearisome arguments, Nancy supplies me with cigarettes to supplement the miserly ration I'm allowed of five a day." Her smile invited me to share her amusement. "Even so, we occasionally get drawn into these little contests of wills."

"Which you always win?"

"Naturally," she said with queen-like serenity. "When you've lived as long as I have your will is either a finely tempered instrument, or so enfeebled as to be worthless. In old age, will and wits are your two best friends."

"At this moment you don't look old." In some extraordinary fashion it was the truth. There was a luminosity about her, an inner zest that in the softening evening light, held age at bay, dimming the memory of the morning's cataclysm of grief.

Her laugh was an enchantment of warm huskiness. "If so, it's because you are here with me." Her voice turned rich with love. "My precious boy's child. A golden child. That's what you are to me."

I laughed, protested: "I'm nearly twenty. Hardly a child!"

"A child!" she teased.

In putting out her cigarette her fingers brushed against the silver box with its blue monogram. She held it out to me. "Ross's Christmas present to me four years ago, when he was teaching himself the technique of enamelling. Now he is one of the most famous enamellers on silver and gold in this country, if not in Europe. Most of his work is bought up by collectors. His most recent is a dinner set with two hundred pieces, for an Arab sheik, his personal setting studded with rubies."

I was more interested in the box in my hand than the extravagance of sheiks. I traced the blue initial. "It's exquisite."

"Of course. He's an artist, a great artist, a superb craftsman." She spoke with emphasis as though I were guilty of underestimating his talent. "By the way, your cousin Marcus has arrived, so you'll be meeting him at dinner. A young man, I'm afraid, who is in no way remarkable. Unfortunately, he has inherited many of the traits of his father, a mediocre little man who married your aunt for her money and as soon as he had lined his pockets deserted her. Marcus . . . well, shall we say he is the type that is doomed to be overlooked in a crowd." She held out her glass for a refill, sipped it, then gave me that richly loving smile. "A fate that is never likely to be yours. You have inherited your father's instant appeal. Do you know what they called him when he was a young man? The Sun King!"

Memory burst over me. For a moment in silence we gazed at the same beloved image. "I can imagine," I said, and I could.

She emptied her glass, passed it back to me. "It is the only wine I drink, so I'm entitled to be a little greedy on this special day. And no one gets drunk on champagne when they've been accustomed to it all their life."

But she became slightly so, in that there was a slackness in her wrist, a vagueness in the focus of her eyes. She talked less, as though she were becoming drowsy, so that the second cigarette I lit for her drooped in her fingers.

I had poured her four glasses, drunk two myself, when Aunt Louise entered, advanced upon the bottle and jerked it out of its nest of ice. "Mama, I ordered Greville to serve half a bottle."

"And I," she enunciated carefully, "ordered him to serve a bottle. Whoever heard of half a bottle of champagne between two!" As Aunt Louise counted the two stubs on the ash tray, opened the lid of the silver box, she added: "You see, I still have three of my day's ration left."

Her daughter's face was a hard clench of anger, but her voice when she spoke was anguished. "Mama, sometimes I think you want to kill yourself."

"On the contrary. Champagne is an excellent tonic for faltering hearts. There are two glasses left, why don't you finish it to celebrate Marcus's arrival home earlier than you expected him?"

My inner ear registered that behind the reasonableness there was a tiny intent of cruelty, but as she stretched out her hand to me, bade me: "Run along, my darling. Have a good dinner and come and see me at ten in the morning, when I hope to have a surprise for you." I chose to ignore it. However fraught and contentious their relationship was, it was no business of mine.

My first impression of Marcus was that my grandmother's description of him had been just. He was no more than medium height, his build slight. His mid-brown hair was of a thinness that left it straggling rattily on his collar. The down-drooping moustache that gave him a look of perpetual melancholy was a disaster, and his brown eyes were of a curiously indeterminate variety that gave no clue to his character. Yet when, a glass in his hand, he crossed the drawing room to greet me, his smile appeared genuinely welcoming. "Cousin Claudine! Good to meet you. You're by way of being a surprise, but a pleasant one."

Trudy sat curled on a sofa, smiled amiably at me and raised her glass. "Hi!"

He gulped down the remainder of his drink. "Just time for one more refill before Greville bangs that blasted gong. Join me?" When I refused, he gave me a mock-comic grimace. "Ah, I forgot, you've been having a state audience with Grandmama. What do you think of the old girl? No, don't tell me. It's too early for you to form a balanced judgment. A day or two hence I'll repeat the question."

As he advanced upon a drinks table, Trudy patted the seat beside her. "Don't take any notice," she said with a fond glance at her husband. "It's a bad habit of his to gabble when he meets strangers."

He turned, gulped from his glass, answered in a slurred voice. "But Claudine isn't a stranger. She's a member of the family. And a very attractive member if I may be allowed a personal compliment."

"Thank you!"

He waved his glass. "That hair, worth a fortune to you!"

"Ginger hair!"

"No," and this time his voice was clear and precise. "Not ginger. Gold. Pure gold." His glance reached for his wife's. "Wouldn't you confirm that, pussycat, pure gold!"

Her answer, if she gave any, was drowned in the hullabaloo of Greville beating the gong.

At dinner Aunt Louise was transformed, the irritation, maybe the pain, she'd been subjected to, ironed away; the reason plain to see: the presence of her son, on whom she poured a passion of love that amounted to idolatry. It must have influenced her fingers while she dressed her hair. It was looser, allowed to follow its natural wave, and her pale lips were touched with lipstick.

But how agonisingly she fussed over him! Why was his appetite so poor? Of course he was tired after the flight, but was he certain he was not sickening for flu? Wasn't there an epidemic rife in West Germany?

Marcus parried her questions with an adroitness I guessed he'd learned as a schoolboy. He could hardly explain that he was suffering from a hangover that rendered speech an effort, eating purgatory and even a smile a calculated act of will.

Trudy tossed in balls of chitchat whenever she found an opening, in an attempt to deflect his mother's overburdening concern, but with little success.

Uncle Conwyn, picking finically at his food, informed me of the exact number of admission tickets that had been issued that afternoon, and the sum of the takings in the pottery shop. Then, adopting a crisp, schoolmasterly manner he took me to task. Why had I run away before he could sketch me a plan of the gardens? Further, he hectored, I had forgotten to buy postcards from the shop. For the sake of harmony, I apologised; whereupon he informed me, as though granting me an enormous favour, that he had bought me a selection and would give them to me, plus the stamps, after dinner.

He did not demand to know how I'd spent my afternoon, which

left me with a niggling suspicion that he knew where I'd been. Yet how could he have kept track of me and sold his horrible mugs and ash trays? Unless there were other servants, outdoor ones who, as devoted to him as Greville, had kept a watch on me. Even in relation to Uncle Conwyn, with his chronically unstable nerves, quickness to take offence—which suggested, maybe, an incipient persecution complex—that was surely too farfetched a theory!

When we went into the drawing room for coffee, he excused himself. As he did not partake—he actually used that word—of coffee, and after a fatiguing afternoon, he would retire to his private wing.

Aunt Louise after, despite his pleas, pouring an extra lashing of cream into her son's coffee, which he could not bring to pass his lips, hurried away to make sure Mama had all she required, promising to return within half an hour.

"Relax!" Trudy comforted her husband. "Take five deep breaths and you'll feel better." She glanced at me. "She can't help it, you know. It's a typical mother-only-son syndrome. That's why we're going to have a minimum of four children. Takes the heat off them."

"Claudine," Marcus said, suddenly coming to a semblance of life, "is an only child."

"I'd forgotten. So you were. Did your mother dote on you, make you her *raison d'être,* or did she let you do your own thing?"

"More or less. She was rather a self-sufficient person."

"Lucky you!" She regarded her husband with amused concern. His head was pressed into a cushion, his eyes closed. "Poor darling, that's what flying does to him, wears him out. While he's napping, I better go and take a peep at Marco. Nancy is off-duty. What about you?"

As I'd been waiting for this hour since early morning I knew precisely where I was going. "I think I'll go for a walk."

"Well, don't get lost. Greville bars and bolts front and back doors at ten-thirty sharp. And if his knees are playing him up, I've known him to get cracking on the job by ten."

There was a board on the open farm gate with the name. Beyond was a ruler-straight tarmac drive, enclosed on both sides by fields on which sheep grazed, so that I advanced towards the house with nothing to impede my view and equally nothing to screen me if someone was looking through one of its windows.

It was a medium-sized flat-faced house, built of the same smooth grey-yellow stone as Saffron, the grazing land flush with its walls, without so much as an inch of garden. Behind it, spreading its grey sapless branches like tentacles over the roof was a spectre-like tree that must have been blasted to death by lightning or struck by disease. Even on a summer night, the air heavy with the day's heat, the house gave forth a chill and unwelcoming air.

I raised the iron knocker, let it fall, though the emptiness within proclaimed itself to me. No one answered, and after the echo of my knock had faded, the stillness was so absolute I could hear the sheep's teeth tearing at the grass. The casement windows were all tight shut. My peerings between the curtains revealed a hall, a functional kitchen and two sitting rooms. The first, conventionally furnished as a dining room had the appearance of disuse.

The other was a living room. A desk was piled with files, and when the open shelves along one wall had proved inadequate for the stock of books, the overflow was stacked on the floor at the foot of a sumptuous black leather armchair. And on a low table, within arm's reach of the chair were some thick account books, newspapers, and an assortment of ball-point pens.

I stood, my nose pressed against the pane for a long time, committing to memory the pattern of the room. Any home tells tales about the character and tastes of its owner. My mother's house, with its locked gate, high blank fence, the calculated simplicity within was, for those with eyes to see, at once a proclamation of her fanatical need for privacy, plus a contempt for possessions for which she had no use.

The room without the grace of a picture or an ornament revealed it was not prized by its owner. Also, that unless he sat his visitors on upright chairs, he did not entertain in his own home.

I tried the doors of the double garage. They were locked. I sat on the shallow doorstep, my arms clenched round my knees, where I had a view of the lane that kept company with the river in both directions so that he could not take me by surprise. As the brightness ebbed from the sky, the dream began to repossess me: the sun-dappled wood, the slow-dawning smile that was like a blessing.

Nine, half-past, and at ten o'clock, when the sky attained a depth of blue nearer to night than day, I pulled myself up from the step where I'd sat so long my legs ached with cramp. A dozen paces along the tarmac, I turned about, and for the space of two seconds I saw a hand at an upper window holding the net curtains apart, what I was almost but not quite sure was a woman's face, before the curtain was released and the window became opaque.

Against reason—since no one had approached the house since I arrived, so whoever was there must have heard and ignored my knocking—I raced back, hammered on the door. No one answered. And though I bent my head against it, I could detect no sound within. The sight had been no more than having a card flashed before your eyes. I could not guess whether the woman had been young or old, but there had been darkness not light about her head, so that her hair had been black or brown. But whoever it was had seen me coming down the drive, let me sit like a beggar on the doorstep rather than admit me to the house. But not him. That I would not believe. A friend, maybe a servant, but not him.

When I reached the lighted courtyard, I could just see by the hands of my watch that it was 10:25. Not wanting to keep Greville out of bed, I ran towards the door, but it was ajar and I found myself thrown forward into the hall.

Uncle Conwyn grabbed my shoulder, wrenched me upright, holding his face so near mine that its white clenched fury momentarily stunned me. "Where have you been? What do you mean by staying out until all hours of the night? I repeat, where have you been?"

The shock of being literally manhandled for the first time in my life, gave me strength to shake him off. "I went for a walk. I didn't know I needed to ask permission before I left the house."

"A walk to see whom?" In the shadowed hall, his pale eyes were made almost luminous with ferocity. "I'll tell you. A devil. For that is what he is, a force of evil that seeks to destroy this house and those who live in it. A devil who . . ." The intensity of his rage had stolen his breath, left him gasping.

His appalling loss of control fixed mine back in place. "I went for a walk during which I saw no one and spoke to no one."

"But not for want of trying. You made it perfectly plain this afternoon whom you wished to see. So he wasn't at home?"

"No."

"But you'll try again."

"Yes."

"Dip your fingers into pitch, the devil's pitch."

Suddenly I lost patience with his hysteria. "We don't have to spell it out. I'm not a child . . ."

He interrupted. "That is precisely what you are, an ignorant, stupid child!"

I recalled the psychiatric clinic, his history of nervous breakdowns, and wondered uneasily whether he was on the brink of another.

"Besides which," he said with extraordinary irrelevance, "I told you that I would see you later to give you your postcards and stamps. Where was I supposed to find you?"

Partly to relieve the tension under which he was labouring, and partly because I was desperately anxious to escape, I apologised twice over. I'd forgotten, and I was sorry. Out of my eye corner I could see a batch of postcards, stamps clipped to a sheet of paper, on a half-moon table against the wall panelling. I told myself except in so far as I was a guest in a house of which he was a quasi master, he held no mite of authority over me. I walked to the table, picked up the stamps and postcards, thanked him again, and began climbing the stairs. When I was three treads from the bottom, he called my name. I turned.

His voice was cold with menace. "You'll serve your ends better by heeding my advice than flouting it. Remember it was I who brought you here. Where is your gratitude?"

"I'm not likely to forget that you fed and educated me, kept a roof over my head. I'll pay you back in money, but in nothing else. As for ends to serve, I haven't any that can be furthered by you or anyone else living in this house."

"You're mistaken. I have the power to place you where your mother wished you to be."

Tremors of shock undermined my calm. I heard myself shout: "What do you mean? How do you know what she wanted for me?"

That he'd touched a raw nerve, put a smile back on his face. "Go to bed," he said as to a child. "And think over what I've said."

"You're forbidding me to speak to my father's son!"

He enunciated slowly: "Your father's bastard who has plotted the downfall of every Delamain since he was old enough to set himself to the task. And that includes you."

I turned my back on him and mounted the stairs. It was an ugly scene on which to end the day. All right, I accepted that he was subject to nerve storms and, at times, tumbled off his mental balance, leaving hate and prejudice to overrule reason. My mother . . . but to believe his boast was to play into his hands which were unclean. I shut him out of my mind. And yet, as I lay in bed, I found my limbs shaking, and it was after midnight when I fell asleep. When drowsiness came at last, for comfort, in my last waking moment, I promised myself that I would make another pilgrimage to the house on the river bank in the morning, early, say six o'clock, before he left it. But I was woken by Marco crying in the night, the opening and shutting of doors, Aunt Louise's voice, held to an undertone but still penetrating.

When sleep came a second time, I overslept and was ten minutes late arriving at the breakfast table. Since no one else appeared, it did not matter.

I tapped on the door and when there was no answer, I opened it. The saffron velvet chair was empty, and as I looked questioningly towards the wide-open windows, I saw him, standing by the parapet, feeding two turtle doves with grain. Grandmother, lying in her bamboo *chaise-longue* watched him. The absolute silence communicated to me a wondrous ease so that on an instant I was saturated with a joy more profound than any I'd ever known.

It was Carlo who shattered the tableau. Tail waving, he danced towards me. The speckled turtle doves, with their white-rimmed tail feathers took flight, and Grandmother turned, held out a hand. She was wearing dark glasses against the shimmering sun, so that as I bent to kiss her, her eyes were hidden from me.

"Now, I must introduce you. Claudine, this is Adam Terson, the mastermind and hand of Saffron. Come, Adam, and meet my granddaughter, Claudine."

He obeyed, that was the verb that flashed through my head, not with gladness, but on a command issued by his mistress, and so cast the first flicker of shadow over my joy. He was even taller than he'd seemed at a distance, leaner too, whip-thin. When he held out his hand, my nerve broke, and I found I could not look up into his face. His voice was strong and even toned but without the depth and resonance for which I'd hoped. "Welcome to Saffron, Miss Delamain. I hope you're going to be happy here."

What did I reply? Probably no more than thank you.

When he'd placed a chair for me by her side, he said to Grandmother: "If we could just get the Farrant issue settled."

"It is. A quarter's notice, and Mrs Farrant arriving here with two babies in a perambulator, won't have the slightest effect on my decision. You might pass the word along to save her a wasted effort."

"He'll certainly plead sickness, produce a doctor's certificate. It may not be easy even with a quarter's notice to evict him."

"Sick, of course he's sick. Anyone who gets drunk seven nights a week is sick." She made an irritated gesture. "So deal with it first thing in the morning." She took my hand, placed it under her own. "After we've had a cup of coffee together, Adam is going to take you on a tour of the estate. Not the gardens, we'll explore those together, but the farms, the parkland, and the woods. He knows every yard, practically every tree. That's true, isn't it, Adam?"

"I hope so." And though she'd smiled at him, he didn't smile back. The likeness and dislikeness between the two men confused me, so that I was lost between the shadow and the substance.

"I particularly want you to show Claudine the waterfall her grandfather discovered. It was one of his favourite places. Where he used to sit and work out his problems."

His glance turned in my direction but did not link with it. "Will eleven o'clock suit you?"

I said it would be fine.

"I'll be waiting for you in the Land-Rover in the courtyard."

At that moment Nancy entered with the coffee tray. He took it from her and placed it on the table by Grandmother's side. For a split second, their eyes met in a hooded, secret glance, and I knew, by some sixth sense that contained no shred of proof, that it was she who had been behind that half-drawn curtain last night. I wondered if it was he who'd driven her to cry half the night away.

Alone, Grandmother asked, as I put the coffee cup beside her hand: "Now tell me what you made of Marcus?"

"I only met him over dinner when he was completely exhausted by his flight. So tired, that he could hardly keep awake."

"For a young man in his twenties he is remarkably deficient in energy. A misfortune, not wholly of his own making. Energy is born in one. But a certain amount can be cultivated. Fatigue, like over-indulgence in alcohol, is a vice."

I did not believe that she cared one way or another for my opinion of Marcus. The introduction of his name was either a delaying tactic or a smokescreen. I was not inclined to let her get away with either. Yet, to avoid embarrassing her, even cause her pain, I sought to find words that would do neither.

"Has Adam Terson been your estate manager for long?"

"Three years. After leaving school he went to agricultural college, then did a course in farm management, followed by two years in charge of a large estate in Norfolk."

A purely factual statement that caused her no shadow of embarrassment. She kept her dark glasses focused on the turtle doves who had returned to their scattered grain, her profile turned to me, ivory except for the brush of rose on her lips.

Very slowly she moved her head, a whisper of a smile touching her mouth, as though she could see through the dark glasses into my head, and was highly diverted by what she read. She said with precise articulation: "He is highly skilled. I value his services. Furthermore, we are good friends." The smile widened into outright amusement at my expense. "Does that satisfy your curiosity?"

Was she implying that she knew and forgave? Or that she blindly refused to know? Motivated by supreme magnanimity or a depthless love for a son she had lost? Did she know or care that another son counted him a master of evil? Suddenly I had a sense of treading water so deep that it was bottomless, plus a stupidity in myself to analyse a situation that was probably simplicity itself to everyone else.

Before I could answer, she gave that entrancing husky laugh. "Don't fret, my darling child. Human relations are complex. Only the years teach you how to understand and handle them. And you haven't lived long enough."

I turned my head as I heard footsteps crossing the room, and saw a stout middle-aged man, with a bright pink complexion.

Grandmother looked round the chair, exclaimed pettishly: "Charles! Who sent for you on a Sunday morning?"

"No one. It's merely a social call."

"During which you'll take my blood pressure and pulse and send me a bill for the privilege! Well, I suppose now you're here, I'll have to put up with you. This is my granddaughter, Claudine. Darling, this is Dr Knox, who has the most abominable bedside manner of any doctor I've ever met."

He shook my hand, gave me a shrewd glance, but no smile, though his face suggested good temper rather than the reverse.

"At least you look nice and healthy," he remarked, "not much hope of you as a prospective patient."

"I'm afraid not. I haven't been ill since I had measles when I was twelve."

I looked at my watch. As it was five minutes to eleven, I took my leave of them.

In the courtyard the Land-Rover and its driver were waiting for me.

8

GLANCE FIXED IN SOME VAGUE MIDDLE-DISTANCE, he cupped my elbow to boost me on to the high bench seat. "I'm sorry the inside is a bit mucky. If I'd had longer notice, I'd have had it cleaned out."

I said it didn't matter. His air of stubborn ungivingness, as though he were committed to a penance, was intimidating. I had to fight to get the words out of my mouth. "Couldn't we forget the drive, just go somewhere and talk?" As he got in behind the wheel, I watched the smile break on his face, not the one I'd seen in my dream, but one of angry scorn. I challenged: "Surely, you'll admit we've got to talk."

"You're not interested in a grand tour of Saffron?"

"Not in the least."

"Then why the hell are you here?"

"To see an old woman who wanted to see me." Through the window I caught a glimpse of Trudy pushing the perambulator through the hall. She posed a threat of delay, an involvement that, in that moment of suspense, I couldn't stomach. "Grandmother mentioned a waterfall . . . I've a picture of it at home. Couldn't we go and see it?"

"Okay, if that's what you want."

After the first mile, which led us back over the route I'd travelled in Friday's storm, we cut down a deep-rutted track where thickets of young saplings whipped across the bonnet, until we emerged into a clearing where there was only a solitary oak, and the ground under the tyres was made uneven by a natural paving of smooth rocks.

When he switched off the engine, I heard the sound of rushing water. Without waiting for him to let me out, I jumped down, left him to follow me or wait, for the moment uncaring which course he chose. I ran across the slabs, following the line of the pulsing stream, and when I reached a cascade of water that threw itself over six feet of jagged rock, I slowed my pace round a curve of the bank, so that I could sit at its feet.

In the sunlight his form behind me threw a shadow over the water. "A touching picture of ancestor worship! Well, does it match up to your painting?"

I answered factually. "In the picture there are trees, an impression of a ruin in the background."

"Artistic licence. A bit of faking."

I stood up, brushed some shreds of moss from my skirt, and now that the crisis of disappointment was behind me, found it possible to look into his face. The wide-spaced cobalt blue eyes were slightly narrowed, and his mouth was a twist of irony. "You don't have to tell me. You hated him, didn't you?"

For a moment the silence between us hung suspended like a high wave that was never going to break, and then he shrugged. "Hate's not the word I'd use, but it will serve for the moment. How old are you?"

"Nineteen."

He scoffed: "With a hang-up about your father who's been dead and buried for fifteen years, obsessed with a child's sugary notion of finding a long-lost stepbrother, who incidentally has never been lost, the setting the background of a picture dear old Dad painted! In this day and age!"

At least the end had been mercifully quick, like a decapitation. "Quite ridiculous!"

Then, when it was too late, he gave me a smile that was near enough to the one I remembered to revive sufficient life to sustain anguish. "Maybe we'd better get a few hard truths established. To you, our father was an idealised daddy-figure. To me he was a man who bought himself out of trouble, or blackmailed his parents into doing it for him. In your memory enshrined, in mine a father who took pains never to be on a street where there was a remote likelihood of his setting eyes on his illegitimate offspring and if, as happened once or twice, he got his timing wrong, he'd deliberately make his eyes blind to the sight of me."

"You're saying he was heartless and cruel to his own child?"

"Cruel? Not according to his lights. And I'm not questioning his heart, only his moral courage. It was a minus quality with him. But he'd enough judgment never to get himself embroiled in a battle he couldn't win. So far as the Delamain code of conduct was concerned, they did not shirk their responsibility. By the time I was six months old, my mother owned the village shop in which she had been employed as an assistant, and her shiftless, impotent husband was relieved of the pretence of looking for work. And I knew my father, at least by sight." He gave a crow of laughter. "He was a great horseman, had what was known as a magnificent seat. Thanks to mechanisation

I've never had to have any truck with the brutes. He put me off horses for life!"

"But it didn't put you off being a paid employee of your grandmother!"

"Ah!" He drew out the syllable with relish. "According to your rule book I should have emigrated on a free passage to Canada or New Zealand, ceased to offend the Delamain clan by my obnoxious presence! But I'm my mother's son as well as my father's. She comes into the picture too. Maybe that's why you went and took a look at her the day after you arrived at Saffron?"

"I went into the shop to buy some stamps and postcards. I saw her but I didn't know who she was, not then."

"Well, you do now." He paused, went on less contentiously: "Coincidence, or rather timing played a part. When I'd obtained the right degrees, the practical experience, old Henderson decided to retire. I applied for the job, got it. It was as simple as that."

Did he expect me to believe the tale he told? Henderson must have been ageing, the date of his retirement known in the village, certainly to his mother. I couldn't doubt that his training had been dovetailed to coincide with the old man's departure. "And Grandmother gave you the job? Why, if she'd never accepted you before?"

"Again, timing. Her husband was lately dead. She was free of his domination, her own mistress, motivated by reason and unreason—like all women. So far as the qualifications went, I came out top of the short list. Also she wasn't averse to administering a premeditated kick in the teeth to her children and grandson. A public show of who held the whip hand, and they'd better not assume too much too soon. Maybe, too, a spot of comfort in her old age, in that in looks I remind her of a son whose fatal weaknesses she chooses to forget. Okay, I agree it's an unusual relationship in that she has never admitted in words I'm her grandson, but it survives. You could even say it flourishes." He turned a hardening glance on me. "Or it did until Friday. Now I have a rival, a girl who was born a Delamain. So what now?" He quipped: "If we'd been cousins, she could have married us off, and all her problems and ours would have been solved."

"What problems? There are none for me. I'm a visitor passing through, not a threat to your expectations or anyone else's when Grandmother dies."

"So that's your cover story, is it?"

"Not a cover story. The truth." For the moment I'd had all I could take. "If you'll go back to the Land-Rover, I'll join you in a few minutes."

He opened his mouth to protest, then thought better of it, and I heard his feet retreating over the rock slabs. I chose a point where I could look back on the silver-blue waterfall, sat on the bank, with the river swirling at my feet. For an isolated moment, it seemed all I had: a picture of a waterfall. I bent my head, pressed my fingers hard into my eyeballs, willing another picture to paint itself in my head. In a little while it did, and in imagination I pulled down the swing ladder and climbed into my attic studio.

When I was sure my calm would not crack under pressure, I walked back over the rock slabs. He came halfway to meet me, and when we were only a single pace apart, he turned about, slid his arm casually about my shoulder.

"I'm sorry I've let you down with a bang, though it is your own silly fault. I've no desire, God knows, to be a reincarnation of my father, but if it had been in my power to become him for twenty-four hours for your sake, I'd have had a damned good try. But not a hope. So you had to find out the hard way. And, honestly, wasn't it all a bit naïve?"

A need, not a dream, that had burst from the innermost depths of the heart. I forced myself to mock what he called naïveté. "All right, I admit I was guilty of sentimentalising. But I've got myself straightened out now, so we can forget it."

"Good! Having cleared that up, shall we get a few other facts straight? Rumour has it that Conwyn ran you to earth somewhere in France, shortly after your mother died, hijacked you to Saffron. True or false?"

"Nothing so dramatic as a hijack. A simple invitation to visit my grandmother, which I accepted. If, as has been suggested, I was persuaded to come to Saffron to fill a vacuum, I had no idea one existed."

His head swivelled, his glance so sharply suspicious my feigned lightheartedness faltered. "And what's that supposed to mean?"

"Grandmother lost a nurse-companion she was fond of, a girl who was drowned."

His hand dropped from my shoulder. "You have a quick ear for gossip, little stepsister."

"Not gossip. Grandmother showed me her photograph. You must have known her."

"Naturally." I felt the weight of his sideways glance. "Isn't it a coincidence that you and her brother should arrive at Saffron simultaneously? A two-pronged attack?"

"An attack on what?"

"The truth. Whether or not the coroner's jury arrived at it."

"Do you think they did?"

"I was an interested party, one of the suspects, so my opinion's worthless."

His aim had been to shock me. Now he was waiting for my reaction, so I was careful not to reveal it. He pressed: "Have you and Andrews been hobnobbing?"

"I've not seen him, let alone exchanged a word with him, but I've been warned not to let Grandmother hear that he is around."

"Who warned you?"

"Uncle Conwyn."

"Ah, Conwyn!" he drawled. "Someone should have put you wise before you accepted his protection. If the ice cracks beneath him, which it is liable to do, he'll abandon you to your fate. So how do you propose to handle the situation? What are your battle plans, little sister?" Alongside the Land-Rover he stopped and we stood face to face, scrutinising each other. His words had been scoffing, his expression deadly serious.

"I haven't any battle plans. I don't need them. You may find this hard to believe, but I covet nothing. But you do, don't you?"

The words exploded out of his mouth. "Yes, by God I do! The earth as far as my eyes can reach." He didn't bother to hide his single-track concentration on a solitary objective; maybe it was beyond his power to do so. "I've earned it. I love it. Can you think up two better reasons?"

"No."

He laughed: "Not the argumentative type, are you? If your disinterest isn't a cover up, what do you propose to do with your life when this so-called 'visit' comes to an end? Return to France and marry some handsome young Frenchman who's pining for you this minute?"

"Wrong guess."

For the first time he grinned with amusement, and for a split second my heart moved before it steadied. "It was a logical assumption. You're quite a smasher, you know. I don't wonder Hermione laid her heart at your feet. But there's a payoff. So don't delude yourself you're going to make a quick get-away, always presuming you want to. She'll work every trick in the book to keep you. If you thwart her, she'll play her ace. Induce a heart attack, so that the house sinks into silence except for whispers as they tiptoe over the carpet to moisten her lips with brandy."

"Are you honestly as callous as that!"

"Not callous, you little innocent, a realist. I've seen her pull that trick with Lorraine."

The inflection as he spoke her name alerted my ear. Not quite tenderness, but some emotion not far from it. "Twice, and on each occasion it was when Lorraine announced she intended to leave Saffron. But no conscientious nurse, and Lorraine was one, abandons a dying patient."

"It wouldn't work with me. All else apart, I've my living to earn."

"Really!" he mocked. "No nice little pension from Uncle Conwyn! How do you propose to do it? No, let me guess. Except it isn't a guess. Where else would you want to tread but in the old man's footsteps: paint! Let's hope you're a better artist than he was. He wasn't all that good, you know. Or didn't you?"

I'd known for years. I was a better judge of the merit of my father's pictures than he was, but I didn't have to prove it to him. "Not a painter." I spoke in the present tense instead of the future which was bending the truth. "I'm a fashion designer."

"Well, I hope, provided you're given the chance, you're a successful one. But I wouldn't bet a penny on it, your being given the chance, I mean. Either you walked innocently into a trap, or Conwyn Delamain lured you into it. Either way, you're caught. It would be interesting to learn what sort of deal you two cooked up between you, but I'd be wasting my breath by asking, so keep your little secrets. One day they'll all come crawling out of their holes."

"There wasn't a deal."

He laughed in my face. "As if you'd admit it . . . to me!" His eye ran lightly over me. "You have the unmistakable air of a girl who's been delicately and expensively raised. How did your mother achieve that? I always understood that the Delamains literally cast her and her child into the snow without a penny piece. So who paid for you to acquire your pretty airs and graces?"

"She was clever with money, naturally thrifty like most Frenchwomen. We managed. Why should it concern you how we managed?"

"Because I have a future to protect; consequently everything that affects it, including you, concerns me. Let's lay it on the line, shall we? Either you are for me or against me. So, little half-sister, which are you, friend or foe? Have you the guts to admit which?"

"If it were true, I'd hardly be likely to, would I? As it's not true, I'm neither. Why should you assume I am?"

"That's the history of Saffron. Permanent battlelines, constant forays. An advantage won there, another lost. So, are you either for me and against yourself. Or for yourself and against me?"

"If I'm honest, I'm for myself, everyone is to a degree. But that doesn't mean I'm against you." And that curiously was the truth. I had survived a bitter-as-gall disappointment, a shattering revelation of my naïve sentimentality, arrived at a point of acceptance. "You can't turn me into a rival or an enemy however much you try!"

"No?" he queried. "Then you're a very rare animal indeed. To most women power is like drink. It flies straight to their heads, intoxicates them. Take Hermione, she's a past mistress of the power game. You say you're not interested. I'd like to believe you. But I don't, not with Conwyn backing you." He opened the door of the Land-Rover. I looked down into his face, he up into mine. We shared a long-drawn-out moment of crisis, a silent duel of wills. I saw a face washed clean of mockery, suspicion, even the glint of cruelty that I'd learned was part of his make-up stripped down to the hard bone of vaunting ambition that only death would destroy.

"So," he said matter-of-factly, "is this where we say goodbye?"

"Won't I see you feeding the turtle doves?"

For the second time he gave me a smile that was a near match to the one that had kept me company for fifteen years, then I stamped out a sentiment that belonged to a dead past. "Maybe, but we can hardly get to know one another chaperoned by Hermione and two turtle doves!" He considered. "Would you be prepared to sup with the devil and throw the enemy into such disarray, you might well have cause to regret it?"

"You mean Uncle Conwyn would disapprove?"

"Strongly."

"How about Grandmother?"

"God knows! You need second sight to divine her motives. Deep and dark, subject to whirlwinds of change. Sometimes there is no motive, it's no more than a game she plays. Other times she dices with human lives. Well, what's your answer?"

"You'd be prepared to feed your enemy?"

"Yes, as a once-in-a-lifetime experiment."

"All right. When do you suggest?"

"Wednesday. I'll pick you up at seven."

We smiled at one another as freely as though there were trust between us, acting out a lie. But for me it was only a half lie in that the idealised image had been replaced by a living human being as compensation for a dream one I'd lost.

The door of my room was ajar. Through it I heard a peremptory male voice demand: "Surely, Mr Delamain, you're not questioning my right to pursue my investigations into my sister's death?"

"Certainly not, but it is my duty to warn you, yet again, that you are wasting your time. Your enquiries will yield no more information than is already recorded on the police files and the transcript of the inquest."

"I hardly count time spent on establishing the exact circumstances of my sister's death as wasted!"

Uncle Conwyn, who, for him, seemed to be maintaining a remarkable calm, gave an audible sigh. "You have already been informed of the circumstances by me, my sister, and the police. You have taken possession of Lorraine's personal effects and her car. This was her room which you expressed a wish to see. You have examined it. No obstacles have been put in the way of your interrogating the inside and outside staff. There is no relevant fact that has been withheld from you. So now, Mr Andrews, I must ask you to leave."

Rather than be caught ignominiously eavesdropping, I stepped into the room and came face to face with the human watchdog who had posted himself at the end of the tunnel. Thick-set not with fat but with muscle, square-shouldered, with short-cropped light hair covering a bullethead, his face a reddish tan, with chalk-blue eyes glinting between the lemon-yellow lashes. My first impression of pugnacity and aggression was underlined.

His hard glare flicked over me betraying no sign of recognition. "I don't think I've had the pleasure of meeting this young lady."

"My niece, Claudine Delamain, who arrived from France two days ago. She never met your sister and has nothing to contribute to this discussion."

"But you'll have heard talk of my sister's death, Miss Delamain? She was found drowned in the river below that window, despite the fact that she was a champion swimmer."

"Yes. My grandmother told me. I'm very sorry . . ."

Uncle Conwyn cut in: "Mr Andrews . . ."

"Mr Delamain," he cut back with heavy sarcasm. "I appreciate your desire to sweep your house clean, to absolve your family and staff of any suspicion of foul play. Also your anxiety that your old mother should not be subjected to the distress of learning that the file on my sister's death is not, as she believes, closed."

"The file is closed."

"There's only one person with authority to close it and that is me. There is still half an hour before you people eat what you call luncheon. So let's use it to run over a few proven facts. My sister was off-duty the day she died. She spent the morning having a lie-in. After lunch she drove in her car to Hastings to visit a friend, Rosemary Scott, who was employed as a staff nurse at the hospital there. That's on record in your testimony to the police. She did not garage her car when she arrived at the house but left it outside in the courtyard. Then, because the front door is bolted from the inside, she should have used her key to open the middle french window of the drawing room. But she never reached that window. She either walked, or was persuaded to walk along the path that skirts the river."

He raised a pudgy hand, splayed his fingers and counted them off. "Point one, no nurse of the name of Rosemary Scott is employed by the East Sussex Hospital Board. According to your testimony she rented a furnished flat in Hastings or St Leonard's. A search, widespread publicity, has failed to locate her."

"Lorraine only mentioned her name casually. It is possible we misheard it."

"Or made it up! Point two, why, on a bitterly cold night, when there had been a fall of snow, did my sister choose to promenade along the river bank, instead of going directly to the drawing-room door?"

"We can't know, only conjecture. The probability is that she slipped, knocked her head and fell unconscious into the moat."

"Point three, my sister was exceptionally sure-footed, in excellent physical shape. And if, by mischance, she'd found herself in such a predicament as you describe, she'd have got herself out of it, or raised such a hell of a racket that someone would have heard her and come to her rescue."

"If she was, as the report on the post-mortem suggested, unconscious when she fell into the moat, she could neither have scrambled out, nor called for help." He paused, then added with an assumption of delicacy: "Having seen the report you will know that the alcohol level in her blood, while not high enough to prohibit her from driving was . . ."

Mr Andrews said menacingly: "You're saying my sister was a drunk?"

"Indeed not. I'm merely suggesting that to leave a warm car for the freezing night air, when you've taken even one drink, can slow down anyone's reactions."

"Are you! By all accounts there was some sort of relationship going on between you and my sister. I don't find the notion palatable, even credible, but since you professed to have some feeling for her, how comes it that you're prepared to stand there and malign a girl who can't speak up for herself? In my language that makes you sort of a rat."

His face stiffened into a frozen mask. "I have no intention of exchanging insults with you, Mr Andrews. Perhaps you would be good enough to leave." He walked to the door, held it open.

Bernard Andrews did not stir. "Off the premises by 12:45. Those were the orders I received from your sister. Okay, I don't aim to distress an old lady with a dicky heart . . . not unless you drive me to it. Meanwhile, there's one fact you should know. Although Lorraine and I hadn't met for four years, that didn't mean we'd lost touch. We corresponded regularly. Three or four times a year we'd telephone each other. What I'm saying is that her life here wasn't, as you appear to believe, a closed book to me. For instance, in her last letter, she said she had a suspicion someone was keeping a tag on her. Some sort of private eye, she hinted, checking where she spent her days off. That's not in any statements your family made to the police. I've got no record of the telephone calls, but I have the letters, Mr Delamain. Or photostat copies. The originals are with my solicitor in London."

He gave me a half nod. "Good day, Miss Delamain. To you, Mr Delamain, it's *au revoir*." He strode out of the room with the air of a man well pleased with himself.

My uncle stared with an hypnotic gaze at the door, then, with an effort, he wrenched his eyes away from it, fixed them on me. "You're to wipe from your mind every word you've heard. I make allowances for the shock Andrews has suffered, the fact that he seemingly finds solace in his bereavement by vilifying me and other members of the family. But there are no grounds for his suspicions, and in due course he will be driven to accept that fact."

I looked at the rose curtains that enclosed the bed. "This was Lorraine's room?"

He answered shortly. "When Nurse Hailey arrived your grandmother preferred that she be accommodated in another room, so the bell was moved. But it was her wish that it should be made ready for you."

The shock was irrational, the drag of superstition mortifying. Both had been triggered off by sheer surprise in that I hadn't known this had been Lorraine's room. Even so, as I moved towards the dressing table, it was her image that looked back at me, not my own.

I had my back turned, when he stepped forward, accused: "So you disregarded my orders, spent the morning with Terson?"

Now it was his face that appeared beside mine in the mirror. I'd guessed his age at about fifty, but I could have added another twenty years. I didn't waste effort on speculating, yet again, whether he'd kept a watch on me, or hired someone else to do it for him. "Grandmother introduced us, asked him to drive me to the waterfall my father painted. His father too . . ."

"He has a mother, don't forget, who was the village slut."

"And a grandmother who thinks highly of him." With an effort I quietened my voice. "I can't understand what all the fuss is about. He lives a quarter of a mile away, presumably he spends a good proportion of his day about the estate. No one who knew my father could doubt he was his son. Even if Grandmother hadn't stage-managed a meeting between us, you hadn't a hope of preventing us from knowing each other. So why the melodrama? The senseless mystery?"

A curious tremor passed over his face, as though the mirror were a sheet of flowing water. I twisted about as it was steadying, and for a split second we stared directly at each other. Like lightning, suspicion shot through my head, hardened into certainty: some plan he'd made had slipped out of his control. Only deep panic could have induced that tremor.

"Why?" I repeated.

Without giving me an answer, he turned, left the room, so extending the areas of distrust between us that were fast becoming impenetrable. He deserved pity, but I'd none to give him; the alienation between us was now total.

9

DURING SUNDAY LUNCH no reference was made to my meeting with Adam. Yet except for Uncle Conwyn, whose face still wore a ghost-like aftermath of the eruption of hate that had torn him apart in my bedroom, they kept a covert watch on me, the questions printed on their eyes. Towards the end of the meal I began to imagine that Greville's gaze was more often focused on me than on anyone else.

Aunt Louise fretted because Marco had developed a cough and upbraided Trudy who, though she had known Dr Knox was in the house, had not summoned him to examine the baby. Imperturbable as ever, Trudy replied airily that Marco's temperature was normal but, as a precaution, she would rub his chest before he went to bed.

As Greville served the ice pudding, Grandmother asked whether, as Chandler was still indisposed, Marcus would drive the two of us through the gardens to the orchid house? She had already telephoned Rigson, the head gardener, ordering him to meet her there at 5 o'clock.

"Are you sure you can trust me with the Daimler?"

She ignored the sarcasm. "I don't see why not. You're a competent driver, and you won't meet any oncoming traffic."

Predictably Aunt Louise reacted by a flurry of anxiety. "Mama, you know that Dr Knox forbids you to climb the stairs more than once a day."

Grandmother's reply was not so much unkind as disregarding. "At my age permit me to be the expert on my own body. I assure you I shall be none the worse for a short drive. If, when I reach the orchid house, I'm too feeble to climb out of the car, Rigson can show Claudine the Pink Queen. And I promise you that no one will have to carry me upstairs."

The Daimler was royal purple, its interior dove grey and walnut. Marcus helped Grandmother in, spread a sable lap rug over her knees. As he returned to his seat behind the wheel, she leaned forward to check that the glass panel separating the car into two compartments was shut, sealing us in a privacy from which Marcus was excluded.

As we climbed through the blazing fire of the massed scarlet and pink rhododendrons, her glance, vibrant with impatience, seized mine. "Did you enjoy your drive with Adam? How did you two get along with each other?" My face must have given me away, betrayed my bafflement. She said in a kindlier tone but without a hint of apology for truth deliberately withheld: "Yes, he is your father's son."

"He couldn't be anyone else's. Why didn't you tell me who he was when you introduced us?"

Roguish amusement puckered her mouth. "It's not the old but the young who have compartmented minds. Black or white. No half-

95

tones. As you grow older you'll learn that no single issue in life is clear-cut. I presume that what you want to know is why don't I either accept Adam into the family or ignore him?"

"Yes. He seems to exist in some sort of no man's land."

She gave one of her husky laughs. "I assure you he does nothing of the sort, and he's certainly never voiced a single complaint to me. So why should I deprive myself of a first-class estate manager, one moreover who has the blood of his father and grandfather in his veins, which affords him an instinctive love of Saffron I'd find in no one else? The alternative is to make him an outright gift of his father's name." Her face drew itself into haughty lines, and her voice took on a cutting edge. "As long as his mother lives that is unthinkable. She was a scheming village girl, who managed, heaven knows by what wiles—she had no looks—to seduce your father. Thank God she never succeeded in tricking him into marriage. It took your mother to achieve that."

It was the first time any reference to my mother had crossed her lips. For once it did not evoke a haunting tide of grief. I was not called upon to unravel a mystery, only accept an age-old commonplace: a mother's undying resentment of any girl who stole a piece of her son's allegiance.

She patted my hand. "Adam and I are in total accord. Both of us accept a situation that works to our mutual advantage. Meantime, all that need concern you is that it is my dearest wish that my darling's two children should become known to each other."

She had virtually told me nothing; yet her wits were needle-sharp. It followed she must be aware that Adam was a time bomb ticking away in the heart of Saffron: that the lives of her son, daughter, and grandson were being eroded by enmity and jealousy. Did she draw some satisfaction that was beyond the reach of my understanding from an exercise in cruelty? There must be another answer, but however I strived, I could not lay my mind to it.

"Fortunately, Adam has inherited none of his mother's qualities."

In that, at least, she deluded herself. He had inherited from her his white-hot fire of ambition. As we purred through a wide gate set into a high brick wall, guarding a kitchen garden and a range of glasshouses, I told her he was taking me out to dinner on Wednesday night. The news won for me that lovely and loving smile that I found irresistible.

Marcus opened the door, gathered up the sable lap rug. "We shan't keep you waiting long," she murmured as though he were indeed a hired chauffeur. Behind her back, he gave her a mock salute, and not quite hidden by the drooping moustache there was an ugly twist to his mouth.

At one of the glasshouses a middle-aged man was literally standing to attention, dressed in navy-blue serge, his high starched collar so tight about his neck I marvelled he could breathe.

"Good afternoon, Rigson. This is my granddaughter. I want you to show her the orchids, especially Pink Queen that won us a Gold Medal at Chelsea this year. Perhaps you would give me your arm."

Marcus, back in the car, watched us through a veil of cigarette smoke, as Rigson steered her reverentially into the almost overpoweringly hot, moist air where sprays of orchids vaulted out of the brown tulip-shaped roots that were cosseted in sphagnum moss. Purple and cinnamon, gold and ice-white, and through every blend of pastel, like hundreds of butterflies poised for flight.

"They were your grandfather's favourite flower. He won his first Gold Medal at Chelsea in 1950. Do you remember that day, Rigson?"

"That I do, madam. We all drank champagne that night."

"How many years did it take you to produce Pink Queen?"

"Eight, madam, that is from seed."

She gave my hand an admonishing pat. "You see, to create a masterpiece demands the expenditure of infinite time and patience. Human beings, if they are to achieve their full potential, require even more. Ah, there's Pink Queen."

Three sprays of apple-blossom pink, suffused at the tips with carmine and primrose. When I'd admired it, she ordered: "Rigson, pick one spray for Miss Claudine, and some white and mauve ones, so that she has a bouquet to put in her room."

We travelled back at the same sedate pace with the exotic bouquet on my knee. She needed a stronger supporting arm from Marcus to help her out of the car and, uncharacteristically, she made no protest when Aunt Louise, who was waiting nervous and flurried in the hall, insisted that she sit down for five minutes before she mounted the stairs, pausing on each one to collect her breath. When the two of them had disappeared Marcus emerged from the drawing room into which he'd vanished flourishing a glass.

"After that touching feudal scene, I've earned an early drink. Come and join me." Without waiting for a reply, he turned on his heel.

When he brought me the gin and tonic I'd chosen, he pointed a nicotine-stained finger at the orchids I was still carrying. "Pink Queen, forsooth! You're highly privileged. I doubt if Rigson would have cut a spray for anyone else. Well, here's to you, Cousin Claudine." He made perfunctory toast, sprawled back on a sofa, as I laid the orchids on a table, sat down in a chair by its side.

"Are you run-in by now? What do you make of us all?"

"I'm beginning to find my way around . . ."

He interrupted: "I wasn't referring to bricks and mortar, but to human beings. How do we strike you? Grandmother, for instance?"

I was still disquieted by her near collapse, the blood draining from her face, and the faintly bemused look as she doggedly worked her way up each stair. Consequently my answer was uncalculating. "The drive, and the half hour we spent in the orchid house exhausted her. I wish she hadn't made the effort for me, tired herself out."

He gave a snorting laugh. "What a clever little dodger of issues you are! Don't break your heart. A couple of hours' rest and a handful of pills will restore her to normal, busy moving us about like chesspieces on a board. A living miracle to be worshipped, though not from afar." He paused. "Coming one place down the list in order of seniority, how do you rate Uncle Con, hardly a cuddly avuncular figure, but presumably your ally-in-chief."

"Only in so far as he made the effort to come and see me in France after my mother died."

"So you said!" His voice was a rasp of impatience. "What would be more informative would be to learn why he put himself to trouble and expense—he hoards his pennies you know—and why you were so amenable to his blandishments. Okay, you'll say you wanted to see Saffron, Grandmother, but didn't you also want to see your father's bastard?"

His attempt to shock me was a damp squib. "If my parents hadn't decided to get married a month before I was born, we'd have shared what you obviously regard as a stigma, illegitimacy."

He drawled: "Not a stigma, more an impediment, socially . . . and legally." He lolled back, regarded me with narrowed concentration. "Well, now you have met the *Eminence Grise* of Saffron, have you two established a touching brother-sister relationship?"

The thrust of loyalty took me by surprise, the hot impulse to defend was no more than a throwback to that early morning shock of recognition. "We share the same father. Did you expect us to hate each other on sight?"

"Equal odds either way. Rivals or buddies forming a common front against the enemy, though in the circumstances it's an alliance foredoomed to fall apart. He's strictly a non-sharer, that brother of yours." He pulled himself upright and his glance shot across the space that divided us, for once totally alert and committed. "Someone, probably Shakespeare, he got around to saying most things, said 'such men are dangerous,' and however long you live you'll never meet a more dangerous man that Terson." He tossed the remainder of his drink down his throat. "A cousinly warning, honestly delivered. And shall I tell you why he is dangerous? He wears blinkers that reduce the men around him—and the women, oh, especially the women—to creatures of no account, so that it costs him nothing to dispose of them, not a pang. Yes, dispose, that's the right word. He reduces them to corpses. Ponder on it, sweet cousin, a corpse is a very cold thing to be."

By now I had reached a stage of rough and ready acceptance of the supercharged emotional atmosphere in which I found myself, so the menace which he sought to convey misfired. It was altogether too absurdly melodramatic, even for Saffron. Also he was halfway to being drunk.

I smiled. "Are you trying to scare me?"

"If you'd a wit in your head, you'd be frightened to death already."

It was then I made the mistake of laughing at him. But the laugh congealed in my throat, quenched by the palpitating hate he emitted, even though I knew it was not for me.

The door opened and his glance flew away from me. "Pussycat!" He stretched out an arm to Trudy, and when she was near enough wrapped it round her waist. "I've been pouring words of wisdom into our little cousin's ear, with the best possible motive, but I don't think she is inclined to take me seriously."

She dropped a kiss on his forehead, winked at me. "I don't blame her. You're as tight as an owl and in one of your boring introspective moods. Anyway, my guess is that Claudine can get along very nicely without your wise words." She confiscated his glass. "You're on rations for the rest of the evening to sober you up for the office in the morning."

I was writing a letter to Jean-Baptiste when Nancy knocked on my door. "Mrs Delamain would be obliged, miss, if you would go and say good night to her. But Mrs Delamain-Powell says would you be sure only to stay ten minutes."

On other occasions when I'd seen her she'd been dressed in the semi-uniform of a navy-blue nylon overall, which did nothing for her. But not this Sunday night. Her mat of jet-black hair had been brushed and tamed and her geranium linen dress and matching jacket, nipped in at the waist to emphasise its slenderness, threw a glow on her sallow skin.

I only stared at her for a couple of seconds, but it was long enough to bring a smile of sly complacency to her lips. Nancy obviously on an evening out. I didn't have to guess with whom she was spending it. As I walked along the corridor I wondered whether she was any more to him than a trustworthy spy he'd placed in the house, and though maybe it should have done, the speculation didn't shock me.

The bedroom led directly out of the saffron room, the door left open for me. Grandmother was propped high against a mound of flounced pillows, billows of swansdown on her bedwrap curling about her wrists and neck. She appeared to be asleep. With make-up removed, her lips pale, shadows like finger marks below her eyes, she was at once an exquisite drawing in pastel chalk, and so fragile that my heart's beats quickened in alarm. As though she could feel my breath as I bent over her, her eyes opened. When I saw that her glance was unclouded and that the old witchery had returned to her smile, my fear subsided. She patted the satin quilt. "Come and sit by me."

When I did Carlo, who had been curled in his basket, assumed that he was included in the invitation and leapt up. "Is he allowed on your bed."

"Only for short sessions when no one is looking. It's nearly time for him to go downstairs, so he can stay." He snuggled between us and I rhythmically stroked his head.

"The heat in the orchid house was too much for you, and all that standing. I feel horribly guilty because you exhausted yourself for my sake. I shan't let you do it again."

She eased herself more upright against the pillows. "Exhausted! What nonsense. I'm perfectly well. And please don't adopt your aunt's manner towards me. I tolerate her fussing and scolding because the habit is so ingrained she can't throw it off. But I am not prepared to accept it from a chit of a girl!" She smiled to take the edge off what had begun as a reprimand.

I laughed. "You certainly sound rested."

"I am. Light me a cigarette, and then there is something I want to say to you before your aunt arrives to the tick of the second hand on her watch to dose me with sleeping pills." She drew the smoke into her lungs and slowly exhaled it, smiling at me. "Tomorrow morning I intend to telephone my solicitor, Alan Brigstock, and instruct him to make arrangements for you to be paid a monthly allowance . . ."

I'd received not a second's warning, so that alarm and indignation struck simultaneously, tied thought and speech into knots. "Please, don't telephone him, make the arrangements. I have sufficient money. I don't need an allowance. I wouldn't know what to do with it. Please . . ."

She countered with the high, autocratic tone I heard her use to others but not to me. "My dear child, don't talk nonsense. Of course you must have your own allowance. There are certainly articles you need." She ran a cool eye over my dove-grey dress. "That is charming, it becomes you, and was admirably suited to the small-town life you led, but as my granddaughter, living with me at Saffron, you must have couture clothes, not reach-me-downs, bought off the peg."

I kept my voice muted. "It was not bought off any peg. I designed and made it myself. That is what I intend to be, a fashion designer."

There was no more belief in her face than if I'd declared my intention of flying to the moon. I insisted: "It is the only career I've ever wanted. That is why I trained at an art school in Paris until my mother . . ."

She cut me off. "That is the past, which has no bearing to your future. You are now my responsibility. Your home is at Saffron. What other home have you?" The flesh on her face seemed to thin, and the swansdown about her throat became alive with the deeper breaths she drew. "The circumstances of your life have been transformed. Your first duty is to learn to adjust to them. In due course, you will be meeting my friends, their children and grandchildren. Clothes have a role to play in your life here. Do you want to look like Trudy! I'll assume not. Tomorrow morning I shall instruct Brigstock to pay you an allowance, so let us have no more childish tantrums. False pride in a girl of your age amounts to a public display of gaucherie which is most unbecoming!"

Anger battled against compassion. Anxiety weakened my resolution, persuading me there was a bluish tinge to her lips, that the swansdown on her breast flew higher every minute. Emotional blackmail? The two words whispered themselves in my head, but I refused to listen, and cravenly chose a middle road I prayed would be safe. "Couldn't we talk about it in the morning? It's late and Aunt Louise told me not to stay longer than ten minutes. Tell me what time you'd like to see me in the morning, and I'll be able to explain it a lot better, make you understand."

To the tick of the second hand, Aunt Louise entered. Obedient to

101

the wave of her hand that dismissed me, I stood up, stooped to kiss Grandmother good night. Her lips were stiff and tightly closed against mine, her breath held in anger. Except for the faint warmth of her flesh, it was like kissing a dead face.

I walked by the open drawing-room door where Marcus was sprawled in an armchair with Trudy sitting at his feet listening to a record player, through the courtyard and over the bridge, and then I climbed between the crossed-struts of timber into the unroofed shell of the Abbey. The birds were no longer in flight, but their last trumpet calls still occasionally pierced the silence. I walked to the far side, leaned out of a high arch of stone that had once been a window and gazed at the water meadows where the geese were settling for the night. River and sky were an exact shade of muted silver. Darkness was an hour away, time suspended between the brilliance of day and the cool secrecy of night, when reason dissolves and small fears grow huge. Again and again I repeated to myself that I wasn't a prisoner, the cost of my freedom the life of an old woman who loved me.

The barest whisper of sound pulled me about. He was standing six feet away, his face so grave and enquiring that it would have fitted perfectly into my mediaeval frieze. He came forward, leant against a buttress and my unsleeping inner eye recorded his body's grace.

"Did you find him?"

"Grandmother found him for me, sent us out on a drive together . . . to get acquainted." After that first swift glance I had to dip my head to screen my face, unable to rationalise the insane happiness that suddenly swamped me because he'd walked three quarters of a mile to find me, terrified it would show.

"I've been wondering," he said thoughtfully, "didn't your mother talk to you about Adam?"

"No. I didn't know he existed until I saw him in the distance early on my first morning here. She probably didn't know either." I persuaded myself that the mindless euphoria was beginning to fade, that I dare meet his eye. But he was looking away from me, his expression puzzled, as though he were trying to equate two opposing sets of facts, arrive at the truth.

"But she did." He altered the angle of his head and our glances linked. "When she lived with us Adam delivered the morning papers. Every Saturday my father used to hand her a shilling tip for him. Sometimes in the holidays I ran the errand for her. Each time he used to look me straight in the eye, doff his cap, say 'thank you, sir!'

A bit of play-acting designed to make me feel a fool, which it assuredly did."

"She could have forgotten him," I protested, as a face saver, though by now I was sliding towards the certainty that there was not the smallest aspect of Saffron that had not been lodged in the deepest crevices of her memory. Sometimes I suffered a dreamlike, eerie feeling that her ghost dogged my heels. I waited for him to agree or disagree, and when he did neither, but stood looking at me questioningly, I asked: "And now Adam is no longer the paper boy?"

"We live in the same village, maintain the relationship required by shared community interests, though I'm only a weekender, and shall soon cease to be that."

Though the answer had been designed to express tolerance, the dislike was barely masked, evoking that irrational loyalty in me that Adam himself would have derided. I heard the heat in my voice, tried to quell it, failed. "If you were treated like an outcast, if your father passed you in the street without recognising you, and an old lady who is your grandmother never admits the relationship but uses you to score off her son and daughter, wouldn't you fight back with every weapon you could lay your hands on!"

To my astonishment he laughed, so that for a moment the ruined shell echoed with a lovely sound. "He certainly did a good job on you! Then he has a perfect right to make his own case good. Did he confide in you what his ultimate ambition is?"

"Yes, to own Saffron."

An eyebrow quirked. "Honest, too! So how did he react to the new competition?"

"Don't you remember we settled that issue on Friday night. I'm strictly a non-competitor."

His smile of mild disbelief, broke my temper. "Inheritances, wills, a safe stuffed with jewels, the assumption that enough money makes you happy-ever-after . . ." Of its own accord, my head shook violently. "Not for me."

"If riches aren't important to you, what is?"

I could have said: "To be loved, to have one's life set on a rock that would never founder. I cheated: "Human relationships, doing the work one's best equipped to do."

"And if I suggested that lack of money can warp human relationships, that grudges held for twenty years can eat every mite of generosity out of a man's heart, and that hope deferred too long can wither the spirit, would you contradict me?"

103

"You're talking about Adam?"

"Yes, though there are others who are as severely penalised. A man with as many old scores as he has, can't afford the luxury of being overscrupulous . . ."

I jumped in: "All right, you dislike him. That's your *right*. You don't have to explain or apologise to me."

"That wasn't my intention," he said blandly. "The idea was to give you a slightly broader and more balanced picture. One that might even come in useful, hold you back from getting out of your depth on a wave of nostalgia. Physical resemblance can be a distraction, even a little dangerous."

This time it was I who laughed. "I've already been warned he's dangerous, an *Eminence Grise,* a bastard, and a devil."

"Sounds like overreaction!" His smile was more tolerant. "Anyway, I'd be surprised if any of those epithets influenced you, probably the reverse." Then between one second and the next his voice changed tone, became imperative. "But don't make the mistake of sentimentalising over him. Above all, don't try to play off Adam against Uncle Conwyn. The chances are it would be you who would get your fingers burnt."

I looked down at the darkening turf. "Doesn't an adventuress, a girl out to exploit a rich grandmother deserve to singe her fingers?"

Unreasonably, deeply, he had been stung. I could feel the anger build up in him as vibrantly as if it were my own, so that I held my breath in fright of what was to come. But it was only a sigh, a sound of exasperation that exploded from his lips. "Don't I get forgiven one error of judgment?"

"It depends on what your judgment is now."

"I was guilty of preconceived ideas, not wholly unwarranted in the circumstances, but probably mistaken . . ."

"Probably?"

"Yes," he said firmly, "probably. I lean towards the theory that Uncle Conwyn pressurised you, even lied, or withheld the truth from you. Is that a fairer assessment?"

Perhaps he was offering me a half apology, one which, had I accepted it, would have marked a turning point. But the mixture of emotions he evoked blurred and ran into one another, so that none stayed firm. Maybe the issue was simpler: pride! Love at first sight, I cautioned myself, was a romantic has-been, a delusion of the eye that destroyed reason. "I've already explained I came to Saffron of my own free will."

There was a pause, and then he said as though to mark the end of contention: "Anyway, you've made Hermione very happy."

I had left her in a cold rigour of anger, her pulses racing towards danger level. "How do you know? Have you seen her?"

"No, I'd hoped to, but I've spent all day packing up the workshop for the move on Thursday, also checking up on an exhibition we're putting on in Edinburgh in a couple of weeks' time, but I've talked to her on the telephone." There was sufficient light for me to see his face that was turned to mine, the disbelief wiped away, and in its place an expression that, if you were credulous enough, you could persuade yourself was the beginning of love. His voice was as comforting and tender as the one he had used to Sue to quieten her fears of her mother's second marriage. "When you're old, sick, to love and be loved by someone young is a renewal of a life force that by a miracle sometimes extends the life that is withering away."

He stopped abruptly, demanded: "What's the matter? You look frightened. What's scaring about being loved?"

Because love in its omnipotence could turn destroyer. I fumbled for words. "Whatever love she gives me has to be subtracted from someone else's share, so it becomes a kind of theft."

"I would question that." I could feel him studying my face. "In any case, wasn't that your prime purpose in coming to Saffron, to win her affection, give her yours in return?" His voice dropped a tone. "Or did Uncle Conwyn win a promise from you that, now you know her, you regret having made? Or is Adam at the bottom of it?"

"No, not Adam. And there were no promises, no pacts between me and Uncle Conwyn. Yes, there was one I made yesterday. Not to let Grandmother hear a whisper that Lorraine's brother is in the neighbourhood, intent on proving that his sister was murdered."

I saw his body stiffen. "Have you met Bernard Andrews?"

"Once. I walked into my bedroom and found him threatening Uncle Conwyn with some letters from his sister he's handed over to his solicitor."

"Letters that contained firm evidence that Lorraine had been murdered?"

"I don't know, but that's what he inferred. Is it likely? Is it possible that she was murdered?"

"After the earlier, very thorough police investigation, not likely. But possible? Yes. If Andrews is in possession of facts that weren't known to the police at the time of the first enquiry."

"Whom did they investigate?"

105

"Everyone in the neighbourhood who hadn't got a watertight alibi from 9 P.M. until midnight, with special emphasis on the male members of the household . . . and Adam." His voice was quietly pondering. "Gossip, a bush fire of wild conjectures, the natural prejudice of a bereaved brother add up to a powerful mixture of emotions." His glance sought mine. "Has anyone been talking to you about Lorraine?"

"Grandmother showed me her photograph. It upset her terribly. And Trudy swore that Uncle Conwyn was in love with her, hoped to marry her. That couldn't be true, could it?"

"Oh, yes it could."

Somewhere in a tree on the slopes above us, a nightingale broke into song, the music so pure and joyous, it cleansed mind and spirit, as the notes climbed higher and higher into ecstasy.

We listened in silence, then he smiled on me. "He's early tonight, he doesn't usually start up until after eleven and in good voice." He reached for my hand. "You're getting cold. Time to take you indoors. In ten minutes Greville will be locking up, and I have to make an early start in the morning."

Even when his flesh had warmed the chill out of my hand, I left it within his. The physical link gave me a sense of being divided in half, two persons: one myself and the other a part of him, so that his thoughts, with their light and shade, the doubts and indecisions he suffered were as plain to me as though they were my own.

When we stepped off the bridge into the courtyard, I drew my hand out of his and that strange unearthly awareness was cut, leaving me isolated. We walked, steps keeping pace, towards the door that was open, spilling its dimmed red light across the stone paving. Without warning, as our feet stopped moving, and we stood face to face, that lovely madness returned and I persuaded myself that he was going to bend his head and kiss me.

But intuition played me false. It remained above mine. "I care what happens to you," he said slowly, "I wouldn't like you to be hurt by Uncle Conwyn . . . or Adam. Will you believe that?"

I could have answered that Adam would have no cause to hurt me because there was no likelihood that I would steal the smallest particle of his birthright; that Uncle Conwyn was rendered impotent by my dislike of him. You can't be wounded by someone you despise, only by those you love. Instead, I said: "Yes."

"Then take care of yourself. Concentrate on Hermione, forget the others. Good night."

He lingered a second, or it might have been two, and then he turned abruptly about.

I closed the door very slowly, watching the swift swinging stride until the dusk swallowed him up.

10

NEXT MORNING Trudy came bounding into my room. "Goody, I wanted to catch you. You wouldn't know, but Monday is Pierre's day." When I looked baffled, she explained: "Monsieur Pierre of Grosvenor Street, who abandons his salon for one day a week to do Grandmother's hair, brings along a slave girl to give her a facial and manicure. Just as Friday is the masseuse's day. Pierre is a prissy old bore who brain-washes old women into believing he makes them ravishing. Ugh, he gives me the creeps. So I had an idea, why don't we skip eating lunch with Uncle Con, Pierre, and his blond slave and have a picnic? I'll fix it with Mrs Harper and Ma-in-law. Provided I dress Marco like an Eskimo, she won't object, and she certainly won't admit you to Grandmother's presence this morning. On Mondays the idea is to keep her in a state of suspended animation until Monsieur Pierre arrives. Bowing and scraping! One of these days he'll forget himself and drop her a curtsey!"

In the hope that I'd see her that morning, I'd been rehearsing to myself phrases calculated to melt that glacial anger. "I'd like to see her, if only for a moment."

"Not a hope," she said blithely. "Coming?"

Reluctantly I abandoned my hope until later in the day. "Yes. It sounds a good idea. Has Marcus gone to London?"

"At the crack of dawn, poor lamb. I'm keeping my fingers crossed he won't fall asleep at the wheel. I had to spread his egg on a slice of toast and feed it to him. He loathes his boss so much that he practically goes into a coma of fright at the thought of seeing him."

I wondered why he didn't change his job, even, since his chronic lethargy suggested he'd find it more congenial, have no job at all.

By now I was familiar with the broad layout of the gardens, and could map my way along the main paths that curved through the rainbow sashes of colour. But Trudy, pushing Marco in a carry-cot mounted on wheels, led me to a hidden garden, enclosed on three sides by yew hedges, their fresh yellow top-growth making a shimmer of gold over the dark lower foliage. The fourth side was a rose-pink brick wall that supported a fig tree. Trudy manipulated the carry-cot down half a dozen stone steps to the level of a sexagonal pool in which goldfish swam in slow motion through the magenta waterlilies.

She stripped Marco of two layers of woollies, and put him in the shade of a tangled briar rose. "And no small change out of you. You've been fed to bursting point, and now you're out of the padding in which your doting grannie smothers you, I expect you to take a nap."

Squatted on the step below mine, she gave a sniff of pleasure. "This is what I call a garden. Cosy! Though I'd swop that fish pond for a swimming pool. Let's see if Mrs Harper remembered the booze."

She lifted out a thermos flask, unscrewed the top. "Ah-ha! Two dry martinis coming up if you can dig out the glasses."

She drank half of one filled to the brim. "Tomorrow I'm going to harden my heart and abandon Marco to his grannie, drive up to town with Marcus." She bit into a chicken sandwich. "I'm homesick for my own six rooms, kitchen and bath, and a nice little whizz round Marks & Sparks. How about you? Is this a home from home for you?"

"Hardly! It's the most unhomelike place I could imagine."

She eyed me shrewdly, took another gulp of martini. "You're a bit of a clam, aren't you? What I mean is, you don't exactly open your heart. Well, I suppose you can't. Reveal all, and you'd have Uncle Con down on you like a ton of bricks."

I laughed, shook my head. "There's nothing to reveal." I countered her look of frank disbelief with a question. "If you're happier in your own home than here, why don't you go back to it?"

"Why?" she exploded. "Because Marcus would lie awake all night worrying what everyone was up to, especially now we've got Bernard Andrews prowling round like a bloodhound that's sniffed a drop of blood! And if Marcus worries, I worry. Not exactly in line with Woman's Lib. Then I'm not a woman's libber!" She reached for another sandwich, parted it to insert a lettuce heart. "I don't fancy spending my life here, but he does. So he's on the jump unless he's keeping an eye on his future. And the more anxious he gets, the more he drinks." She challenged me with a hotly accusing glance. "If you and Adam both dropped dead, I'd wean him off gin for good."

The boast was an empty one. Drink was not an occasional prop to Marcus, it was a permanent crutch. "You can hardly ask us to drop dead to pacify Marcus, but you could make a start by persuading him that as far as I'm concerned he can throw all his worries overboard."

She gave me a look so spiced with venom that for a second I had a feeling I was looking at her for the first time. "Everyone here puts on an act. So why not you! Just as you're not as innocent as you make out, I'm not as dumb as I look." Her speech quickened, became a gabble. "A dumb little would-be blonde, half a stone overweight, bulging out of her clothes, that's how you see me, isn't it?"

"Trudy," I shouted, "stop it! You're talking nonsense, worse, making it up as you go along, and feeling sorry for yourself."

The impact of my voice quelled her rising hysteria.

She gulped, then started to giggle. "Anyway, for the moment you're stymied. Mr Brigstock has had the audacity to take himself off on a holiday to Spain without informing Grandmother he wouldn't be there to come running down to Saffron when she tweaked her little finger. Ma-in-law told me. It will be a week before he can present himself for the ceremony of The Will. So you've seven days to keep yourself firmly on your pinnacle. Quite a balancing act! Be careful you don't topple."

I matched her mood, left her to believe what she chose. "With an effort I may be able to manage it."

After lunch she went to sleep and while she slept I did a charcoal sketch of Marco. "But it's good," she pronounced with unflattering amazement when she woke up. "Can I have it?"

I handed it to her.

"Where did you learn to draw? It's the image of him!"

"At school. But I'm no good at portraits. The line of his left arm is all wrong."

"It looks all right to me. I might even have it framed. Thanks. Your father was an artist, wasn't he? Is that what you are, or would have been if you hadn't opted to be a comfort to Grandmother in her declining years?"

"No. I'd like to have been one, but wanting, even giving it all you've got, isn't enough, if the talent isn't born in you. My job's fashion designing."

"Crikey!" She eyed my plain cotton blouse and seersucker pants. "You know, I'd never have guessed it. There are thousands of them now, running up dishy clothes with what my Mum calls a red-hot needle and a burnt thread, so you'll be up against a hell of a lot of competition. Now I suppose we'd better take his lordship back to his grannie, otherwise she'll send out a search party." She sighed as if a sudden darkness had descended upon her volatile spirit. More likely, I decided, she was still sleepy from the sun and three outsize martinis.

There was a message, I guessed written by Nancy, on my dressing table asking me to go and see Grandmother at six o'clock. Relief and foreboding were equally balanced, and I found myself tapping at the door with the same queasy feeling that had accompanied a summons to Mother Superior.

She was sitting in the yellow velvet chair, her dress an airy silver-grey chiffon patterned with shell-pink roses. As I crossed the floor I searched her face for any lingering remnant of the anger and stress that had set her pulses racing. I could detect none. In their place was a look of quizzical appraisal. "Do you know what you remind me of, a young colt that has not been schooled."

"I was clumsy. I'm very sorry."

"So you should be." The brilliance of the smile was immensely reassuring. She held out her hand. "Come, no more quarrelling. Life is too short and too precious. You are a very pretty child. In time you will become a beautiful woman. But beauty is an empty shell unless it is accompanied by grace. And that is what you must acquire, my darling, grace of heart and grace of spirit. So it behooves us both to be patient with each other." She looked deep, almost sternly into my eyes. "And, above all, you must trust me."

"I do," but as the words left my mouth I wondered if they were the truth. I loved her, but love and trust, I'd discovered, were two separate elements that did not necessarily fuse.

"Then all will be well. Open the champagne. I'm afraid your aunt has rationed us to half a bottle, but we'll make the most of it."

As I put the champagne glass in her right hand, she ran her left through a strand of my hair. "When Pierre comes next Monday, I shall ask him to take a look at your hair. It needs shaping, perhaps a restyle, and Mirabelle is bringing with her a full range of cosmetics. That eye shadow makes you look like a hollow-eyed, hungry orphan."

"But isn't that what I am, an orphan?"

She laughed, joyously from the heart. "You are my grandchild, and within a month we'll have you looking the part."

I stayed with her until Nancy brought Carlo back from his walk.

There was, as she had wished, calm between us, no clash of wills because I had deliberately put mine to sleep.

At breakfast next morning, I found two letters beside my plate. One was from Jean-Baptiste, the other, the one I'd been waiting for, and which Mademoiselle Greux had readdressed, was from Lisette. I couldn't bring myself to read either under Greville's attentive left eye that maintained a constant watch on the level of the coffee in my cup, on every mouthful I swallowed lest I ran short of toast or butter. When the telephone rang and he left the room to answer it, I ripped open Lisette's envelope, but before I had time to unfold the sheet, he was back at my side.

"It's a call for you, Miss Claudine. I'm sorry there's no extension in here. It'll mean you'll have to take it in the morning room or the library."

Because it was nearer, I chose the library, a sombre room in which the air tasted stale. The voice that met my ear was warm and rippling with excitement. "Claudine? This is Emmy Heron. I arrived home last night, and I'd simply adore to see you. Could you come here today, say for tea? Or any other time. I have to shop this morning, otherwise I'm free all day. Could you?"

When I said I'd like to and that tea would be fine, she cried: "That's wonderful! Come as soon as you can after lunch. The door will be open. Just shout for me."

But she was in the hall, arranging a silver bowl with sugar-pink roses which, on seeing me she dropped to the floor, ran forward. She was a medium-plump woman, with hair that had once been the colour of her son's, but fading now and streaked with grey, his marvellous tawny eyes, and a radiant smile of welcome.

"Claudine!" She held me at arm's length and then pressed her cheek against mine. "You'll never know how exciting, and oh, so good it is to see you after all these years. I can hardly believe it is really you." Without a backward glance at the scattered roses, she steered me into the room I knew. "The wind is blowing every which way today, so I thought we'd be more comfortable having tea indoors by the window." She raised her voice: "Marty!"

The middle-aged woman who answered the call was dumpy with a calm, tolerant expression on a smooth pink-cheeked face that was framed by straight grey hair I guessed she cut herself, and which was pinned back with a sky-blue slide.

111

"Marty, this is Mrs Delamain's granddaughter, Claudine. And this is our darling Marty, who keeps us all in order."

Mrs Martin gave me a smiling nod. "Tries to, more like."

Emmy Heron laughed. "Give us five minutes, Marty dear, and then we'll have tea.

"There"—she plumped up a cushion in one of two armchairs on either side of a low table by the french window—"let's make ourselves comfortable. You'll never know what it meant to me when both Sue and Ross telephoned and told me you were coming to live at Saffron." Before I could contradict her, she ran on in her gay, fast-flowing voice: "How like your father you are! That gorgeous hair. Hermione must be overjoyed to have you with her. I'm nearly as delighted for her as for myself." Her voice quietened to a deep sincerity. "You see, despite the age gap, I counted your mother one of the dearest friends I ever had. Does it grieve you to talk about her? Is it too painful so soon after her death?"

"I'd love to talk about her, especially about the time when she lived in this house with you." As Mrs Martin brought in the tea, my eye moved about the room, striving to visualise my mother with the head in my father's portrait superimposed on a young, lithe body. Imagination failed me.

She filled my cup, put a plate of buttered scones between us. "She was with us for over two years. The prettiest, gentlest-tempered girl who ever lived. Within a month of her arrival she was part of the family. I can never decide whether I regarded her as an elder daughter or a younger sister. Even after all this time, I wept when Ross told me she was dead. But I'm not going to upset you by talking about her death. She would have hated that."

Even if I'd been able to describe my mother in her sealed house in the rue de Paris, nurturing—maybe unconsciously—a death wish, I would not have distressed Mrs Heron by the telling. "Did you see her after I was born?"

"Yes. Three or four times a year when I was in London, I spent an afternoon with you both." She gave me a questioning glance. "Did she ever tell you about those days?" When I shook my head, she gave a sharp little sigh. "They weren't easy for her. As often happens, two people, poles apart temperamentally, fall deeply in love. Your father and mother remained in love until he died, but their reactions to any given set of circumstances were diametrically opposed to the other's. Your mother was a practical young woman, concerned with maintaining a roof over your heads, paying the bills. While your father . . ." She paused, began to pick her words with more care. "Perhaps the explanation lies in his youth. He was literally a young god, with the world at his feet to dispose of how he chose. Old Mr Delamain was strict, almost a Victorian parent, but such was Marcus's charm, and let's admit it his guile, that however deeply he displeased or angered his father, ultimate forgiveness was as certain as the morning sunrise. Then, as you know, he eloped with Michelle and a week later the girl to whom he was engaged killed herself. But by then the belief of the infallibility of his charm was so impregnated in him that he was convinced it would only be a matter of time before he was welcomed back to Saffron. So, with riches just over the horizon, he shrugged off unpaid bills, dunning tradesmen which constituted a burden that literally made your mother ill with shame." She paused, her grieving glance lingering on me. "How well do you remember your father?"

"Very well. I remember the day he brought me to Saffron, a hot summer day when we had tea in the Abbey."

"You do! Yet you could only have been four. I happened to be there with Sue and Caro and the Harris twins who were staying with us. You were so pretty, so winning and your father was so enormously proud of you."

"But not winning enough!"

"That's not true. I mean the fault was not yours. Old Mr Delamain was willing to receive you and Marcus back at Saffron but he imposed a condition that your father would not submit to: either he divorce or secure a legal separation from Michelle. The appalling mistake he made was to tell Michelle of his father's terms. Men! It was wicked and downright cruel to burden her with the knowledge that but for her the two of you would have been surrounded by comfort, luxury with never a care about money. I still find it hard to forgive him for not holding his tongue. If she became embittered, and I am afraid she did, who could blame her!" She looked deep into her teacup, her face strained with grief. "I don't judge her because I loved her, and you don't sit in judgment on people you love. Sometimes bitterness breeds a need to repay in their own coin those who have cruelly wronged you. Whether that was her intention, or whether it was that she was distraught with grief, I don't know. But she never told the Delamains that Marcus was dying of cancer. He'd been dead twenty-four hours before her letter reached them." She leaned across the table, grasped my hand between both of hers. "Darling, if anyone accuses her of heartlessness, and they may, old memories die hard, remember it was the Delamains who taught her to be merciless."

For a moment the pretty room, with its notes of gleaming silver, blanked out. Flickers of doubt coalesced into ice-hard certainty. Using the Grey Man as her accomplice my mother had schemed for fifteen years to put me where I was now. It seemed in that black moment that I was being manipulated by a dead hand.

She went on: "What was so appalling was that on the day your father was buried, my husband was abroad and I was confined to bed with pleurisy. I wrote Michelle explaining and begging her to come and see me. She didn't, and I've never understood why. Instead she returned to London from the churchyard. As soon as I was on my feet I went to see her. I was too late. She'd gone and left no forwarding address. All I could find out from an old crone who lived in the basement was that a gentleman had come to see her on the day after the funeral." Her voice began to tremble. "I failed her at the time when she needed me most, and for that I'll never forgive myself. I never even knew where you both lived until Ross told me that Conwyn had found you in Northern France. I've always worried how the two of you managed. How did you? Did Michelle have to work?"

"No." I hesitated for only a second. "We lived on a pension paid by Conwyn Delamain. He must have been the visitor the old woman mentioned to you."

Astonishment made her face comic. "Conwyn! But she was so proud, so independent. She'd never have accepted a penny from any of the Delamains." She stared beyond me in stunned bewilderment, then very gradually I saw her reach acceptance. "Yes, I do understand. What was pride balanced against providing you with a home, an education! In a like situation, I'd lie, cheat, and humiliate myself, trample my pride to death to keep my children from want." For a moment doubt or distaste came alive again. "But Conwyn . . . of all people, Conwyn!"

Mrs Martin opened the door, stood on the threshold. "There's a Mr Andrews asking to see you."

"Now! When he telephoned this morning, we arranged that he should call this evening at six-thirty. What's he doing here in the afternoon?"

"Something about an emergency. He has an appointment in London this evening and he'd be obliged if you could see your way to giving him ten minutes of your time. He's waiting in the hall."

"How inconvenient!" She looked at me. "This wasn't what I planned at all. I'd like to send him away, but in the circumstances, it would be rather unkind. Marty, dear, could you drop him a hint before you bring him in to be as brief as possible?" Again she glanced at me. "He's the brother of a nurse who looked after your grandmother. She was drowned last March. A most appalling tragedy. He was in Australia. Now he's come to England and is anxious to talk to everyone who knew her. It's all very sad. I really can't ask him to go away."

I got up. "I'd love to walk round your garden and say hello to the pony, and when Mr Andrews has left you can give me a call."

"No, no. There's nothing private about it."

Anyway, I was too late. Bernard Andrews's stocky figure was already striding into the room.

His cotton shirt was a perfect match to his hard chalk-blue eyes, his lemon cropped hair seemed to bristle, and though he was not so aggressive in Emmy Heron's drawing room as he had been in the bedroom at Saffron, he wasted no words. "I apologise for altering the time of our appointment, but it was unavoidable as I have an urgent consultation with my legal advisers in London this evening." His bullethead moved, noted my presence, dismissed me with a curt, "Miss Delamain."

"I see you two have met. Now draw up that chair, Mr Andrews. You'll have a cup of tea, won't you?"

"I think not. I'll be as brief as possible. Were you a friend of my sister?"

"Not a friend, though of course we were on friendly terms. I met her when I visited Mrs Delamain. She was a churchwoman, so am I. I saw her at early morning communion and at social occasions to which we were both invited. But she was a young woman; I am a middle-aged widow, so it was hardly likely that we'd be intimates. What I do know is that she was a very charming girl and an excellent nurse."

"Did she ever discuss with you her relationships with various members of the Delamain family?"

"She did not," she said with a degree of firmness I'd not imagined her capable of.

The rebuff had no effect. "But you've lived on the doorstep of the Saffron estate for twenty-five years, Mrs Heron. You and your three children have the free run of the place. Are you telling me that you remained unaware that my sister and Conwyn Delamain spent a considerable amount of time in each other's company, that according to some rumours, they were on the brink of becoming engaged?"

"Mr Andrews, all villages are hotbeds of gossip, breeding grounds for rumours. One learns to disregard them until they are proven fact. Your sister and Conwyn Delamain lived under the same roof. He is devoted to his mother and would therefore be grateful to your sister for her excellent nursing. If there were rumours of a closer relationship, they never reached my ears."

His eyes hardened to belligerency. "Unlike you, Mrs Heron, I set a value on rumour. Not all rumours are ill founded. Did you ever hear my sister's name linked with that of Adam Terson?"

"No. And if I had, your sister's romantic affairs were no concern of mine. She was twenty-four, I understand, and a most attractive girl. It would be unnatural if she hadn't had boy friends. But who they were, whether she developed a serious attachment for a particular one, I simply do not know."

"Your son, Ross Heron . . ."

She laughed sweetly into his face. "Not Ross, Mr Andrews. I really can cross my heart and swear to you that Ross and Lorraine were not having an affair."

"If you'd allowed me to finish, you'd have learned that I was not going to suggest they were. But on the Friday night my sister was drowned, he drove down from London, arrived here at approximately 11 P.M. Did he see my sister's car, or any other one for that matter, near here?"

"No," she said firmly. "And if you've read the statements made to the police, of which his was one, you already know that. My son is not a liar. Mr Andrews, I hate to sound ungracious, but I do have a guest. And there is really nothing else I can tell you."

His lips curled at one corner. "I realise that I am trespassing on your valuable time. My excuse for doing so is that a small, closed community automatically clams up on a stranger, only talks under pressure, even duress. Let me give you an instance, it was only yesterday that I learned Conwyn Delamain had, on three separate occasions, been a patient in a psychiatric clinic. A nut case living in the same house as a girl who met her death in highly suspicious circumstances, and no reference was made to that fact in any statement I've read!"

"Conwyn Delamain suffers from occasional nervous collapses. One such occurred shortly after your sister's death. Not unnatural in that it was he who found her body! I thought nowadays all of us held more enlightened views on mental health. But you do not seem to share them. Conwyn Delamain is not a psychotic case. Under severe stress, his nerves occasionally crack, and he needs rest and treatment in a clinic that specialises in such illnesses. I assure you it has no sinister overtones. Now, if you would be good enough to excuse me."

He had, perforce, to accept his dismissal. On his feet, he turned his hard brick-dust countenance on me. "Now you have met your half brother, Miss Delamain, I imagine I would be wasting your time and my own if I asked you if you were aware of any intimate relationship between him and my sister!"

"I didn't know your sister. I've only met my half brother once. He didn't confide in me. I'm sorry, I can't help you."

"Thank you!" The irony constituted an insult. "Thank you both for putting yourselves at my disposal for fifteen minutes. It's lucky for me that I don't have to rely on what you, your buddies and relations are prepared to tell me. What people like you never take into account is that in any wall of silence there's a hairline crack somewhere. Or to put it more plainly: someone who bears a grudge! That being so, feudal estates, sick old ladies who would be terrified at the sight of me, don't scare me. Thank you, I'll see myself out."

When the door closed on him, Emmy Heron sighed. "Oh, dear, what a very distressing scene, but I don't think we should hold him wholly accountable for his abominable manners. It could be he obtains some relief from his grief in making his so-called investigations. There may even be a basis of guilt in that he didn't keep in closer contact with his sister. I can't imagine what grounds he's got for his horrible suspicions."

"He told Uncle Conwyn he has some letters from Lorraine that he's handed over to his solicitor."

"Well," she said with relief, "Lorraine was hardly likely to write and tell him she was about to be murdered! She was a first-class nurse, but though I wouldn't have said so to him, she was what in my young days was called a flirt, even a tease. Of course, she had boy friends. Girls of her type attract them in shoals. There was a certain amount of talk about her and Conwyn and, to a lesser degree, the same goes for Adam, but Ross!" Her good humour, lightness of heart returned. "Well, you've met him, haven't you?"

"Yes." I found myself smiling. "He collected me from the airport."

She smiled back and for a moment the pulses of our hearts were in accord, and then she said: "I'm glad you like him," though I'd said no such thing.

"Now, let's forget that poor wretched man, shall we? Did Ross tell you I'm going to be married again, to an old family friend, Arthur Blakeley? We've known each other since our teens, so we shouldn't give each other too many shocks, even though he is a bachelor. He's coming to spend next weekend with us and on Friday night, when Ross and Sue will be home, we're having a party, nothing elaborate, just close friends. And then in a fortnight we'll slip in and out of a registrar's office and be married without any fuss. You'll come on Friday, won't you? Your uncle has promised, and I'll telephone Trudy and Marcus, now I hear they're at Saffron. With Nurse Hailey away I doubt if your aunt will leave Hermione, but I'll ring her too, to make sure. You will come, won't you?"

"I'd love to." And the date held at bay the darkness that would engulf me the moment I was alone.

"And another scheme of mine, when we can coax Hermione to part with you for a day or two, is to kidnap you. We'll stay at Ross's house in Chelsea, and do the sights and shops together. Would that appeal to you?"

"What a lovely idea. I was planning to stay in London when I leave here, but now I'm not sure that I'll be able to." At her look of puzzlement I explained. "I'm afraid everyone's jumped to the wrong conclusion. I'm here on a visit, a short one, not to stay permanently."

She looked shocked. "But your grandmother believes you're going to make Saffron your home."

"She's misunderstood. I'm terribly sorry. I don't know who told her that I was going to live at Saffron . . ." I contradicted myself. "Yes, I do. It could only have been Uncle Conwyn."

She pleaded: "Wouldn't it be rather cruel to run away almost as soon as she's found you?" When I made no reply, she went on: "I know it's not a very congenial household, that, well, not to put too fine a point on it, your aunt and uncle are more often than not at loggerheads, and that Hermione hasn't much use for Marcus and less for Trudy. But you're young, all your life before you, couldn't you spend a month or two making Hermione happy? Her health really is very precarious. It isn't Louise who's guilty of overfussing, it's Hermione who with her amazing will power bluffs people into believing she is stronger than she is." She wheedled: "Couldn't you take that into account?"

I fingered the letter that was in my pocket. I thought of the meeting between my mother and uncle the day after my father was buried, the tool into which they'd fashioned me. I said slowly: "I can't cheat her, pretend that I'm prepared to live at Saffron indefinitely." A need to justify myself rose up hot and strong. "To her I'm a child to be dressed up, shown off. It's a very long time since I was a child; I can't turn myself back into one even to please her, however hard I try. Can you understand?"

She nodded ruefully. "As the mother of two daughters who were hardly in their teens before they were convinced there was nothing about life they didn't know, yes." She smiled at me, light flooding the topaz eyes she'd given to her son. "She loves you, and I can understand why. You're instantly loveable, as your mother was. It is a marvellous gift to possess. So be generous to Hermione, promise you'll come back and see her, that you won't ever lose touch with her."

It was an easy promise to make, one which I would keep.

As she led me, her arm linked through mine across the hall, she remarked: "From what you said to Mr Andrews, I gather you've met Adam."

"Yes. Grandmother introduced him to me as her estate manager, then sent us out on a drive, presumably to discover for ourselves that we possessed the same father! I didn't need to be told." I waited for her reaction.

It was simple and straightforward. "That's the bit of the devil in her. She adores to keep people guessing. Even so, I'd be prepared to bet whatever motive she had was sound. Until you get to know her better, some of her whims, what Ross calls her 'queenly moods' may throw you, but I shouldn't worry. I'll telephone her and see if she'd like me to look in tomorrow morning. And afterwards, it's only an idea, but as I want to drive in to Canterbury to buy Jonathan, he's Caro's son, a birthday present, I wondered how you'd like to come with me, have lunch and a wander round the cathedral. Would you?"

I saw the pictures in the book at home: *Cathedrals of England*. I said in a rush of intense pleasure: "Oh, I would. Very much."

"Good! I'll fix it with Hermione."

As I walked back I thought that Emmy Heron's natural instinct was to flip over any coin to show its bright side. Her kind heart, anxiety to act as a protector against pain, would lead her to play for time. But I could no longer believe that time was my friend.

11

AFTER DINNER I went and sat on the seat that encircled the Judas tree to read for the third time the two letters that had arrived that morning. Jean-Baptiste's, written in French instead of the stilted English of which he was so proud, struck a note of black despondency. My departure had spurred his parents into action. By the time he'd returned from the airport his second cousin, Marie-Thérèse, had arrived on a supposedly surprise visit. I'd met her: raven-haired, lissome, soft-voiced, a girl with the trick of lowering her lids as a blind over her eyes; the only child of the owner of a plastics factory in Lille. I could envisage Monsieur and Madame Mouchard gilding the pill of marriage by a promise of capital to modernise the "hotel," which they'd never fulfil, and Jean-Baptiste, lacking subtlety and guile, betrayed into marriage to a girl who had, with the blessing of both sets of parents, selected him as her husband when she was in her teens.

I'd made him no promises, given him not one vestige of hope, but that didn't weaken the poignancy of his appeal, my yearning to love where I had no power to love, to protect the goodness in him that bitterness might wash away.

For comfort I reread Lisette's written from Rome where, for a year, she had been working for an Italian couturière. We'd been friends at the College of Art. Even then her future, in which she had allocated a niche to me, was a finite, detailed plan in her head. To realise it she needed the backing of her father, a man who was both astute and cautious in money matters. Her letter was typewritten, concise, no words wasted. She had, at last, wrung a promise from him, that provided he approved the terms of the lease, he would buy the shop in the rue Tronchet on which she'd had her eye for six months. And provided her purchase price was met, the elderly owner, Madame Durand, was prepared to vacate the premises at the end of July. This would give us the whole of August to reorganise, throw out the old stock and introduce our own. Lisette suggested that for the first year I should be a paid employee, and thereafter we could reconsider the setup, decide whether or not I wished to buy and she to sell a share of the business. There were two empty floors above the shop, one of which we could use as workrooms, the other as living quarters. Appointments with her father, his lawyer, and Madame Durand were fixed for the weekend after next. Her flight would arrive at Orly at 20:15 on Friday the 25th, and as soon as she reached her parents' apartment she would telephone me.

As an afterthought she added she'd been sorry to learn of my mother's death. Lisette was endowed with a mind that never wasted energy on a backward glance. Defeats—she hadn't experienced many—and disappointments she erased from memory.

With a beat of excitement, a definite sighting of the longed-for new horizon opening before me, I replaced the letter that spelled out my future into its envelope. If it had reached me before the Grey Man had stepped across my threshold, there would not have been a single reservation in my mind. But the interlude had introduced two. In my head Lisette's emphatic voice preaching common sense. "Oh, for Heaven's sake, all you have to do is get up and go. An old lady who's dying anyway, a dishy man who suspects you're after her money or in league with a wicked uncle who sounds as though he should be certified! Crazy, unless you are dead sure you can persuade her to leave you a fortune."

When the dusk thickened and the bird calls dwindled into occasional isolated notes, I thought how simple it would be if one possessed a magic filter that would subtract love; even persuade oneself that love was no more than a brilliant mirage that temporarily blinded the eye, maddened the senses.

The house I entered held an abnormal stillness. After dinner Trudy and Marcus had driven to have a drink with some local friends, leaving Marco in Aunt Louise's care. Uncle Conwyn had not chosen to eat with us, and I imagined him toiling at his self-imposed task of recording the history of Saffron for posterity. At the top of the stairs I hesitated. Turn left, bang on his door, demand an accounting of his double-dealing? My heart packed solid with hate cautioned me to turn in the opposite direction. My rage, a spume of accusations flying from my tongue would only drive him deeper into the icy depths of his monstrous arrogance. If I was to succeed as an inquisitor, my calm must be tempered to a point when it shattered his.

The hours between midmorning and early evening gave me what I desperately needed: a respite from Saffron, in which I could temporarily ignore what loomed ahead of me. Perhaps Emmy sensed my need; more likely, familiar with its passions, secrecy, and fratricidal infighting, she decided to shut Saffron and those who lived under its roof from sight and memory as we drove through the gates. The time we spent at lunch, wandering through the cathedral and its cloisters, shopping for Jonathan's birthday present and a diminutive boiler suit for Samantha was an easement of spirit, all the more precious because it had a time limit.

Standing beside her car, I asked: "How do you say thank you for a perfect day? It's been marvellous, every single minute of it."

"You don't even try." She kissed my cheek. "Anyway, if you start, I'll have to. I've enjoyed it just as much, even more. To me it's been something rather special. We'll do it again, and meanwhile, if I don't see you before—I must get things in hand for the party, and Ross will be down on Thursday—I'll see you Friday."

I watched her car disappear. The lovely buoyancy remained with me even after I'd entered the house. Grandmother had waved us off, said: "Come and see me when you get back," and so I knocked at her door without the smallest premonition of what lay waiting for me on the other side.

She was sitting in her yellow chair, a cigarette burnt almost to the butt between her fingers. For once, her glance did not fly towards me as the door clicked. For a second I wondered if, despite the cigarette, she was dozing, but when I whispered her name, she heard me, twisted her head. The shock was light but distinct when her eyes meeting mine betrayed no glint of recognition. Then, as if surfacing from some hide deep within herself, she gave me a nod that acknowledged my presence. "Will you feed the turtle doves while Carlo is out with Nancy?"

She handed me the Chinese porcelain bowl that was filled with seed for them twice a day. I scattered it on the parapet, waited until they began to circle. As I advanced towards her I was conscious of a gaze of such alarming intensity that fear jabbed, and I cried: "What is it? Is something the matter?"

She pointed to an upright chair immediately facing her. "Sit down." When I was seated the silence was so absolute that I could hear the hard little beaks of the turtle doves pecking the seed.

She spoke in a cold voice, the enunciation slow, the grip of her eyes that were impenetrable never wavering for a second from mine. "I want to know if you have met Lorraine's brother, Bernard Andrews."

The cells in my brain seemed to spin. It was an ultimatum with only seconds allowed for a decision: the truth or a lie? I'd made a promise to the Grey Man but I would have broken it without a scruple if I could have been certain that the truth would not harm her.

Before I could stumble towards a judgment her voice rang out in fierce command. "No, don't answer me. From you silence is less painful to bear than a lie. And that's what you were about to do, to lie to me."

She averted her face, leaving me with a profile on which the colourless flesh was sealed rigidly to the bones.

Alarmed, I pulled a low stool to the level of her knee, seized her hands. She tried to wrest them away, but I would not let them go. "Lies can be prompted by concern, even love. If I had lied, and I'm not certain I would have, it would have been out of concern for you that you should not have to suffer that terrible grief all over again."

"Lies," she whispered, her head angled against me, her eyes fixed on the picture in the silver frame, "are stones that build up into a tomb. My tomb. I'm being slowly put to death by lies. I'll be buried under them. And as for grief, it has been a close companion all my life, my familiar."

I felt my flesh shiver. She sensed it and turned her face that was remote with outraged pride. "An old friend, Lady Vanley, came to take tea with me." Scorn touched her mouth. "No one apparently had the forethought to swear *her* to secrecy. So it was with considerable relish that she discovered I was ignorant of Bernard Andrews's arrival in Meads Cross, his numerous calls on people who were acquainted with his sister including, so Meg's spies informed her, two visits to Saffron." She drew deep on the seemingly bottomless well of her wrath. "While I, its mistress, have been kept in total ignorance of his presence in my house. And you have allowed yourself to be used as an accomplice in a monstrous and quite unforgiveable deception."

"But it was a deception to protect you from suffering a second time the grief of Lorraine's death, reliving it. I didn't see myself as an accomplice . . ."

"*But* willingly or unwillingly that's what you were. How many times have you met him?"

"Twice. I went into my bedroom when Uncle Conwyn was showing it to him. That was the first time, and we didn't exchange more than a couple of sentences. The second was yesterday when I was having tea with Mrs Heron. He had made an appointment to see her in the evening, and then found he had to return to London . . ."

"London! You mean he's no longer in Meads Cross?"

"I don't know."

"Did he say in which hotel he would be staying, how long he would be in London?"

"No."

"What did you talk about?"

"He asked Mrs Heron how well she had known his sister. She explained they'd been friends, but not close friends because of the age gap between them."

She said contemptuously: "One question, one answer, it could have been exchanged on the doorstep."

"He wasn't with her for more than fifteen minutes. He was in a hurry to get away."

Her eyes bored into me. "He didn't question you or Emmy about the timetable the police compiled of the day before and the night Lorraine was drowned?"

No lies, so far, but now I made the mistake of hesitating a moment too long. She snapped her lids, as though she could not bear the sight of me. "Enough, I refuse to catechise a child who has had words put into its mouth, been bullied into withholding the truth." On a sigh of great depth she opened them. "We will put this matter straight between us. It is my wish, indeed my order that Bernard Andrews, as Lorraine's brother, should be made welcome in a house that was her home for two years. That he should be treated with every courtesy and consideration due to him, and have any questions which he wishes to raise answered. So I expect, if you learn he has returned to Meads Cross you will tell me of your own free will. Or, if you see him, you will convey to him a message from me that I would appreciate his calling on me. At least it will afford him an opportunity to see that, as he has no doubt been given to understand, I'm neither crazed nor senile! I'm not asking for your promise. I am assuming you will obey me. Without trust between us, there is nothing. Do you understand?"

"I understand." She had issued an edict. At the moment I believed I could obey it. "You can trust me."

She reached for an envelope on the table beside her. "Now I want you, some time this evening, to take this letter to the Old Rectory for me. It is for Ross. I wish him to have it when he arrives home tonight or tomorrow morning. Will you do that for me?"

"Of course. I'll go now, this minute."

She pressed the bell. "Any time this evening will do." She looked into my face, and a faint ghost of the old, loving smile touched her lips. "I do not blame you, but I do blame those who would deprive me of my rightful authority in my own house."

Nancy opened the door, Carlo on a leash at her heels. "You rang, madam?"

"Yes. You can let Carlo loose, and be good enough to ask Mrs Delamain-Powell and Mr Conwyn to come and see me, at once, if you please."

I did not go downstairs until Greville sounded the gong. Trudy and Marcus were already seated at the table. "Ah," Marcus said, "so we are not to be condemned to a dinner *à deux*," and with an exaggerated gesture he rose and pulled out my chair.

Trudy scowled at me. "What's been going on while I've been having my day at home? Ma-in-law is in an awful flap, all scarlet about the gills. You've been here, so for Heaven's sake give us a clue."

"Grandmother had a visitor this afternoon who told her that Bernard Andrews was in Meads Cross, that he'd actually called here without her knowing he was in the house."

"For God's sake," Trudy exploded. "That's all we need!"

"Lady Vanley!" Marcus crowed. "I'd bet on it. The self-appointed town crier! How did she react, Grandmother I mean: Off with their heads or an attack of angina?"

Before I could answer the door opened and Uncle Conwyn entered. He spoke first to Greville, who was limping hurriedly to set another place. "I'm not dining downstairs, Greville." He touched his shoulder, bent his head towards the old man's ear. "Would you leave us for ten minutes. There is a family matter we need to discuss."

When the four of us were alone, he moved to the head of the table, theatrically took on his most arrogant stance, addressed us as though we were a class of children, his pale, soulless glance darting from one to the other. "You are all aware that, to protect your grandmother from distress, when Bernard Andrews took it upon himself to reopen the investigation into Lorraine's death, we decided, for her sake, to spare her this knowledge. We could not foresee that Andrews would spread his net so wide that his mischief-making would become the subject of common gossip. This afternoon Lady Vanley called and passed news of his meddling to your grandmother. Fortunately Lady Vanley either did not know, or shrank from telling her, of the abominable tactics Andrews is employing. Her anger and resentment arise solely from the fact that she has been prevented from receiving Andrews at Saffron as a welcome guest."

His glance pinned itself on me. "I understand when you met him at the Old Rectory yesterday, he was on his way to London?"

"Yes. I gained the impression on a short visit to consult his legal advisers. Those were the words he used."

"No matter. So far as your grandmother is concerned, she is to be informed he has left the district and cannot be traced. Initially we acted solely in the interest of her health and well being, and we will continue to do so."

Marcus queried: "Orders to lie our heads off."

"Orders to protect your grandmother from a painful encounter with an unmannerly, brutish inquisitor."

"And lie to the police when they come calling?"

"The police? I'm not with you."

"The boys in blue with notebooks and forms on which they write down charges. Why else should Andrews have turned sleuth if not to lay a charge against a man or . . . a woman."

"Facetiousness is singularly inapt at a time when our sole concern is to ensure that your grandmother is not subjected to a harassment that might well kill her."

Trudy wailed: "No one's immortal. We've all got to die some time, even her," and then covered her face with her hands.

"Belt up, pussycat," Marcus said.

Uncle Conwyn's incensed glance swivelled from one to the other, before he widened its range to include me. "My orders to the three of you are to hold your tongues and keep holding them."

Marcus laughed. "Why, when we've nothing to lose but our chains, and maybe if the charge sticks this time, a hell of a lot to gain."

He sneered: "You're in your usual state of inebriation."

"Drunk!" Marcus corrected.

"Oh, for God's sake," Trudy screamed, "let's grab Marco and clear out."

Marcus smiled into his uncle's face. "With the throne of the co-favourite tottering, the old queen a-dying! Hardly the moment, I think."

Wordless, no spring in his limbs, he moved like a marionette to the door and out of the room.

Trudy whispered despairingly: "If the police couldn't prove it was murder in March, what better chance have they now?"

"A dirty little thing called money. If it doesn't talk, it acts as an irresistible persuader. And that's Andrews' trump card, a nice thick wad of ten-pound notes."

Simultaneously they both became aware of my presence, as though after the Grey Man had left the room, I'd been invisible. As Greville eased himself through the door, Marcus said in a soft voice: "It would appear we're shocking Cousin Claudine. Perhaps murder is an ugly word to her!"

"Isn't it to everyone?"

"No," he said, his smile alight with malice. "Not everyone, little cousin, not by any means. It can be a beautiful word if it's applied to the right person."

After dinner, with the letter in my hand I went into the sweet-scented dusk, across the bridge, and up through the interlacing paths, pausing only once to look back at the fading silhouette of the Abbey.

When I reached the main gate, I leant against one of its pillars. Not a glimmer of light showed in the house, and it gave forth no whisper of sound. I thought by this time tomorrow he may be there, and the beautiful image that had taken root in my heart burst into clarity, and in my ears I heard the notes of his voice. I stayed listening and looking, passion burning yearningly until, with knowledge of its futility, I had, physically, to shake myself back to sense. I wondered how long it would take me to win back my freedom.

I trod the path with stealth, dreading having to speak a word, to assume a normality of manner I did not at that moment possess. The door was flung back, the hall empty, and not a sound stirred in the whole house. I tiptoed in, laid the envelope on the table under the silver bowl of pink roses and tiptoed out.

Next morning when I stepped into the corridor, Aunt Louise and Dr Knox were talking at the top of the stairs. Step by step, as I advanced, their words became audible.

"I assure you, Louise, it was no more than a very mild attack. Thank God, we can now control angina. Keep her in bed, though if she expresses a wish to do so, she can get up to tea." His hand gripped her shoulder, "And for everyone's sake, try to relax. I'll leave you some mild tranquillisers. Take one before you go to bed. If you don't have more rest, you'll break down. With two patients in the house, I'm not anxious to have a third."

She burst out: "There's this other wicked business . . ."

"I know," he soothed, "but in all probability it will die down in a day or so. You must not worry; and neither must she. Stress is the prime killer of the age."

As her eyes registered me, she announced: "Your grandmother had a heart attack in the night . . ."

"How is she now?"

Dr Knox answered: "It was a minor one. There is no cause for alarm, at least at this stage."

"She must have absolute quiet, see no one," she insisted.

Again he touched her shoulder. "Oh, I don't know. If she asks for Claudine, it will do her no harm to see her for half an hour this afternoon. We have to balance exhaustion against frustration and boredom. One is as dangerous for her as the other. It is a delicate balance, but we can only do our best. Confiscate her cigarettes for twenty-four hours, disconnect her telephone, and no stairs for at least a week."

He gave me a kindly nod of dismissal, and stood aside for me to pass. As I descended the stairs, I heard him say: "I'll look in on Conwyn before I go, see how he is."

For once I found Trudy sitting at the table spooning up cornflakes. Without a touch of make-up, minus her false eyelashes, she looked wan and plain. "Did you sleep through all the commotion, or did you decide to lie low?"

I said guiltily: "I must have slept. I didn't wake up until half-past seven."

"Lucky you! Marco was on the grizzle from midnight, and then at two, when he fell asleep, Grandmother had an angina attack. Panic stations, and by the time all the fuss had subsided, it was time to get Marcus off. I wanted to phone his boss, say he wouldn't be in, but he wouldn't let me."

"Couldn't he have taken the day off?"

"No," she snapped, "he couldn't because whatever excuse I'd dreamed up, short of producing a doctor's certificate, his boss would have assumed he'd got a hangover. And he'd be a little farther on the skids than he is now." She glared at me. "You know what you are, don't you? The last straw!"

"Not intentionally. How many more times do I have to swear I don't pose a threat to Marcus or anyone else?"

She gave a ghost of her old grin. "But you'd say that anyway, wouldn't you? Lie in your pearly teeth. Oh, what the hell. You're only a puppet. Uncle Con pulls the strings."

Anger flared. "You're wrong there, too. He does not. Even if he pulled one in the beginning, he doesn't now."

She shrugged her disbelief. "Well, he won't be dogging your heels today. After a night standing guard over Grandmother his ulcer is playing him up and he's retired to a bed of pain." She shoved back her chair. "And I am getting out of this damned place. It's going to be a scorcher, so I'll take Marco to a beach where there will be a breeze. If anyone asks, we won't be back until five." She added grudgingly: "You could come too, if you wanted. At least I'd know what you were up to."

I thanked her but declined.

"Okay." As she reached the door, she tossed back over her shoulder: "Take care of yourself when you keep company with the devil tonight. He doesn't concern himself with a little thing like principles, you know."

"You mean Adam?"

"Who else! Who do you think had most to gain by Lorraine's death! Work it out for yourself. And remember you're a threat too, the biggest he's ever faced, sprung at him out of the blue, the enemy's master stroke."

"I'll take care." My promise was so lightly given that the final glance she threw me was loaded with a pitying contempt.

After lunch I took a sketch block and sat under the umbrella of shade cast by the big balcony. A little after half-past three I saw Aunt Louise advancing on me with her purposeful but ungainly stride. "Nancy will be serving tea to your grandmother at four o'clock. You may drink it with her, providing you do not stay longer than half an hour, and during that time do not touch upon any topic of conversation that will either excite or distress her."

"I wouldn't dream of doing either. How is she now?"

"Her condition is slightly improved from what it was this morning, but it is still critical. In my opinion Dr Knox is far too sanguine."

Her dressing gown was a brocade mandarin coat, with a narrow stand-up collar, its extravagant bronze, ultramarine and silver flowing one into the other, on her feet gold kid mules. While Nancy fiddled with the elaborate tea service, I exclaimed: "How I'd love to paint you in that heavenly coat. Only I wouldn't be able to do you justice."

She smiled, but her eyes weren't quite focused, and her voice was a little breathy. "So you shall, but on a day when I've not been robbed of half my faculties by doctor's pills." She looked beyond me to Nancy. "Thank you, Nancy. Miss Claudine will pour. Would you please bring me a packet of cigarettes from behind the books on the third shelf in my bedroom?"

When Nancy had left us, I said: "Are you allowed to smoke today?"

"No. But I intend to. To preserve your aunt's peace of mind we will destroy the evidence." I was ordered to tear the cellophane off the packet, and mould her an ash tray out of the foil, which I held in the palm of my hand. She stroked the brocade, savouring its texture. "One of Kitty's happiest choices. Kitty Langton who shops for me now that I can no longer travel to London. She was a well-known Mayfair hostess before the war, famous for her exquisite dress sense. Alas, she lacked all sense with men. Her last husband was a compulsive gambler who shot himself and left her nothing but debts. In reduced circumstances, she capitalised on her talent for fashion, taking a percentage on the clothes she selects for women like me who can no longer visit the couture houses. She is an agreeable creature. Knox confirms that Chandler should be fit by the end of the week, so he can drive you to London to meet her. She knows my taste and will soon learn yours."

I felt my teeth grit, but the wavering of her fingers towards the foil ash tray in my palm, poured the love and pity back into my heart. Even weakened and, I suspected, slightly drugged, her perception was still sharp enough to sense my reaction. She gave one of her husky laughs. "You have spirit, and I would not have you without it, but it will not diminish that spirit to take advantage of the expertise of a woman with a flair for recognising style and elegance. Tomorrow when my telephone is restored to me, I will telephone her and arrange a day for you to shop together. Not Tuesday, my solicitor will be here that afternoon and I want you to meet him. I suggest we make it Thursday."

Thursday was the day I'd picked out to return to Paris. Now I must advance it to Tuesday. I counted the days between and they were terrifyingly short in number.

After she'd sipped her tea, she laid her head back and drifted into a doze, breathing evenly, her body relaxed. I crumpled the makeshift ash tray and put it in my pocket; the windows were open so the scent of tobacco had been washed away by fresh air. With her usual sleight of hand the packet of cigarettes had vanished. Then I sat and watched her, enduring the conflict of love and prickling resentment she engendered in me. After ten minutes or so her lids parted, and the eyes that gazed at me were perfectly focused.

"What a sinful waste of time to sleep while you are with me! You must blame it on Knox's pills. They reduce me to a comatose, mindless body."

"Not now. You look better, as though that little sleep refreshed you."

"Do you know why? Because I spent it dreaming of you, my darling."

"What were we doing?"

"What we are now, sitting quietly together at peace with each other. Peace," she repeated, "is one of the most beautiful words in the English language."

"Yes it is, nearly as lovely as tranquillity," I said, and thought except in this room, between the two of us, peace and tranquillity did not exist at Saffron.

Nancy, after her usual perfunctory tap, entered. "Mrs Delamain-Powell said you'd be wanting to get back to bed now, madam. Shall I help you?"

"Yes, in a minute, Nancy." She smiled on me. "You look altogether too solemn today. It will do you good to be taken out to dinner, and Adam, I promise you, is an excellent host. Come and see me in the morning, and you will witness what Charles Knox calls my miraculous powers of recuperation. Now, Nancy, you may give me your arm."

As she stepped forward I was conscious of Nancy's glance of blinkered hostility. I could only assume this evening was one she counted her own, and resented my depriving her of it. Why otherwise should she hate me?

12

ADAM WAS FIFTEEN MINUTES LATE picking me up. As he opened the door of his maroon E-type Jaguar, he said, breathing impatience, his attention only lightly pinned to me: "Sorry I'm late. Dickson, one of the men, took a tumble from the tractor late this afternoon, and I had to run him to hospital."

"Was he badly hurt?"

"Mild concussion and a broken arm. It was his own fault. He's a careless young devil who thinks he knows it all."

He drove fast up the drive, ignoring the speed limit, his profile tense, temper smouldering. When we stopped outside the gates to give way to a car towing a caravan, I said: "I'm being a nuisance, aren't I, and probably a bore? Why didn't you telephone me and cancel the date?" I nearly added, but checked my tongue: "And if it is a bore, let's call it off now."

"Stand you up! Not likely. Defeat my own interests! My trouble is that I'm three drinks under par, but we'll soon put that right." He gave me a lightning side glance, a half-mollifying smile. "Anyway, dressed-up you're an ornament to any car. Everyone must keep remarking that you're the image of dear old dad, but you've got a look of your mother too. I remember her. What did she die of?"

"Heart failure."

"Speaking of hearts, how is Hermione?"

"I had tea with her. She was tired, but improving. Planning to buy me a wardrobe of new clothes picked out by an old friend of hers, and having Monsieur Pierre restyle my hair."

His nod was vague, uncaring. "Good for you." I thought he didn't have to glean his bulletins on Grandmother's health from me. Nancy, his spy inside the citadel, would relay them to him. His lover? Yes, but not in running for a wife. He'd set his sights higher than a village girl with rough hands, who didn't wash her bushy hair often enough. With the wind tearing at mine, the speedometer touching 90 on a narrow winding road, I yelled: "Are you always such a reckless driver?"

"Not reckless," he shouted back. "Just a damned good one. What's the point of paying for speed under the bonnet if you waste it dawdling? Don't worry, you're not going to get a scratch on your pretty face."

The dining room of the inn was low, its ink-black ceiling beams only a few inches above Adam's head. We were escorted to a table in an alcove formed by a semicircular window by the head waiter who addressed Adam by name as he presented the menus. "A large drink first, Alex." He cocked an enquiring eyebrow at me. I chose a cinzano. I looked over my shoulder at the cavernous fireplace, the pitch blackness of the ship's iron-hard timbers. "How old is it?"

"Foundations probably go back to the sixteenth century, but there's a lot of fake tacked on top. It was an old coaching inn and a hideout for smugglers. You know: 'Brandy for the Parson, Baccy for the Clerk, Laces for the lady . . .'"

"And Letters for a spy!"

"Kipling in a French convent!"

"Why not? Didn't you ever learn any French verse?"

"God forbid! More important than the olde English bric-a-brac, is that they employ a French chef, keep an excellent wine cellar and, if you stipulate one of three tables, you can eat and drink without anyone breathing down your neck. For these parts, the best to hand. Which probably leads you to suspect I'm stepping out of my station!"

I laughed. "Do people still have them? I thought they became obsolete after the war."

"Depends on your age. Over forty they most certainly do. Not stations so much as cages! Now what are you going to eat for the main course? Steak? Lobster?"

I chose the lobster thermidor. He ordered steak. During the meal he was at pains to keep the conversation impersonal, manipulating it with a practised ease, which I found both enlightening and amusing.

We had coffee on a terrace overlooking an unending stretch of green pasture on which sheep and lambs grazed. I said: "There must be millions of them."

"A few hundred thousand, Romney Marsh is the richest sheep grazing in the country, and the most expensive." He leaned so far back in the white metal chair that its two front legs left the ground, and dropped his pose of amiability. "Suppose," he suggested, "we get down to business."

"By all means. But what business?"

A rage of impatience almost beyond control seized him. "Oh, for God's sake, you're a bright girl, I don't have to spell it out. An old lady who's dying, bequeathing a fortune for the last of the contenders to win her heart. That's the trick, you know, to be installed as the last favourite before she dies."

"And you're scared it might be me!"

"With good reason."

I found myself smiling. "What on earth do you imagine I'd do with an ancestral home, a garden so huge I haven't been able to walk round it yet, and thousands of acres of land! Pen myself up for life in what amounts to a shrine dedicated to the past?"

"You could use it as a base to take off for the jet set, buy yourself a Greek island, and a yacht to take you there. Milch Saffron until you'd drained it dry . . ."

With a kind of disbelief I saw his black anger spiralling, said quickly: "I've got a job lined up in Paris. A girl friend with a rich father to back her is in the process of buying a boutique. I'm joining her. When I've saved up some money, I'll probably have a stake in it too. That's my future."

"And that's what you've told Hermione?"

"No, not yet."

He laughed in high glee. "I didn't suppose you had. Not with Brigstock putting in an appearance next week!"

"When the right moment arrives, I'll tell her what I intend to do, also that every week or so I'll fly back to see her!"

He eyed me with cynical delight. "So you are as young as you look, and naïve to boot." He leaned across. "She's had eighty-five years to learn her guile; you've had less than twenty. Even if I believed you, which I don't, why should you shop around for a partner with a rich father? If you're so mad keen on a dress shop or whatever, you've only got to sit it out, behave yourself prettily and within a year the chances are that you'd be able to buy a whole one for yourself in the rue de la Paix. Don't tell me that hasn't crossed your little mind?"

"It hasn't." Our faces were close. The dream image of my father dead, his own character was building up brick by brick, steely, merciless, enslaved by an ambition that had set hard when he was a schoolboy. Curiously I felt no revulsion, only the birth pangs of empathy, and a sense of closeness as though I'd known him all my life. "My guess is that we've one other characteristic in common besides the colour of our hair. Since you were old enough to plan your life, you've known what you wanted. Well, the same goes for me. You want Saffron. And though it may sound absurd to you I want a fashion boutique." Treacherously, I was brushed by an anguish of love. I thrust it aside. "Not even for Grandmother, can I transform myself into a docile little handmaiden."

"Not even for a year?" he mocked.

I pounced. "How do you know? How can you calculate the length of a life?"

"By taking expert, professional advice."

"Doctors don't talk about their patients' expectation of life."

"But nurses do."

Nurse Hailey, the frenetic knitter, was middle aged, what Grandmother described as a poor conversationalist, heavy in the hand. She didn't sound like a gossip. I saw him watching me, speculating whether I'd work it out.

"Lorraine Andrews!"

"Who else!"

"I still don't believe that the best nurse in the world can put a date stamp on when a patient is likely to die."

"A rough estimate, by someone with a stake in the outcome."

Involuntarily my mouth shaped itself into a grimace of distaste. "Marriage to Uncle Conwyn!"

"Maybe." He suddenly switched subjects, began to speak at speed, only just above his breath, his cobalt eyes as hard as flints. "Okay, you propose to turn yourself into a weekend commuter between Paris and Saffron. If you are to keep your lead that's what it would add up to, leaving five, maybe six days a week for those in possession to annihilate you when you weren't there . . . no matter what steps Conwyn Delamain took to protect your interests and his own." The cigarette burnt so low between his fingers that it must have scorched the skin, but he hardly noticed, stubbing it out without taking that hypnotic gaze from my face, the whole of his being compressed into the quick-flowing words. "Listen, for as long as I can remember I've walked a tightrope. I'm not going to be tumbled off it by Conwyn Delamain or his protégée. You see, unlike you, my upbringing hasn't been one to persuade me that blood is thicker than water."

A moment before I'd been proud that I was beyond being hurt, that I could accept and understand the wild ruthlessness in him. Now I wasn't sure. "Grab some money, get rich and live happy ever after."

"Money plus power equals happiness or as near as you're likely to get on this earth. Next Tuesday afternoon, at two fifty-five precisely, a black saloon car will arrive at Saffron. Out of it will step a drab little man who looks like an undertaker's assistant. In fact he's a solicitor. Hermione's. At three o'clock to the tick he'll be shown into the sanctum. They'll spend an enthralling hour discussing a new will. After which he'll be served with tea. Then, with salaams, he'll drive off, having made a date, approximately one week later, for a second visit, when the will will be signed and witnessed by the two clerks he'll bring with him. Let's say ten days from now. And the chances are it will be the last will Hermione makes. Conwyn Delamain will take good care it is. So now do you follow me?"

"I'd have to be deaf and blind not to. But I don't want . . ."

He flattened my protest. "What you want or don't want is of no consequence. What you're given is. You could be given the lot . . .

depending on the terms of the deal you and Conwyn Delamain hatched up between you."

"Which I repeat doesn't exist. So that aside, why should Grandmother disinherit a son, a daughter, a grandson, a great-grandson and you in favour of me?"

"I'll tell you. Her son suffers from what are delicately described as nervous collapses, flies to pieces in a crisis and has to be cosseted back to health in a clinic. Her grandson will be an alcoholic before he's thirty. Her daughter is automatically disqualified because she'd leave what she inherited to the aforesaid alcoholic."

"That leaves you."

"My point. The current favourite until you appeared on the scene. Now she could leave me a farm and a few thousand pounds. It's narrowed down to a name on a birth certificate, hasn't it?"

He was wrong. It narrowed down to his mother. The potent blood link, regard for professional skill even love were of no account when weighed against the spectre of Alice Terson entering Saffron as mother of the owner, maybe moving into the balcony suite. For all his shrewdness he had no inkling that the stumbling block wasn't me, wasn't even the name on his birth certificate, but the existence of his mother. My summons to Saffron hadn't arrived until my mother was dead because Grandmother was willing to accept the progeny so long as their mothers were no more than a heap of bones under the earth. For a moment I was wrenched out of the present, chilled by a grief so overwhelming that he faded out of sight. Had my mother sensed that, and knowing it, willed herself to die? But surely not all those years ago. Then I blinked, and his face came back into vision. He'd never inherit Saffron unless his mother, who could only be in her fifties, died before Hermione. All that vaunting ambition would be spent without return. I was filled by emotion like tears . . . pity or affection, or a combination of both.

He had leaned away from me, a half smile touching his lips. "So, if you don't see yourself as mistress of Saffron, all you have to do is walk out before Mr Brigstock makes his second appearance in ten days' time. Simplicity itself!"

I would probably have given him a precise date if I had not been certain he'd confide it to Nancy. "I will, but in my own time."

The smile remained but its quality changed. "So now we come down to the crunch. Just sweet talk. Our father was a master at the art, with a genius for walking round ugly situations and pretending they didn't exist. Once my mother told him she was pregnant he never addressed another word to her, but communicated with her through a solicitor." There was a tiny pause, and he spoke not to me but to himself. "One day when I was ten, watching a village cricket match, Conwyn Delamain swore at me, called me a filthy little bastard because I didn't hop respectfully out of his way. My mother was with me. A boy who had no right to exist. A mother who had no right to bear a child!"

"A grown man now with every right."

The shutters lifted from his eyes. "Every right. All earned. But my mother has earned compensation too. And I intend to make sure she gets it, with interest."

I stared at him, as my heart mourned for the boy he had been, who'd fight as long as he breathed, only to tumble headlong into defeat.

But with me he appeared, momentarily at least, to have given up the fight. Impatiently he clicked his fingers for the bill.

The car park was a walled enclosure that made darkness seem nearer than it was. Adam's Jaguar was parked in an angle. From a distance of ten yards the shape of a man was visible bending over the door, fiddling with the handle.

Adam took a leap forward, grabbed his shoulder, wrenched him upright. Simultaneously the overhead lighting system in the car park was switched on and I recognised Bernard Andrews.

Adam shouted: "What the hell do you think you're doing snooping round my car?"

Bernard Andrews jerked backwards to free himself. "Better a snooper with a right to snoop than a liar, and that's what you are, Terson, a liar and a perjurer." His thick-fleshed face gleamed with cruel exultancy. "The reason why nobody could trace Lorraine's girl friend was because she never existed, but she had a boy friend, hadn't she, who took her to dinner at an hotel where the head waiter identified you from a photograph . . ."

"You haven't got a photograph of me."

"I took it two days ago, admittedly without your permission. Telescopic lenses come in very handy at times." He jeered. "Are you so wet behind the ears you don't know that alibis provided by wives and mothers are highly suspect! Swear their little souls away, especially mothers of illegitimate sons with expectations. Coached by you, of course, she swore you'd spent the evening with her, never stirred from her side. But you spent it with Lorraine. I've a witness who saw you in her car. Reginald Farrant."

137

"The village drunk!" Adam gave a roar of laughter. "Blind drunk by 10 P.M. seven days a week."

"That night he wasn't too drunk to recognise both of you, which makes you a lying, murdering bastard . . ."

Adam's fist exploded, connected with Andrews's chin, and he slithered cumbersomely to the ground as a girl approaching a car alongside Adam's screamed and the boy with her ran forward.

"Oh, my God!" he breathed in a scared voice. "Di, fetch the manager."

Adam threw open the passenger door, pushed me. "Get in."

I swayed but stayed where I was. "He's unconscious. Hadn't you better find out how badly he's hurt?"

"I said, get in." This time the force was harder, but it came too late. The manager who'd greeted him in the foyer laid hold of the door to prevent it being closed. "Mr Terson, please. I must ask you to stay. Mr Andrews has been a guest at this hotel several times during the last fortnight, and is staying here tonight."

The young man who had Bernard Andrews's head propped against his shoulder exclaimed: "Thank God, he's coming round."

Adam jeered: "You didn't think you'd got a corpse on your hands, did you? I caught him snooping round my car. He got what he deserved: a sore head. That's the beginning and end of it."

The manager's hand was still on Adam's arm. "I have to hear Mr Andrews's side of the story. For all I know he could bring a charge of assault . . ."

"Let me get up." Bernard Andrews mumbled, and heaved himself up on knees that nearly but not quite buckled under him. By now a crowd hemmed us in. Through it a glass of brandy was passed. The boy held it to Andrews's lips. He sipped, pushed it aside and looked dazedly about him. Then in slow motion he blinked twice, like a punch-drunk boxer, and took a deep breath as awareness returned to him.

"Okay." His blurred gaze found Adam, and an ugly smile licked his mouth. "Married to Lorraine, you'd have won a fortune. But she turned you down, didn't she? That's why you murdered her, threw her into the river . . ." He gulped, shouted: "As though she were a stray cat! Tomorrow morning the letters she wrote me about you will be in the hands of the police. It's my bad luck that they don't hang murderers any more." He squared his muscled shoulders, bull-dozed his way through the ring of spectators, who in stunned silence parted to give him passage. The manager followed him.

For the first ten minutes Adam drove like a maniac, then gradually he eased off, took a glance at me, and drew into the nearest lay-by. "I didn't take you for a girl to be thrown into a panic by the huffing and puffing of a bully-boy like Andrews!"

"I'm not in a panic."

"Then what are you in? You're shaking like a jelly and you've gone as pale as a ghost. Afraid I'm heading for a life sentence for murder? No, I'd be flattering myself. More likely scared out of your wits that I'm going to knock you over the head, throw you into a ditch! So try and use your little brain: approximately fifty witnesses saw us drive off together, which means only a madman would attack you. And whatever else I may be, I'm sane. So pull yourself together. Within half an hour you'll be cosily tucked up in bed."

"Stop lecturing me. I'm a good deal steadier than you are. What I'd like to know is whether you did commit perjury, give the police a false alibi?"

"Among other things, Andrews is an ignoramus. Perjury is lying while you're under oath in a court of law. A false alibi? Okay. Any man in my shoes would have provided himself with one. Lorraine and I had dinner together in an hotel in Hastings on the night she died. The Jag packed up, and she drove me back to Saffron, in the light of a full moon! Somewhere along the road Farrant must have stopped being sick in a ditch for long enough to spot us."

"Why didn't he say so at the time?"

He shrugged. "Maybe he distrusted his fuddled memory, wasn't sure, or more likely remembered I was his master and Hermione was fast running out of patience with him. Then along comes Andrews, rustling crisp notes in his ear, and Hermione slaps a three-month eviction order on him, and he's nothing to lose."

He turned his head, his smile cynically amused. "Stop shaking in your shoes. I don't make a habit of murdering my girl friends. I got out of the car in the courtyard and went straight home. Not a hair of her head was harmed." He joked: "Honour bright!"

"Honour bright," I mimicked, "did she turn you down that night?"

"No. She was in the process of making up her mind."

"Between you and Uncle Conwyn?"

"Yes. Weighing the odds. So why should I murder her?"

Only if he were lying. Slowly I turned my head and found his glance waiting for me. He nodded. "I could, of course, be lying, giving you the story in reverse. That depends on whether you can convince

139

yourself a girl of twenty-six would have preferred to be married to Conwyn Delamain rather than to me? Can you?"

"It's hard to believe."

"But not impossible?"

I saw the face looking out of the silver frame close to Grandmother's hand. Beneath the smile there was strength and intense powers of calculation. Lorraine had the look of a girl who weighed all the odds and placed her bet on the man most likely to win. Maybe she was emotionally dry, reducing the issue to the man who would give her Saffron.

I said not "did you love her" but: "Was she in love with you?"

"Love isn't a precise science, not between consenting adults. You'll learn that someday, or maybe you'll be lucky, and won't. We understood each other." For a moment he clasped my shoulder, then he laughed. "I seem to be fated to bring you down to earth with a bump. Maybe it's an extension of your education, I wouldn't know. What I do know is that a delicately raised convent girl shouldn't be riding round in the dark with a man suspected even by an idiot of battering women to death."

"Don't joke. Please don't make a joke of it."

"Why not? What's Andrews but a windbag bursting with jokes?"

"Will he go to the police, show them the letters Lorraine wrote?"

"Sure. He'll probably be there by now, hot-footing it in case I make a run for it." He leaned forward to turn on the ignition, then paused, mused. "Somehow I can't see Lorraine committing herself to names. Not on paper. There was a canny streak in her. She'd boast about the number of men who'd chased her, yes, like telling me she'd had eight proposals of marriage and turned them all down . . ." His voice dropped and he seemed to be talking to himself, culling the depths of his memory. "Their professions, bank balances, luxury flats, names of restaurants or hotels where they ate, but never their names. Just nick-names: Bunny, Daddy Longlegs, Charlie-boy." He grinned. "Wonder what she dubbed me. Let's pray it wasn't Ginger!"

I tried to speak, but the words wouldn't come out. "Listen," he said in the gentlest voice I'd ever heard him use. "I've fought since the day I was born. Sometimes clean, sometimes dirty. That's me, a fighter to the death. A bloody sight better fighter than bully-boy Andrews. So spare me the tears, there's a good girl."

"There aren't any. You don't need them or deserve them." Instead I demanded an explanation of a query that had been hanging in my mind for days. "Since Uncle Conwyn's main objective in life is to have you disgraced in Grandmother's eyes, thrown out of Saffron, why does he obstruct a man who is trying to dig up sufficient evidence to have you charged with murder? Logically he should be working hand and glove with Bernard Andrews to bring about your downfall."

"Logic! That's a laugh. It isn't in him. Not that it would make any difference if it was, he's got no guts either. He knows that I'm not only a fighter to the death, but something even more dangerous, a natural survivor. That's what scares him rigid, keeps him awake at night, my gift for survival against all odds. On a battlefield strewn with corpses, I'd be standing upright, a sword in my hand. To aid and abet Andrews in his dream of murder, Conwyn has to be certain the charge will stick, or with me roaming free, he'd never again draw an easy breath."

"I don't find that theory very convincing."

"No, you wouldn't because you don't know Conwyn, his split-personality, split plumb down the middle, so he's always fighting himself. Engaged in a battle between the devil, me, and Saffron. To have Saffron smeared with scandal, the family's dirty washing spread across the newspapers, particularly the Sundays, with banner headlines would send him whizzing back to the clinic. The locals being treated to rounds of drinks in The Cock Pheasant by London reporters in return for information about the bastard's love life, and me having my 'life' ghosted by a professional writer to provide me with a nice little nest egg when I came out of jug . . . Not Conwyn. A woman on her beam ends with a kid to support, or a girl who has ambitions to set herself up in a fancy dress shop, that's more his mark, strictly undercover tactics, no dirt for the world to peer at."

"Now there's a witness who saw you driving home with Lorraine, will you be questioned by the police?"

"Fortunately they know Farrant. Drunk or sober he'd swear the moon was made of green cheese for a five-pound note." His voice tightened. "Of course, there's you. Why did I open my big mouth? You could nip along to the police in the morning. Is that the bright idea that's brewing in your little head?"

"You know perfectly well it isn't."

"Yes, I guess I do. Odd, that."

"I'd like to know what happens to you, about the police, I mean."

"If I get a chance I'll telephone you, but I'm not promising."

"Or you could ask Nancy to pass a message."

"Nancy!" He laughed. "What sharp eyes you have, sister!"

141

"Not particularly sharp, just eyes. She'd die for you, literally."

"Oblige me by keeping your nose out of my love life."

And this time he did turn the ignition key.

When Greville closed the door behind me, Uncle Conwyn stepped out of the morning room into the hall. "That will be all, Greville, thank you. Good night." As Greville walked towards the green baize door, I moved quickly in the direction of the stairs.

"Claudine, in here, please."

Because he uttered an order, I didn't have to obey it, but since he had disappeared inside the room, I was forced to advance as far as the threshold to make my excuses.

It was a less formal room than the others, the furniture casually assembled. There was a litter of women's magazines on the sofa, a pile of records on a central table, evidence that it was used by Marcus and Trudy as a bolt hole.

He posed himself in front of the fireplace, his hands clasped behind his back. Before I could utter my excuse, he demanded: "Are you hurt? Injured in any way?"

"No. Why should you imagine I was? But I am rather tired, so I would like to say good night."

He reverted to his habit of rendering his ears deaf to any speech that he counted irrelevant to the one he was about to make. "I'm very relieved. Now that Terson has involved you in a public brawl, perhaps you'll be prepared to heed my warning. Or don't you find it objectionable when your host resorts to thuggery?"

For once, he'd succeeded in astounding me. All right, I accepted that he checked on my movements in the house and gardens, but it was less than an hour since we'd left the hotel car park. Was it conceivable that he went to the length of having me followed? I heard the rage in my voice, made no attempt to suppress it. "How do you know what happened? How could you know?"

"If you are going to shout, please close the door. There is no need to wake the household or for anyone else to know of this scandalous affair."

"Tell me how you knew. Tell me."

"The proprietor of The Lamb Inn is an acquaintance of mine. That your father's daughter is staying at Saffron is common knowledge, and rightly after Terson's abominable exhibition in the parking yard, the accusations which Andrews made, the fact that on returning to the hotel he telephoned the police, laid charges against Terson, he considered it his duty to contact me, reasssure himself that you had arrived home unharmed. He acted with the greatest propriety."

"His concern, and yours, was quite unnecessary. He must have given you an exaggerated account of the incident. Mr Andrews was tampering with Adam's car . . ."

"Which," he interrupted, "gave Terson the right to punch him unconscious. At the very least assault and battery which means that you, as a witness, may be called upon by the police to make a statement. Doesn't that shock you to your senses? Or had you both had so much to drink, you were too fuddled to be aware of what was going on?"

"I've never been drunk in my life. I certainly wasn't tonight, and neither was Adam. As I said, I'm tired, so if you would excuse me."

"You may retire to your room when you have given me your word that you will not see Terson again."

"You should know the answer. Of course we'll continue to see each other. How could it be otherwise? It was crazy to imagine, having brought me here, you could keep us apart."

He stared over my head, his face sealed in riven anguish. When he spoke it was in a thin, remote voice. "It was my hope and intention that you should remain outside his sphere of influence until you had time to learn what manner of man he was, the threat he posed to you and Saffron."

I said quietly, not as an accusation, but a simple explanation surely within his grasp: "Children grow up, and when they are adults, as I am, they don't automatically obey orders they find unreasonable."

With a sharp movement, he angled his face away from me, the cold venom seeping back. "You obviously have no regard for me; you've been at pains to make that abundantly clear. I'm not asking for gratitude, but an acknowledgement that you have received from me advantages you would not have received from anyone else. However, I will not labour that point. What I find beyond comprehension is that you utterly disregard your mother's wishes."

"Perhaps because I was never consulted about them. They were imposed on me without my knowledge."

"A child of five, ten, even fifteen! An infant! Your mother's health was already deteriorating to a degree that it was not beyond the bounds of possibility that you would be left an orphan. Who would have cared for you? Nuns in a convent? A charity child! It was her first duty to make provision for you. She chose the wisest course. When you were four years old, in the event of her death, she appointed me your legal guardian. A deed was drawn up, signed and sealed in the presence of a notary in Paris."

So that was the false base of his assumed authority over me. It was so ludicrous an anticlimax that I heard myself laugh aloud. "A deed that is null and void, a worthless scrap of paper! I'm well past the age when I can be put under anyone's guardianship."

"But not past the age when you have a duty to respect and honour your mother's wishes: that your life should redeem the misfortunes and penury that ruined hers. Unlike you, I keep my promises. Mine to her was that when I am dead, you will inherit Saffron."

His pomposity was not only insufferable, it was past human belief, it drove me to cruelty. "A promise you'd have broken if you'd married Lorraine Andrews."

He made a manic gesture. A drop of spittle escaped his lips. He was an ugly, frightening sight. If I could I'd have withdrawn the words, but it was too late. "Mind your own business, you impertinent child."

I said, my voice schooled to implacable reason: "The impertinence is yours in claiming a right you don't possess, to manage my future. If my mother did, as you maintain, when I was a minor make you my legal guardian, that is a dead issue now."

He said sweepingly: "You talk of matters of which you are ignorant. I find that offensive."

"And I find it . . ." the exact word wouldn't come to my mind; I borrowed his, ". . . offensive that when she was penniless and ill you exploited my mother, that you visited her the day after my father's funeral, exercised some sort of duress over her . . ."

He laughed a little madly in my face so that an involuntary shiver passed over my flesh. "There was no duress on my part. Once I had agreed to pay your father's debts which amounted to over a thousand pounds, it was she who suggested the deed of guardianship. At any time by destroying it, or drawing up a new one, she could have annulled the original. She never, on the five occasions on which we met in Paris, expressed a wish to do so. Of course, though no reference to it was made by either of us, we were both aware that the basis of her negotiations with me, was the satisfaction she obtained from exacting retribution for the rightful position that had been denied her after her marriage to your father. So, I suggest you sweep from your mind the picture of me as a wicked uncle using pressure on a sick woman. I intend, despite your ungrateful and graceless behaviour, to honour my promise to her. On Tuesday your grandmother's lawyer will draft a new will. After my death Saffron will be yours. I hope this will induce you to mend your manners and to cease consorting with a man who is corrupt . . . evil."

That my mother had travelled secretly to Paris to see him on five occasions, was a betrayal that temporarily numbed me. The rest of his words were meaningless, no more than idiot mumblings. I turned my back on him.

"One moment. You are to tell your grandmother nothing about the disgraceful brawl in which Terson involved you."

I spun round. "I don't accept your authority to issue any order to me. But as I wouldn't willingly subject her to shock or distress, you're pretty safe. But how do you muzzle newspapers, people who may visit or telephone her?"

He said with lofty arrogance: "That will be taken care of. How is no concern of yours. If the police charge Terson with murder . . ." For a second his eyes glazed with inner horror . . . "I will deal with that situation."

Literally not able to look upon him a moment longer, I spun round a second time. On the stairs I met Trudy taking a warm bottle up to Marco. "Golly, you look like the wrath of God, not someone who's been supping with a long-lost brother. What did he do, unleash his fiendish temper, give you a taste of it? Well, I did warn you, didn't I?"

13

I SLEPT IN SNATCHES, barely aware that I slept. When the bird song broke upon the air, I gazed at the damask canopy over the bed. For once the chalk drawing of Ross was momentarily blotted from mind. Somewhere on the periphery was a memory of Bernard Andrews shouting threats at Adam, and my curiously unblaming acceptance that, under stress, he was capable of lying. It was my mother who absorbed all my thoughts as they tracked back as far as that snowy day in the churchyard.

Disconnected scenes from childhood flickered through my head: one, the twenty minutes she devoted each evening to brushing my hair, the strokes slow and firm—how she must have relished the task, not merely for love of me, but because it was one of the underpinnings of the retribution she'd planned so secretly, her ally a man whom she could only have hated and despised. I made myself feel with my heart and nerve ends the penury, the cruelty she had borne, the immutable grief that had cleft her life in half, her will to live until I was, legally, an adult, but still I could not forgive. Yet, paradoxically, I raged for her that, if Lorraine had not died, Uncle Conwyn would, in the end, have cheated her. As I would.

Soon after nine Aunt Louise came in search of me. She appeared less taut and exhausted than on the previous day—perhaps Dr Knox's tranquillisers had acted on the ferocious anxiety complex that gave her no respite. Her pale, shrewd eyes probed my face. "If you've been crying over Terson, you should have more sense. Like everyone else in England he is accountable to the Law. You might as well know that a police car called to take him to the police station at eight o'clock."

In fact, I hadn't shed a tear. It was sleeplessness that had swollen my eyelids. She gave me a bracing look that ordered me to pull myself together. "Sympathy is wasted on him. He has no mercy, not a grain, not even for Mama. If he's made himself agreeable to you, it's only to further his own ends. Well, now it would seem that he's been guilty of lying to the police. Not that that should surprise anyone who knows him."

"A liar isn't necessarily a murderer!"

"True," she conceded punctiliously with that regard for truth to which she attached supreme importance. "I count no man, not even Terson, guilty until that is the verdict of a jury. I hope your grandmother doesn't ask to see him today, but should she do so, she is to be told that he is at a cattle sale in Ashford. Meanwhile Greville will be monitoring all telephone calls, so that no one who isn't to be trusted not to upset her will be put through. She is a little better this morning; her pulse is stronger, so you may spend half an hour with her at ten-thirty. I am having two guests for lunch, old friends . . ." She looked with meaningful disapproval at my shirt and slacks. No one could have failed to get the message.

"I'll be sure and wear a dress!"

"If you would."

She was up and dressed in the blue Chanel suit she'd worn that first morning. "And you're not," she bade me when I kissed her, "to enquire how I am! That implies I'm ill, or recovering from illness. I'm neither. And I find the subject of my health boring."

I went through the daily ritual of feeding the turtle doves, while she held Carlo by her side. As I walked back, she said with concern: "How pale you look, my darling. I've been keeping you too much indoors. You must get out more into the air; Saffron air is the most invigorating in the world." She patted the chair beside her. "Did Adam give you a good dinner?"

"Very splendid. Lobster thermidor. Maybe I ate too much, that's why I look pale. We had coffee overlooking Romney Marsh, watching the sheep."

"He's an expert with sheep. Last year we had the highest total of live lambs in the county! Ah, here's Nancy with your coffee"—she made a face—"and my eggnog. A nauseating drink. If you serve it to me tomorrow, Nancy, I shan't drink it."

"Dr Knox's orders, madam."

"It's his *quid pro quo* for smoking. One uneven pulse beat, and the eggnog appears!"

I tried, before she left the room, to catch Nancy's eye, to gauge from its expression her degree of distress or alarm. She refused it.

After two sips of eggnog, Grandmother handed me the glass. "Be a good girl and pour the rest down the lavatory. And if you look in the second drawer of my chest, in the left-hand corner, under a pile of nightdresses, you'll find a packet of cigarettes."

When I uttered a mild protest, she cocked a mischievous eye at me. "You giving *me* orders!"

I laughed. "I wouldn't have a hope, would I."

"Not one, my darling. So let's not waste time arguing."

She smoked two, put the packet in a crocodile handbag on the table. Before closing it she drew out a manila envelope. "A present for you, darling."

I knew what it contained before I slit the flap, drew out the contents. Ten pound notes, most likely ten of them.

"Now," she said briskly, "I don't want another exhibition of your silly pride. It's most unbecoming. Kitty will charge the clothes you and she choose to my accounts. What you have there is pocket money for the bits of nonsense young girls deck themselves in nowadays, only please keep the more bizarre pieces out of my sight. It would pain me to see you in the glass beads and hooped earrings made out of painted tin that Trudy wears."

With my head bent over the notes, I knew she had been at pains to compromise, that the money was a gesture of conciliation that did not come easily to her. That I wouldn't spend a penny of it, had no intention of being led round couture salons by Mrs Langton, she wasn't to know, because I had not yet built my courage to a sufficiently high peak. As I smiled, thanked her, and tucked the flap over the notes, I counted the days, checked the deadline imposed by Mr Brigstock's arrival.

After I left her I went for a walk, turning my back on the extravaganza of the gardens, following the river bank where it was cool and green, unlandscaped by human hand. Blue-greens and yellow-greens, ferns and fronds, and long skeins of black-green weed swaying in the scarcely perceptible current. I had walked less than a mile, when I saw Trudy and Marco ahead.

"Two miles a day. To slim down my waistline and pump pure fresh air into his lungs. Since your waistline doesn't need paring, and you haven't got a baby, what's your aim and object?"

"A walk, out of sight of anyone looking out of the windows of the house!"

She grinned companionably. "He's a terrible peerer, a proper Peeping Tom." The grin vanished, and she said: "So Nemesis has struck. Unfortunately Marcus left before I'd heard the news. No wonder you looked a bit wan when I saw you last night on the stairs. You the centrepiece of a vulgar brawl!" She chortled. "With Adam's alibi busted by Andrews, the police, as the saying goes, may this time have got their man. And the best of luck to them. Personally, I'd like to see him guillotined. I told you the other day I've got a one-track mind. I'm for Marcus. Devoted little wifie, that's me. A pretty rare breed of female!"

"He's lucky, very lucky to have you." And I meant it.

"I'm his only bit of luck," she mourned. "There's always been Adam lurking in the wings ever since he was a kid; Uncle Con tripping on and off stage, then Lorraine, and now you. Hell, he's never had a chance. Oh," she cried, suffering one of her instant changes of mood, "look who's calling. On a weekday too. Do you suppose Grandmother summoned him posthaste to scour the countryside for Andrews? There's no love lost between him and Adam, you know. Or maybe you didn't."

I had delivered a letter, but I had no knowledge of its contents. The blue Mercedes had crossed the bridge, was beginning its climb. He was driving within the prescribed speed limit, and if Trudy hadn't been with me, I'd have tossed my pride to the wind, taken to my heels and caught him up.

"You know, it's pretty creepy when you work it out, but Grandmother still has an eye for a dishy man. She dotes on Ross. And he wouldn't be human if he wasn't busy grinding his own little axe. Marcus says he exerts undue influence over Grandmother. And he's dead right, but what the hell can you do about it while she's in her right mind!" She heaved a sigh. "Visitors to lunch, the Denisons, a couple of dreary old has-beens; he lost a leg at El Alamein and if you don't watch out he'll grab all the knives and forks within reach and build a plan of every desert battle there ever was. Ugh, Monty and Rommel, I've suffered twice!"

He drew no maps of El Alamein for me, but a little pedantically discussed the regions of France, his knowledge being infinitely wider than mine. Whether he was naturally incurious, or was motivated by delicacy of feeling, he did not ask me a single question. To him I was simply a granddaughter paying a visit to her grandmother. No matter whether it was tact or disinterest, I was grateful to him. His wife was a jolly butterball of a woman who, when not sharing reminiscences with Aunt Louise, chattered proudly to Trudy of her latest grandson, who was the same age as Marco.

Uncle Conwyn, who ate perhaps a dozen small mouthfuls of food, drank water instead of wine, did not address a syllable to me. He played his role of host in the lowest possible key. He looked physically ill and as though the ordeal of a modest lunch party was almost past his bearing. Remembering that day I'd climbed down the swing ladder to let him into the house in the rue de Paris, I could not force out of my heart one single drop of sympathy. He was the first person in the whole of my life whom I actively hated.

The Denisons stayed on to take tea with Grandmother. And they, Aunt Louise pronounced, were the last visitors she would be allowed that day.

During dinner the front door bell rang and Greville went to answer it. He was away so long that Aunt Louise's patience jumped out of control and she opened the door as he was about to do so from the other side.

"A gentleman to see Mr Conwyn, an officer from the police, I understand. I went upstairs and enquired if Mr Conwyn wished to see him so late, or whether I should ask the gentleman to postpone his visit until the morning, but Mr Conwyn said I was to show him up."

No one but Trudy spoke a word until we went into the drawing room for coffee. Marcus moved restlessly about the room, occasionally emitting bursts of brayish laughter. "Now you appreciate what it is to be a member of the younger generation of this house. You're reduced to the status of a kid in a nursery. Uncle Con closeted with an officer of the law who's investigating a possible murder charge against a member of the family, albeit born on the wrong side of the blanket, and we're not as well informed as any yokel swigging beer in The Cock Pheasant. We won't hear a word until Terson is hauled before the magistrates, as I pray to God he will be."

His mother protested: "Darling, I keep nothing from you."

"Yes you do. If you consider it will dampen my spirits, drive me to the bottle!"

Trudy gave him a glare. "And who can blame her, sweetie. Sometimes you seem hell-bent on pickling your liver. So one more brandy all round, and that's it for tonight."

"Not for me." Aunt Louise looked hurt by her son's accusation. "I must go and check on Mama. It's a relief to know that Nurse Hailey will be back in a week. She's much cleverer at finding where she hides the packets of cigarettes that wretched girl, despite all my warnings, still buys her. Bribed, of course!"

"Not for me," I said with equal promptitude, and picked up the thin shawl I'd brought down from my room.

I had to gamble. Nancy took Carlo for his last walk of the day between eight-thirty and nine. I knew from seeing them that she varied the direction. I looked up the twisting gravel paths, across the bridge, towards the dreaming ruins of the Abbey but I could see no sign of them. I opted for the narrow road along the river, and when I had been walking for ten minutes, I saw them coming towards me.

As the distance between us lessened, and Carlo, recognising me, pulled on his lead, her steps quickened. The expression on her face was flat and mutinously ungiving. She would, if I'd allowed her to do so, have passed me with a nod, maybe not even that. But Carlo barked, pranced on his hind legs, and she had to slow down.

I said, almost breathlessly, as I stroked his head and held onto his collar: "Is Mr Terson back at the Estate House?"

Her "No" was so grudging that her lips hardly parted.

I stood up, my fingers gripping Carlo's lead, actually heard myself begging: "Can't you understand why I ask, why I'm concerned about him?" Because I could not imagine why she assumed I posed a threat to her, I added: "He's my brother, or rather my half brother."

"I know that," she snapped churlishly. "Everyone knows it. You have your rights, I suppose, or that's what some folks say. But so has he and as likely as not you'll do him out of them, put the old lady against him."

"That's nonsense, absolute nonsense, but I'm not going to argue, put my case to you . . ."

"I've no time to listen, I'm late as it is. Let go of Carlo."

"I will, just as soon as you tell me where he is. Is he still at the police station being questioned?"

"It seems so." She jerked Carlo's lead free of my hand. "So you can make of it what you please, even though he never murdered that nurse creature or anyone else."

I turned round to watch her running walk, with Carlo skipping by her side. Love, I thought, love that possessed, half crucified, so that in that last second before she parted the distance between us, the humiliation of tears had overtaken her.

Next morning Ross flung open the front door as I reached the foot of the stairs. An automatic spasm of sheer joy was followed by a jarring bafflement at his sudden appearance at that hour of the morning.

"How's that for timing! I came in the hope I might beg a quick cup of coffee from Greville, drink it with you."

Somewhere deep in his green-bronze eyes there was a flash of appeal and beneath it an uncertainty I'd never seen there before. "How about it? Can you stand my company for ten minutes at this uncivilised hour?"

"Why not! But Greville would be much happier if you ate a three-course breakfast."

"No time. Ten minutes and I must be heading for Lambeth. I want to oversee the off-loading of the lorry myself."

He came towards me, held out his hand, and it was the most natural gesture in the world to place mine in it. "Does that mean you won't be back for your mother's party tonight?"

"No, that's a must. Arthur will need all the moral support we can muster. Sue is driving him down this morning, so she'll give Marty a hand with the food, etc. I'll try not to be late, but I may be a little."

At the sight of Ross, Greville's face lit up with pleasure. I said quickly, before he laid on kidneys, eggs and bacon: "Greville, Mr Heron just wants a cup of coffee."

"Why, certainly, sir. But couldn't I get you something more substantial?"

Ross gave him a firm refusal, and when Greville had poured the coffee, put the pot, cream, toast, and marmalade between us, he left the dining room.

I stared after him. "Normally, he stands guard over me, watching every sip I drink, every mouthful of toast I swallow."

"Exquisite tact!" He smiled on me and the love that I had resolved to knife to death, brimmed up in me. "The first requisite of an old-fashioned butler, plus honesty, physical stamina, and one hundred per cent loyalty to the family! A way of life that's practically self-immolation. No wonder butlers are becoming extinct."

Greville's loyalty was given to Uncle Conwyn, and of the eight minutes left to us, I was not disposed to waste one on him.

"Why did you come? So early, when you're in a hurry to get to London?" The pause, while he contemplated his coffee cup, extended itself so long that I repeated: "Why?"

He looked up suddenly, held my eyes with his and said with naked simplicity: "To see you." Again there was a pause. "I was afraid you might have been upset by what happened on Wednesday night when you were at The Lamb with Adam. Plus the fact that the police have pulled him in for questioning."

I chose my words carefully. "Yes, I was concerned. I still am."

He gave me a doubtful, slightly cautious glance. "Aren't you being a little overprotective, a bit mother-henish! No one is less in need of a substitute mother than Adam!" As a protest parted my lips, he raised his hand in a gesture of apology. "All right. What you feel about Adam is your own concern. Who knows, he may reveal to you a side of himself no one else has ever been privileged to see. What you want to know is what's likely to happen to him. My father's closest friend was the Chief Constable hereabouts. He retired last year, but once a policeman you never lose your aura of authority and, even more important, your contacts. I telephoned him an hour ago. Adam is still under interrogation, but they haven't charged him, which suggests they haven't got a watertight case. They'll have to do that in the next twelve hours, or release him."

"You mean, they've been questioning him all night?"

His smile mocked me. "This is a rural area, the police aren't Chicago-trained. I doubt if he would be persecuted by any of the local lads, or the inspector!"

"I didn't imagine they were inserting red-hot needles down his fingernails. I was thinking of exhaustion and hunger."

"There's a canteen. He may suffer from a surfeit of sausages and tea, lack of alcohol, but he shouldn't starve to death. Look, for your sake, if I could say he's innocent, I would. But I can't. No one can. Whether he's charged or not depends on the contents of Lorraine's letters to Andrews, copies of which are in the hands of the police. Not even Archie Ware was prepared to be explicit about what was in them. Maybe he didn't know, or maybe he developed a conscience about divulging confidential information." He gave a sigh, regarded me quizzically. "You know I've got a horrible feeling I haven't made it any better for you, though that was my intention."

"But you have." I nearly said: by coming, by wanting to come, and panicked because it was a giveaway. "I'm grateful to you for ringing the Chief Constable."

"No trouble. What about Hermione? She knows nothing about this latest development, does she?"

"No."

"Well, let's hope she never has to."

"He's so like her," I said, feeling my way to a truth I'd never acknowledged. "Much more her grandson than his father's son." His look was so astonished, disbelieving, that I laughed. "Yes, he is. You thought I was guilty of sentimentalising over him; all right, in the beginning I was, seeing him, his likeness to my father. But once we'd talked . . . it died, a neat clean death. All I wanted to do was to know him."

"And do you?" he asked.

"Yes. He calls himself a survivor. I think he is one, a natural survivor. Again it's a quality he's inherited from his grandmother, isn't it?"

"A survivor!" he repeated slowly. "A survivor implies someone else has been defeated. A victor with the vanquished lying at his feet, is that how you see him?"

"Of course not."

"It's how he sees himself." He looked at me meditatively, the concern edging back into his eyes. "Now, though I hate to go, I must. But I'll see you tonight." He reached out and brushed a finger along my cheekbone, and then he was gone.

I examined myself in the long mirror in the bathroom. Violet print skirt with a minute all-over white flower design; white chiffon pintucked blouse with a high neck and long tight cuffs. Hair which I'd spent an hour pinning up. The amethyst suspended on its delicate glittering chain. There was nothing much wrong with me except that my face was too hollow-eyed to take to a party.

As the masseuse had been with Grandmother all the morning and she had rested in the afternoon, this was the first time that day that I had seen her.

Paradoxically, I found myself hoping she would find fault with my appearance so, at one and the same time, lower the pressure of my love and guilt.

But all such thoughts flew out of my head as I opened the door and heard that instantly recognisable laugh. They were sitting together on the balcony, she on her *chaise-longue,* Adam in a wicker armchair. On an upright one hung a sapphire mink jacket.

Their heads turned and they focused upon me two almost identical smiles of welcome. For a moment I felt myself a part of a warm and tightly enclosed trio and my heart swelled with content. I thought: maybe that is the secret of happiness, love without passion.

Adam rose. "My, nobody else is going to have much of a look in with you around! I can see you ending up as the belle of the ball."

"You look very pretty, darling." She pressed a fold of my skirt between her fingers, discovered it was cotton and quickly relinquished it. "And the blouse is charming."

Across the space his eyes mocked me wickedly. "If that outfit is a sample of your dress designing, that shop of yours should go like a bomb."

She chose to take the remark as a joke. "Shop! What are you talking about!" Her smile brimmed again. "Kitty is going to be thrilled at having a young figure to dress instead of fat old women or skinny hags like me. I thought you might like to borrow my mink jacket. Try it on, darling."

When I stood ramrod straight before them, Adam pronounced: "No." She frowned and he repeated: "No. Why gild the lily or the rosebud! Anyway it's much too hot for furs, even mink."

"Perhaps you're right," she admitted grudgingly. And thankfully I slipped my arms out of it, laid it on the back of the chair.

Standing between them, so that our faces were hidden from her, I risked one question. "Nancy mentioned you were at a cattle sale yesterday. Did you have a good day?"

"Reasonably satisfactory." His face maddeningly told me nothing but the fact that there was nothing he wished to tell me. But wasn't his presence proof that the evidence in Lorraine's letters had been inconclusive? And the lines of his body, the shape of his mouth, the brilliant light in his eyes suggested an inner exultancy which could only mean that the survivor had, once again, survived.

"Have a happy time, darling. Chandler will be waiting for you with the Daimler from eleven o'clock onwards. After three hours of party drinking Marcus isn't to be trusted with a car."

"Enjoy yourself," he said and walked through the room with me to open the door.

"What happened?" I whispered.

"Damn all . . . for the moment." He gave me a sardonic, faintly patronising smile. "So don't lose any beauty sleep over me, little sister."

"I won't," I promised.

Uncle Conwyn had decided not to excuse himself from the Heron party. He sat in the front of the Daimler beside Chandler. Trudy and I were in the back, Marcus facing us. Trudy wore an orange dress too tight across the bust and pink scuffed sandals. Her hair was so newly shampooed that the strands across her shoulders were damp, and as usual the left corner of one eyelash looked a bit insecure.

Marcus said: "Our sweet coz is a very glamorous little bird tonight, isn't she, pussycat?"

"Yes," Trudy answered dutifully, with a look that suggested she found the outfit dowdy. "Actually, except for a few of Emmy's old pals in floral brocades and stiletto heels, it's likely to be a bit of a mishmash. If Ross has brought along any of his designers, they'll probably be in jeans and sweat shirts."

Marcus looked behind him to check the panel of glass. It was closed. "It would seem since Terson's been celebrating with Her Majesty that he's managed to wriggle himself off the hook, at least temporarily. Do you remember last time, when we were all hauled in? Usher you politely out of the door, thank you for your co-operation sir or madam, and wham, forty-eight hours later you're back answering the same questions with them checking they matched up with the replies you'd given them the first time. The cat and mouse method. That's what they're probably playing with Terson."

"I should remember!" Trudy said laconically, "the state you got yourself into. Thank God, this time you're a spectator on the sidelines."

We climbed slowly, with Chandler keeping scrupulously to the speed limit. Marcus went on talking to Trudy, but my ears didn't absorb their words. Adam, Grandmother receded until they seemed to belong to another time zone. My head was filled with the thought that tonight might be the last time I should see him.

At Emmy's side stood an elderly, compactly built man, an inch or two shorter than she was, his silver hair emphasising the ruddiness of his complexion, his smile warm, but set as though he'd had to keep it in place too long.

She held my hand as she introduced me, calling over her shoulder to Sue. "Darling, find Ross. That young man you brought along to help with the drinks seems to have vanished. And tell Marty we'll start eating soon after eight."

Ross said: "Hello, Trudy. Marcus. Uncle Conwyn. And Claudine." It was only because I was last, I told myself that I merited a deeper smile. "The bar's in the study. Just follow me." Sue said: "See you in a minute. I better find Gershwin. Poor lamb, he gets shy fits, when he's apt to cower."

We were latecomers, and the hall, drawing room and study, the terrace and garden were covered with a drifting pattern of guests who'd arrived before us. To me the scene possessed the eerie tempo of a dream. It was only after the third person had come up and introduced him or her self, I became aware that I possessed a high curiosity value that kept glances covertly flicking in my direction. The latest to present herself was a tiny, very old woman, in a red wig who gazed at me over her champagne cocktail through bird-bright eyes— her name has slipped out of my memory. "I knew your father. Practically everyone over fifty who's here tonight did. It's very easy to pick out his daughter from a crowd."

"So I've been told." On the periphery of the terrace, my eyes, without turning in his direction charted Ross as he moved with drinks from one group to another. "How is your grandmother?" she demanded. "It is a week or two since I've seen her."

I said she'd suffered a slight heart attack, but was now almost recovered. "She must be a very happy woman to have Marcus's daughter at Saffron. After suffering so many tragedies, so much grief, she's earned the joy of having you with her. Is it true that you were brought up in France?"

I became aware that the nearest groups had fallen silent as an aid in the delicate operation of eavesdropping. Before I could answer, Uncle Conwyn touched her elbow, drew her away. A few minutes later, I saw threading his way towards me, the man who was to be Emmy Heron's second husband.

Released from his duty to smile, his expression became anxious, though when he reached me, he turned the smile on again. It was as strained as though he were suffering from stage fright. He even stuttered slightly. "I'm by way of being a g-guest of honour . . . this p-party is to introduce me to Emmy's f-friends as her future husband. She tells me that you, too, are a s-s-stranger here, though I'm sure you won't be one for long." He cleared his throat, which halted the stutter. "Though there is a wide disparity in our ages, she suggested, if you find it agreeable, that I should escort you to the dining room where there is a cold buffet to which we help ourselves."

I held out my hand. "That sounds just like her. Though I've only known her for a few days, I can understand why she suggested it. We're both on trial, being looked over! She means we'll support one another."

This time the smile was genuine. "And you don't find being on trial a little demoralising?"

"You'd be surprised how quickly you get used to it." Across the length of the room Ross's glance stretched itself over twenty, maybe more people, to reach me, evoking that insane feeling of happiness, and I missed a word or two of what Colonel Blakeley was saying ". . . not good enough for her, that I'm either marrying her for her money or a home in my old age."

He looked so woebegone, that I clowned to make him laugh. "I'm much worse, a nasty scheming little hussy out to worm myself into my grandmother's affections, so she'll leave me all her money when she dies. *And* I'm the half sister of a bastard son who's suspected of murder!"

"Good grief!" He burst into chortles of laughter. "And I was feeling sorry for myself. Let's head for the food. You certainly need some sustenance."

For half an hour we sat side by side on the terrace eating cold salmon, Marty's superb chicken pie, and strawberries and cream, while he confided in me his fear that the rheumatism in his left thigh might worsen and make him a burden on Emmy. When Marty collected our empty plates, he looked at his with astonishment. "I haven't eaten so much for months." He apologised. "I've made a glutton of myself."

She beamed on him. "It'll be a great pleasure having you in the house, sir, with Mrs Heron on and off her diet, I never know where I am. And the same goes for Sue. Eating like a horse one weekend, picking like a sparrow the next. It'll be a real treat to cook for a gentleman who enjoys his food."

He glowed. "That's very handsome of you, Mrs Martin."

As though gifted with extrasensory perception, I recognised his footsteps behind me, accompanied by a lighter pair. I waited, feeling the breath pass in and out of my lungs. I thought it might be a girl called Harriet to whom he was about to introduce me, and my joy—without excuse—was diminished.

It was Emmy. "I have to spread you round a bit." She touched Arthur Blakeley's hand. "The Radcliffes haven't met you yet." She looked at me. "And one of the Harris twins who came to that children's party you remember is here and wants to say hello to you. She's Imogen Rogers now. Ross will find her for you. Oh, and Ross darling, could you spare a moment to go up and switch on the floodlighting?"

"Right away." As the two of them moved away, he said: "It was installed for Caro's twenty-first birthday party. For some reason known only to themselves the electricians put the switch in an attic, and we've never got around to having it moved. Will you come with me, and when we come down, we'll find Imogen."

I had a sensation of gliding up the stairs, so ridiculous that I laughed under my breath. On the broad square landing, he drew me round to face him. "That's the first time I've heard you laugh out of pure joy. Are you happy, really happy?"

"Yes. Perfectly happy . . . as a lark!" And it was true. I'd learnt that you could snatch a moment from time, isolate it from the one that had gone before and those to come, hold it like a jewel in your hand.

He laughed with me in loving delight. "I've watched you. You seemed to float with feet that never need to touch the ground. Ethereal, like a fairy princess . . ."

"Complete with wand . . ."

"You don't need one." His glance lingered on me, then he said: "Let's get those lights switched on."

He guided me into a room in which camp beds, piles of trunks, tables and chairs tipped at odd angles, jostled one another, went to the cupboard beside the rusting fireplace.

I smeared the cobwebs off the window. "Will it startle Silas, finding himself bathed in floodlight as though he were a circus pony?"

"Probably. He's getting a bit neurotic in his old age."

You couldn't see the lamps, only the pools of milky radiance that returned trees and flowers to the brilliance of their daytime lives. On the terrace Sue and the young man who'd been too tardy a barkeeper, were setting up a record player. As the first note of music sounded, Ross's arm very slowly turned me round and with slow absorption he kissed my lips. For a long moment I had a sensation of falling, then I reached a level space, where I drifted along a sweet, gentle current.

His face lifted. "Look at me. Please look at me." And gradually, as though they were weighted with dreams I could not bear to shatter, I forced my eyelids apart. More gently this time he kissed my mouth, as I breathed out my love. Time stopped and I wanted to keep it so, not to have to trust the spoken word, destroy what could not be despoiled, silence. Love should have faith, love should have certainty. But I had neither.

As I stepped back, he reached for my hand, never doubting that it would grip his. "The mortal hurt would have been if I'd had to apologise for kissing you. But I don't, do I?"

I shook my head.

Joy and urgency shook his voice. "Will you be with me, stay with me, always?"

For a moment I felt nothing, and then freezing and faint I was ripped out of a world that had never existed except in my imagination. To make them audible I had to enunciate each word carefully. "I'm going back to France. I have to."

"You can't." His voice was appalled. "You can't run away, not now."

"I have to," I repeated, and added: "I want to."

He turned away from me. The floodlighting whitened one cheek with its high bone, wide, deep-set eye. "Because of Adam? Is this his doing. Has he persuaded you into making some grandiose sacrificial gesture? Because the police have let him go home, it doesn't necessarily mean he's in the clear."

"No. I'm not the sacrificial type."

His eyes, in anxiety and anger, probed deep. "Then what? Why?"

A deal that had been made when I was four years old that reduced me to a pawn, or bait on the end of a fishing line. At that moment it was a fact that seemed to encompass some flaw in myself that I could not bear to reveal to him. "If I stayed at Saffron I'd have to learn to act, play a part, remember my lines. It's beyond me."

"What part? What lines? Why are you talking in riddles?"

I was conscious of space widening between us, so that emotionally we were losing contact. Like a doom I couldn't avoid I knew that soon, however loudly I shouted, he wouldn't be able to hear me.

"A part I don't wish to play."

I heard the chill in his voice. "Are you saying that before you came to Saffron someone schooled you in a part, taught you your lines?" He answered himself. "No, I don't believe it. And what about Hermione, does she know you're leaving her?"

"No. I haven't told her yet, but I will."

He spoke with an anger harder than any I'd believed him capable of. "Have you taken into account the effect of your walking out on her?"

His blind devotion to her sparked off an anger that shamed me. "A month ago she hadn't seen me since I was four years old, had never expressed a wish to do so. She's lived eighty-five years without me . . ."

He cut in: "A month ago I'd never seen you, expected to see you. Time and love seldom match up to a tidy, predictable pattern." He shook his head. "I'm sorry. Shouting at you . . ." He waited a second, then asked: "Are you saying that you find life at Saffron distasteful, insupportable?"

"It is so to me."

He turned away from the window, paced the length of the room, twice stumbling over the heaps of furniture, and back again to my side. Now his voice was gentle, as though movement had washed him clean of anger. "Does the fact that I don't want you to go carry no weight? Five minutes ago, I would have sworn it did. Were you acting a part then?"

It came to me blindingly that I could renounce my pride, the bitterness of disillusion, I could forgive the dead, even to a degree the Grey Man, allow Grandmother to exercise the right to dispose of her property any way she chose, even if it was to me. I could cheat Adam out of an inheritance that would probably never be his as long as his mother lived, but might come to him when she was in her grave. I could remain my grandmother's darling, with hair to be styled by Pierre, my choice in clothes dictated by a woman called Kitty. By renouncing myself, becoming the quiescent tool of my mother and Conwyn Delamain, I could be my love's love. I stared at the breathlessly beautiful vision until it faded. I could not make myself over into a girl who had never existed.

From somewhere inside me I found the strength to laugh. "In a way, I suppose I was. I'm sorry but I think I had one too many champagne cocktails."

The door opened and Sue cried: "There you are! I hate to interrupt but everyone's asking for you." As a band of floodlighting caught her profile, one eye gave me a wink. "Truly sorry; cross my heart."

"Coming." I walked heavy-footed down the stairs I'd glided up. The first trickle of guests were leaving, shaking hands with Arthur and Emmy. Among them was Uncle Conwyn, which meant that the Daimler would be waiting. Escape became my single objective.

Emmy protested: "Claudine, darling, you're not going already? It's only those with a long way to drive who are leaving."

I said I must. I thanked her, shook Arthur's hand, and as if I had a second pair of eyes in the back of my skull, I could feel Ross standing at the foot of the stairs, saying goodbye to me.

Uncle Conwyn sitting beside me, was visibly exhausted to the point where he appeared on the verge of collapse. Callously, I hoped it was a condition that would render him speechless. But within a minute he had summoned enough strength to address me. "In the circumstances in which you find yourself, it is only fair that you should be advised of a fact that may bridle your impatience and subdue your resentment of me and the control I have, with your mother's consent, exercised over you." He paused, announced: "It is unlikely that you will have to wait overlong for your inheritance."

"I hope you're wrong," I said, because I could think of nothing else to say. Whatever the state of his health, I suspected he was guilty of overdramatising its gravity to browbeat me.

"I assure you I'm not." He was vexed I had not treated his declaration with due solemnity. He struck back. "There is something else you have a right to know. Whatever the outcome of the police interrogation of Terson, and at the moment it appears to hang in the balance, I intend to take the management of Saffron out of his hands."

"You mean, dismiss him?"

"Yes."

"Is it likely Grandmother would agree!"

"She will accept my advice."

"Do you honestly believe that?"

"Certainly I do." His voice shook. "He has been guilty of grave misjudgment, if not outright dishonesty, in earlier positions of trust he held before he was employed at Saffron. And, how do you imagine she would countenance his making her serving maid his mistress?"

I could not even make a conjecture. I had not the faintest inkling of her moral attitude to sex. I thought it likely that Adam would, somehow, make his tale good. And Nancy would never betray him.

161

All I knew for certain was that Uncle Conwyn was possessed by two passions: love of Saffron, hatred of the man who, for thirty years had hovered threatening in the wings, and now he believed he could appease both. For the first time he evoked in me not the dislike that had swelled into hate, but a tremor of fright, as though he had drawn one of his bony ice-cold fingers down my spine.

14

PIERRE, gnome-like, wearing a puce velvet jacket, violet-tinted glasses, pirouetted about me, reaching for strands of my hair, weighing them, then tossing them into the air, all the while keeping up a running commentary in English and French, not addressed to me, but to Grandmother. A girl with silver hair, whom he called Mirabelle, hovered reverentially.

"Too thick about the face, a bit like . . . what do you call it . . . ah, yes, a golliwog. A most enchanting golliwog, but a golliwog nonetheless." He took out a magnifying glass, put a hand to his mouth in exaggerated horror. "*Quel désastre!* Every end split. They will only heal with my special oil treatment and conditioner. And because, dear madam, you did not warn me, I have neither with me."

Grandmother ordered him to bring his unguents the following week, and meanwhile to do his best. I emerged an hour later with my hair four inches shorter, and razor cut so thin on my crown that my scalp shivered. Putting my head into Pierre's hands, which would have the effect of rendering it hideous to me for months, had been a kind of atonement in advance of what was to come.

All Saturday and Sunday a discreet surveillance had been kept on Grandmother by Uncle Conwyn and Aunt Louise, with Trudy and Marcus acting as relief minders. I never once saw her alone, her telephone calls were monitored, and only trustworthy well-primed visitors such as Emmy, Colonel Blakeley, and Sue were admitted to her presence. Both days were breathlessly hot, so still that not a leaf or a blossom stirred and the massed scarlet and pink of the rhododendrons and azaleas seemed to sleep in unending languor. Time moved so leadenly as to tempt me into the belief that the waiting would last for ever.

After Pierre and Mirabelle had left, I found her alone, lying on her *chaise-longue* on the balcony, Carlo snoozing at her feet. She was wearing her reading glasses, studying a foolscap sheet of paper. She appeared both alert and relaxed, her glance as she dropped the paper into her lap, one of loving approval. "That new style of Pierre's suits you. Next week, after an oil treatment, it will be perfect. Nancy forgot, either accidentally or because she was ordered to do so, to bring me any cigarettes." Her eyes sparked with mischief. "It's as well I have a secret hoard. In my wardrobe, in the left-hand compartment, there is a sable coat. In one of the pockets you'll find either one or two packets of cigarettes. Be a darling and fetch them for me."

I was, I'd convinced myself, in the state of calm that begets calm. My carefully prepared speech withholding nothing but actual servitude, lulled me into a sense of complacency. The sable coat was swathed in cellophane. I had to unwrap it before I could feel in the pockets. She called impatiently: "Have you found it? Are they there?"

The first pocket was empty. In the second my hand closed over a single packet. For a moment I was trapped in indecision. Deny they were there, even confiscate them? But unappeased she would be restless, even fractious, when I needed her to be aglow with the small triumph of disobeying the rules laid down by Aunt Louise and Dr Knox. When I peeled off the cellophane, handed them to her, held the monogrammed gold lighter, I had put my conscience to sleep.

"What would I do without you!" She pointed to a stool. "Draw that up, and then we can go through this list together. I've decided it's high time to give a small presentation party for you. Next Sunday afternoon. In the Abbey. If the heat wave returns, it will be shady, and if it is windy, it is sheltered." She took off her glasses, handed me the list. "I've written down fifty names, old friends, their children and grandchildren who are your generation. Some, of course, may be away, and I shall probably remember names I've omitted, but fifty is the number we're likely to end up with. Mrs Macfarlane, the farm secretary, can send the invitations off in the morning."

Every word of the prepared speech dissolved, leaving my mind as blank as though it were a slate that had been wiped clean with a wet rag. Dread and fear turned me into a coward who rushes with blind recklessness toward a fence in order to reach the safety of the other side.

163

"I can't be here next weekend. I'm terribly sorry, but I have to be in Paris, from Friday until Monday. I have a date, one I can't cancel."

"A date!" She looked mystified. "You mean you have made an appointment to see someone in Paris?"

"Yes. Lisette Petit. She is a friend of mine. We were at art college together. We made plans then: to have a boutique for the clothes we designed. But first Lisette had to find the right premises, ones that her father would approve as he is going to advance the money to buy the lease. It's not been easy, but she's finally managed it, and she's flying to Paris next weekend from Rome where she's been working, and I've promised to meet her . . . That's why I can't be here. I'm very sorry about the party . . ."

While I'd been dragging out the tattered shreds of my prepared speech, I had not once looked at her, only been aware that the air I breathed grew heavier. At last I could defer the challenge no longer. To my relief she was shaking her head in mild remonstrance.

"Darling child, I'd be the last person to tread on your little dreams, but this one . . ." She laughed. "My granddaughter a shopgirl! Of course, even though your life style has changed, you may rightly feel a sense of loyalty to your friend. But I promise, if she suffers any financial loss from your not being able to join her, I will see she is compensated." She made an exaggerated moue of distaste. "A shopgirl, selling the hideous, shoddy clothes that Trudy wears! Darling, you have no time for such absurdities. Saffron is not only a joy, but a responsibility that you must learn to shoulder. Once and for all, your home is here with me, not in some tawdry little shop in a back street."

I said carefully: "I do realise that the whole idea seems frivolous, absurd, and trivial to you. But it is important to me. I have a talent, or if that sounds too grand, a knack that I want to use, must use. It lives inside me all the time, spinning around in my head. To me it's not tawdry or demeaning, it's the only job I've ever wanted to do. So I have to go to Paris but that doesn't mean I won't come back, as often as you'll have me."

In quick succession her face underwent a whole range of expressions. It flowed through astonishment, blank disbelief and outrage, before it steadied into deadly incensement.

I could not make myself believe that she could regard me with such naked, shameless hate, with a coldness that was more terrifying than anger. Her voice withered me with scorn. "You dishonour your promise, toss it aside as of no account to satisfy a silly child's whim?"

"What promise?"

"The promise you gave your uncle, that you would make your home at Saffron with me?"

Shock stilled my tongue for seconds. "I gave no such promise. He never asked me for one. A visit. That is what he proposed, and what I accepted." On an impulse I reached for her hand. She snatched it back as though my touch burned.

"Then why, may I ask, didn't you declare your intention when you arrived instead of remaining here under false pretences, living a lie?"

Had I? There had been no intent to deceive, only procrastination, a dreamlike inertia, and a dread of forfeiting a gift of love that was precious to me. The images of myself were so intensely painful, I was made dumb.

"I'm waiting for an explanation."

"I loved being with you. I didn't lie, I kept putting it off . . . afraid you might be hurt . . ."

She seized the word out of my mouth with savagery. "Hurt! Offered a choice, Saffron or a catchpenny existence in what the newspapers, most aptly, call the rag trade, you reveal your true nature by opting for the cheap and shoddy. Hurt! You flatter yourself. I am not hurt. I merely deplore my error of judgment. My mistake was that I trusted you." The bitter laugh cut my heart. "Trusted you, for instance, to tell me if Bernard Andrews returned to this neighbourhood! Trust between us never existed. That was yet another of your lies."

She reached for a cigarette, and snatched the lighter from my hand when I offered it to her. The pearly smoke laid a merciful veil over the face that was made rigid by that exalted pride of possession that was satisfied with nothing less than total subjection to her will.

Yet still I could not convince myself that I could not recapture some precious fragment of her goodwill. I began to speak fast, almost in a gabble. My words, the pleas I used have been wiped from my memory; all that remains is my passionate desire to communicate directly to her heart before it iced over.

She heard me out, though she did not listen. When there was silence between us, she narrowed her eyes to blue slits of malice. "Or could it be that you are attempting to threaten me, that you have issued what amounts to an ultimatum to make sure you win the highest price? Maybe you're not only an ignorant, stupid child, but a greedy one too!"

Anger blazed in me, its white heat reducing love, compassion, and penitence to a dead ash. "Why should I threaten you? What have I to gain?"

"Riches," she said laconically. "A life of splendour when I am dead."

It was the last word that quenched my anger. Suddenly, like a blaze of light I saw a path that might, no must, carry us through the eye of the hurricane to the calm that existed on the other side. I would tell her of the pact Uncle Conwyn had wrung from my mother, of its effect on me, reducing me to a tool he'd use without scruple against Adam, Marcus, even the baby. I leaned forward, hope giving me a new base of courage. "My mother . . ."

The ice-voice scythed through my words. "Your mother by criminal neglect wantonly killed my son. I will not have her name spoken within this house. I suggest you pack your bag, and, as early as possible tomorrow morning, you will leave Saffron. If at any time in the future you return, you will not be admitted. I never wish to see you again. Those are my orders. Please make sure you obey them."

I would have told Trudy and Marcus that I would be swept clean out of their lives within twelve hours, if a school friend of Marcus's, and his wife, hadn't come to dinner. I assumed in the hour that had passed since she'd ordered me out of the room, that Grandmother would have made some announcement to Aunt Louise. But from her manner towards me, the usual reluctant acceptance of a distasteful presence in the house, it did not seem to be so. In my half-stupefied state, I acknowledged that Uncle Conwyn had a right to be informed that I would be leaving tomorrow. But he did not put in an appearance, and I had insufficient physical and mental stamina to seek him out and suffer an outbreak of shattered nerves or a violent storm of abuse. That was one errand I could leave until morning.

As soon as Marcus reached for the brandy, I made an excuse and left the drawing room. I turned my back on Saffron and my feet, of their own accord, chose the river road. If Ross had been at the Old Rectory, I believe I would have found courage to climb upwards through the torrent of colour and seek him out, but Emmy, who had brought Colonel Blakeley to have tea with Grandmother on Sunday, had mentioned he had driven to London immediately after lunch.

I had covered half a mile when Adam's Jaguar overtook me, drew into the side of the road. He gave me a flat unwelcoming glance. "An evening stroll? Or were you about to visit me?"

"I might have looked in on you if you'd been at home."

"Home! Hardly that!" There was an edginess to his voice that suggested unease or a collapse of confidence. "I suppose you want the latest bulletin on the Terson affair?"

"If you can spare the time!"

"To use a hackneyed phrase I'm still helping the police with their enquiries. There's probably a squad of junior detectives padding round after me to make sure I don't take off for Tangier or the Bahamas. I wouldn't know what the police methods are in France, but here on a murder enquiry, they don't hand out information, they suck it from you, like blood, needleful by needleful. Tends to make some suspects jittery. So far they haven't had much luck with me."

"What about the photostat copies of Lorraine's letters?"

"Oh, those." His grin had a lick of triumph. "As I thought, no names, only lots of heavily underlined insinuations, vague chitchat that can be interpreted in half a dozen ways. Despite the infamy of my false alibi, as of this moment my impression is that the evidence against me isn't firm enough to guarantee it won't drop to pieces when attacked by a brilliant young barrister. Of course, they could change their minds around midnight, pull me in again."

"Have you ever wondered if you didn't murder Lorraine, who did?"

For a moment he looked startled, then he shrugged the suggestion away. "No, I haven't. Who else but me would have benefited by her being dead! No," he repeated, and stared in hard concentration through the windscreen, speaking aloud, but recapitulating to himself, rather than confiding in me. "She was tight, oh not drunk, but on the verge of the permissible level of alcohol. The latter part of the evening hadn't exactly been a riotous success. I'd tried to push her to a decision, and each time she wriggled out of it. She could, when she set her mind to it, be an infuriating bitch. When we got back to Saffron, I'd had enough. I let her out of the car, kissed her good night and left her to find her own way to the drawing-room door." He turned his head, looked at me. "Not very gentlemanly, perhaps. Then I'm not a gentleman, thank God! I don't claim to have a conscience, but knowing she was tight, I wish I'd spent a couple of minutes, making sure she didn't lose her footing on a slippery path.

If for no other reason than if I had I wouldn't be a mouse in the cat's game the police are playing, with Andrews egging them on." He paused, grinned. "Don't look so doleful, capital punishment was abolished years ago, and with me given a life sentence, Marcus will be your only competition, and don't tell me you can't handle him."

I think I would have told him then. After all, that's why I had gone in search of him, believing that the news would be a present to him, the first and last I should ever give him: Saffron.

But his impatience to be rid of me acted as a brake: his fingers were tapping the steering wheel and he took a flying look at his watch. Even so, I made one more attempt. "Have you had your supper? Or would you like me to cook you something?"

His smile, at last, was sheer amusement. "That, little sister, is all being taken care of. And incidentally getting burned to a cinder."

Taken care of by Nancy. "I'm glad. And I don't think you'll have to eat cinders for your supper."

He laughed, then for the first time since he'd stopped the car, he really saw me. "Is anything up? You look . . . well, different. Conwyn hasn't been browbeating you, has he?"

"No, I've hardly exchanged a word with him over the weekend. And all that's happened to make me look different is that Grandmother let Pierre loose with his scissors on my hair."

"Can't say it is an improvement." He switched on the ignition. "So long. If I'm charged with murder the news will spread like wildfire, so you'll be kept informed."

"Goodbye," I called, but he never heard my last word.

I dreamed that I was being torn from my bed, that my face was being slapped and my limbs pulled, that there was a blinding light shining in my eyes. But it wasn't a dream. Marcus was fighting with the damask curtains to set me upright on the floor. I felt the stinging impact of his palm against my cheek. "Fire," he shrieked. "Damn you. Wake up or you'll never get out alive. Don't you understand, the house is blazing round you." He thrust slippers into my hand, hung my dressing gown round my shoulders and half smothered me with a blanket he ripped from the bed. Then he shoved me towards the door and opened it.

Smoke whirled in my face. Enough of my senses had returned for me to recognise the direction from which it came: Grandmother's balcony suite. I screamed, I tried to wrestle out of his grip, but his muscle-power overcame mine. "I've got Trudy and Marco out, and you're next on the list . . . Damn you, stop struggling, can't you!" Again he slapped my face before he manhandled me towards the stairs. I stopped fighting for as long as it took me to count twenty, and then when his grip slackened, I managed to struggle free. I had reached the top stair, when he pinioned me from behind, twisted me round and half flung me down the stairs. "I can help . . ." I shouted.

"No, you bloody well can't. There's nothing anyone can do to help until the fire engines get here. They're on their way, and the ambulance . . ." Such was the force he used that I found myself out of the front door, sprawled on the courtyard, the pain in my knee so excruciating that it was a moment before I could stand upright. Trudy, sobbing hysterically, grabbed the blanket from my shoulder, wrapped it round Marco, who was wailing piteously. I stared in stunned disbelief at the great banners of scarlet that were climbing up the windows, making the courtyard as light as day. It was the sound of pounding feet that turned my head. Adam, with three men at his heels, was racing towards us. "Well, that's two women and a child clear . . ." He called an order to one of the men. "Lex, get these two and the baby into the Abbey. That's about the safest place . . ."

This time it was Trudy who fought, screaming over and over again she wouldn't leave Marcus. I took Marco from her and the man whom Adam had called Lex picked her up and carried her along the stone path beside which the waterlilies were turning pink.

The crying baby in my arms, I walked at his heels. By now I had worked out Marcus's list of priorities: Trudy, his mother and his grandmother before me. I tried to persuade myself that, with sleep-blurred wits, the answer I'd arrived at was incorrect.

The man put us on the seat under the Judas tree, addressed me: "You'll be acting in everybody's interests if you stay here, keep an eye on Mrs Delamain-Powell and the baby, miss. We'll do our best, but it's fire engines we need . . ." He looked over his shoulder. "There's the siren . . . I best be getting back . . ."

I grabbed his cuff as he turned. "My grandmother . . ."

"Now, miss, I don't know nothing, except about Nancy. She's all right because she wasn't in the house. As soon as the fire's under control, I'm sure either Mr Marcus or Mr Terson will be here to take care of you . . ." It was then, looking into eyes that refused to meet mine, that I suffered the first icy touch of the guilt that was lying in wait for me.

As though attacked by a spasm over which she had no control, Trudy jerked upright. "Can you see Marcus? Can you?" And the

169

coat she had draped round her shoulders fell to the ground on to the froth of tiny blossoms, and she stood naked in the pink glow of light. I picked up the coat, buttoned it across her. "That old witch, smoking like a chimney . . . Where's Marcus, can you see him?"

In a moment of naked truth, I saw the 4 A.M. waking, the hand that when frustration or grief struck grabbed for the release of a cigarette. I looked at the sky to guess the time, and in the east, a faint flush of rose touched the horizon.

I pointed. "There, by the side of the ambulance, to the right of the farthest hose." In the hope that the physical touch of him might stem her hysteria, I laid Marco in her arms. "Maybe he'll stop crying if you hold him." Her arms curved, rocked, but she did not take her eyes from Marcus.

Emmy, breathless, struggled through the arch from which the man who had thrust us to safety must have kicked away the struts. She laid an arm briefly round my shoulder, then took Marco from Trudy's unresisting grasp. "I'm sorry I can't get the car any nearer; the police insist the road across the bridge is kept clear for the ambulance and the fire engines. If I carry Marco, can you bring Trudy?"

"If she'll come. I'm not sure she'll leave Marcus."

But it was as if the screaming, the agony of anxiety had drained her to the point where sheer physical exhaustion took over, and she made no protest. Hanging on my arm she cried quietly and ceaselessly until we reached the car.

The house was flooded with light, normal light, not the light of billowing scarlet flames bursting the windows we'd left behind. Mrs Martin was waiting at the open front door. "There's tea and brandy in the drawing room, a pile of blankets and every warm dressing gown I could lay my hands on. Give me the baby, I've got a cot ready for him."

Trudy was hunched in a chair, with Emmy pouring brandy between her chattering teeth when Marcus, his face smoke-blackened, the sleeves of his dressing gown scorched to rags came in. He put his arms round her. "It's all right, pussycat, so be a good girl and stop crying."

Emmy stood up. She did not speak and neither did I. We waited like supplicants for him to tell us. But it was the figure who entered behind him that spoke. Dr Knox wiped the sweat and grime off his face, shared a half-stupefied glance between us. "I'm afraid she didn't have a chance. Nor did Conwyn. It was he who smelled the smoke, roused Marcus, Louise, and Greville. He did his best, but by then the smoke was too thick for him to reach the bed. That's where the fire must have started." He paused, closed his eyes tight, either because they stung, or to pull his thoughts into a more coherent order. He looked first at Marcus. "I'm glad you managed to get your mother into the kitchen quarters," and then at Emmy. "If I could clean up, I'd like to get to the hospital and see what sort of state Louise is in."

"I'll come with you," Marcus said.

Dr Knox nodded agreement, and as he went towards the door added: "Terson is putting up Nancy and Greville for the night. Apart from some degree of shock, she seems all right. He's not too good. I'll look in first thing in the morning. Oh, and they took the dog with them."

When I woke memory did not lag or jumble the time sequences. The pattern of the last twenty-four hours was minutely recorded, including the seven hours of tranquillised sleep behind me. On the top surfaces of the bookshelves were displayed a collection of small animals—one a miniature teddy bear with its head rubbed bald, which told me I'd been put to sleep in either Sue's or Caro's bedroom.

The door had been left ajar, and some time while I'd slept Merlin had leapt on to my bed, and curled himself into a ball at my feet.

Emmy coming in, said: "So that's where you are, is it?" and stroked his back. "You only have to heave him off if you don't want him." Her face seemed a little unfamiliar, in that though her mouth smiled her eyes were dark, sunken deep into her skull with grief, and probably sleeplessness.

"I like him. Cats are so peaceful. All they ask is to be made comfortable."

"Then he'll like you. Marty's making you some tea." She looked about her. "This is Caro's room. When she got married she took none of it with her. She said she wanted it to remain exactly as it had always been."

"A little piece of the past that you can run back to if you need it."

"Yes, something like that. Ah, here's Marty."

"Indian," she announced. "Pulls you together better than China. Take your time, but since no one had a bite of breakfast, lunch will be on the table at twelve-thirty sharp."

"Thank you, Marty. Ross may be here, but I told you that. I'm sorry I keep getting a bit muddled." She punched the pillows to make a firm backrest, pushed Merlin farther down the bed, and put the

171

cup and saucer in my hand. "Marcus has driven Trudy and Marco to Wimbledon. I think it was best. She'll recover from the shock more quickly in her own home, with the baby to look after. And there's nothing she can do here."

I wondered where they had taken her, where she was lying and, as though it were a penance I must impose upon myself, whether the flesh had been burned from her bones. I asked: "How is Aunt Louise?"

"Still under sedation. Her arms and hands are badly burned but they say at the hospital that she's not on the critical list. Marcus was going in to see her on his way back, and Dr Knox has promised to look in at the hospital this afternoon and telephone me."

As I replaced the cup and saucer on the bedside table, she suddenly leaned forward and wrapped me in her arms. It was her tears that wet my cheeks, not my own. "What can I say to comfort you? All I can think of is that at least she had the joy of knowing and loving you. Will you try and keep hold of that?"

I promised, though any comfort was light-years away, because it took away a little of her hurt. "Did you go to bed at all?"

"I put my feet up for an hour. If I find myself wanting to nod off, I'll have a nap this afternoon when Ross is here to take over. Oh, there I go, forgetting again. Adam telephoned to enquire how you were, and also to say he was coming over after lunch. He said something about Greville, but stupidly I can't think in what connection. Anyway, he'll be able to tell us how he is." She paused, then added with puzzled astonishment: "Do you know, it will be the first time he has ever been inside this house!"

Emmy and I were halfway through lunch when Ross drove in. In a curious way time had expanded, so that an immense amount of it seemed to have passed since the night of the party.

He kissed his mother, held her to him, and over her shoulder raked my face with a glance that beneath its surface anxiety and grief, was wise and deeply kind. When she released herself, he came and sat in a chair beside me. My hands were in my lap and he enclosed them in one of his. "Thank God, you're not hurt. That's one thing to be supremely thankful for. There are others, but it is too early yet for you to accept any comfort. Will you believe that beyond the anguish and shock of this day, you will find it?"

"I believe you." I said it to release him from the burden of anxiety on my account.

When Emmy went into the kitchen to see Mrs Martin about his lunch, he said gently: "Did she know you are going to leave her?"

The coward in me could not face confession. Staring straight ahead I felt like an assassin. I heard the lie pass my lips, his sigh of quiet thankfulness, and then the horror images struck again. "I see her terrified, in pain . . . the flames . . . the burning . . ."

His grasp on my hand tightened. "But there would have been no pain. I swear that and Dr Knox will tell you the same. She'd have been unconscious long before the flames touched her. Smoke is a swift and merciful killer. The same goes for Uncle Conwyn. He never reached her bed." He paused, added: "There are worse ways of dying than sacrificing your life to try and save someone else's. Locally, he'll be accounted a hero. That would have pleased him." His eyes moved over my face with depthless solicitude. "And you were Hermione's golden child; her last blessing on this earth."

I looked up into that marvellous face, listened to the dying echoes of his voice that would haunt my ears. I wanted to hold time still, to feel the clasp of his hand over mine, his gaze so close that I could feel his breath upon my cheek. But I had forfeited the right. I freed my hand. "Was the fire caused by her smoking in bed?"

"That appears to be the conclusion of the fire experts. I looked in to see them on my way here. Though how they can be so definite when all that remains of the south end of the house is four walls filled with burnt rubble that was flooded by the hoses, I wouldn't know. But they seem sure."

Mrs Martin came in, Emmy behind her. "And don't you dare send any of my good food back to the kitchen!"

"I'll try not to," he promised, though it was a promise he failed to keep.

The three of us were drinking coffee on the terrace, when Mrs Martin announced: "It's Mr Terson. You said he'd be coming. I've shown him into the drawing room, along with Greville. I thought the sooner he was sat down the better, Greville, I mean. He's in pretty poor shape, poor old man."

Ross looked at me. "Do you want to be in on this? You don't have to come."

"Yes, she does," Mrs Martin said. "Mr Terson specially asked for her. And for Mr and Mrs Marcus, only I told him they'd driven back home."

Adam was standing by the fireplace. His elbow propped on the mantel had knocked the dolphin on its side. Greville was in an armchair, his two hands folded across a stick sandwiched between his knees. His normally immaculately disciplined hair stood up in tufts, and his jaw shook.

Emmy took one look at him and suggested to Adam: "A little brandy?"

"He's already had two shorts. A third might knock him out. What he needs to do is to clear his conscience."

Ross said tersely: "He needs a doctor."

"Knox examined him this morning. He made no objection to this visit. So, first, we'll deal with his conscience."

Emmy appealed: "Adam, show a little mercy. Forgo the theatricals for once."

He looked from Emmy to Ross. "Ah, the quality of mercy! Rare, very rare indeed in my experience. Not much of it's come my way."

"Get on with what you have to say," Ross ordered. "My mother and Claudine, not to mention Greville, are in no state to play games."

"Then no one's playing them, not today." He took out of his pocket a spiral-backed notebook. "When twice in four months you've been suspected of a murder, you're in no mood to play games. *Mr* Heron." He turned over the stiff cover of the notebook. "I have here a statement that Greville voluntarily made to me at 9:10 this morning having been warned by me that if it contained information that was of interest to the police, I would be obliged to pass it on to them. That proved to be the case, and we'll be driving to the station as soon as we're through here." He began to read. "We start on the night of March 10th, a Friday . . ."

"Wait a minute," Ross interrupted. "Greville can't hear you. How are we to know what you're reading is a true account of what he said?"

"You've missed your vocation, Mr Heron. You should have been a barrister, not just the executor of old ladies' wills! However, we don't want to leave any loopholes, do we!" He went and stood by Greville, bending his head to the level of Greville's ear. "Mr Heron wants to make sure that every word I read out is what you dictated to me, not something I'm making up, so would you tell him that you can hear me?"

"Yes, sir. I'd be obliged if you'd go over it, sir."

Adam began again: "'On the night of March 10th, a Friday, I was woken just before midnight by an attack of indigestion. I went to my bathroom to get my bismuth tablets, and from the top floor

I saw a light coming from the open door of Mr Conwyn's wing. I thought he might be feeling ill and want me to heat him some milk. But he wasn't there. I went downstairs. There was a light in the hall, but all the other rooms were dark. He wasn't one for late nights; his health couldn't stand it. I began to get worried. I was coming back from the kitchen, wondering whether I'd best go and wake Mrs Delamain-Powell, when I heard a noise, a sort of moaning coming from the drawing room, though I'd already looked in there. It was Mr Conwyn, sir, crouched so low by the windows that, with a chair in front of him, I hadn't seen him the first time.

"'I persuaded him to lie down on the sofa, and I was just about to ring for Dr Knox, when he grabbed my hand. "Get me upstairs, Greville, back in my bed." Not once, sir, but over and over again. Almost like a dying wish, sir. Well, I did manage to get him back, though a hard job it was. It was only when I was helping him undress that I found that the bottoms of his trousers and his jacket sleeves were soaking wet. I stayed with him until he fell asleep, then just before six next morning, he came to my room and started shaking me. "We've got to go and find her," that's what he kept saying over and over again. I couldn't make head nor tail of it, but I humoured him. That was always best when he had one of his nervous bouts. Well, that's what happened, sir, we found her: Nurse Andrews. Drowned she was, caught up in that great patch of weed down by the Abbey. The shock, with her lying there with her eyes open, it knocked my legs out. But with Mr Conwyn, it's hard to explain, sir, but the sight of her seemed to steady him. Calm, he was, in complete control of himself. He sent me to my room, and then he told Mrs Delamain-Powell, telephoned Dr Knox and the police. He stood up to everything until after the funeral, then his poor nerves went to pieces like they have done before. The night before he was taken to the clinic, he rang for me. Past midnight it was. There was something on his mind, he said, that he wanted to tell me in case they never let him out of the clinic. That I'd know he was innocent . . . that's how he put it. Because it was such a bitter night, with snow around, he'd waited up for Nurse Andrews, and with a full moon seen her get out of the car with you, sir. He said you put your arms round her and kissed her. I'm not saying that you did, sir, only what he told me. It seems he startled her when she turned the corner and she shouted at him. She could have an edge to her tongue when she was angry, and sometimes he couldn't control his temper. I gather, though he didn't go into it in detail, that they had a bit of a

175

set-to, and then she tried to get by him, and it would seem he pushed her. After that, he got confused . . . I couldn't make it out, not clearly. But it was about her falling into the water, and him not being able to get her out though he kept on trying . . . That would account for his clothes being all wet.'

"At that point I asked him whether he hadn't considered it his duty, when he knew the police were enquiring into Lorraine Andrews's death, to pass on to them what Conwyn Delamain had said to him. This is his reply.

" 'No, sir. I'd sworn to respect his confidence, and I did. My duty was to protect him and Mrs Delamain. But now they are both dead, and knowing that you're in trouble with the police, sir, I couldn't rest easy with my conscience until I'd repeated to you what he told me. Not that I can swear it is the truth, sir. When he came home from the clinic, he only mentioned it once. He explained when people suffered from shock, their memories weren't reliable, and sometimes they imagined things they'd dreamed had actually happened. I don't know which it was; whether it did happen like he said before he went into the clinic, or whether he'd had a bad dream. That's all, sir.' "

Adam closed the notebook. "Now, Greville, will you tell Mrs Heron, Mr Ross Heron, and Miss Delamain that this is the statement you made to me, and that you understand you must go to the police who will question you and ask you to sign your name to another statement they will take from you."

"I understand, sir."

"And that you volunteered this information of your own free will?"

"Of my own free will, sir. I'm glad to have got it off my conscience."

Adam looked around. "Any questions?"

"Yes," Emmy Heron said. "You propose taking an old man who is ill, still in a severe state of shock and should be in bed, to the police. What do you propose to do with him after they have finished with him?"

"Temporarily, at least until after the funeral, he will stay with my mother. Dr Knox will keep an eye on him."

"That is arranged?" Ross said.

"Don't sound so suspicious. She's not going to put arsenic in his tea." He burst out laughing. "I hardly expected congratulations . . ."

"Good!" Ross said. "This is hardly the day for them."

"Depends rather on where you stand. Now, there's the matter of securing the house against vandals, making sure that every Tom, Dick, and Harry from a hundred miles around doesn't come to gawp. And I don't imagine you'd welcome trippers swarming over the gardens on Wednesday! You being the executor . . ."

"One of two. Brigstock is the other. He'll be here in a couple of hours. On the matter of securing the house, can you lay on some men?"

"As many as you like provided you don't mind paying overtime rates."

"I don't, and Brigstock's not likely to make any objection."

"I'll round them up." Slowly and with intent he rested his gaze on each of us individually. "And I'll deal with Andrews. I've earned that privilege . . . and pleasure." He crossed the silent room, put his hand under Greville's arm. "Up on your feet, old fellow. The sooner we finish with the police, the sooner you'll be tucked up in bed."

Ross said: "I'll give you a hand with him to the car."

When they'd gone, Emmy said softly: "Poor Conwyn, the torture of mind he must have suffered."

The ice over my heart stifled pity. She went on with a note of indignation: "Adam enjoyed that scene, wrung every ounce of satisfaction out of it. He shouldn't have gloated because he'd won."

"Then he hasn't won very often, has he?"

"No," she conceded, "I suppose not. He means a lot to you, doesn't he? That's why I wish he was a more generous-natured man."

As Ross stepped into the room, she asked: "Did you believe it? Do you think that's how Lorraine died?"

"I don't think it likely that Greville made it up; more important, implicated a man to whom he was devoted in being, maybe accidentally, the cause of Lorraine's death. I'm inclined to accept Adam's theory: Greville did want to clear his conscience."

"Yes," she said and smiled and sighed both together.

"By the way, can we put Brigstock up for a couple of nights? It'll simplify everything to have him on the spot, especially with the inquest coming up."

"Of course. I'll tell Marty."

His glance moved to me. "Adam wanted to know if you were going to stay here. I said we very much hoped you were. I'm right, aren't I?"

I looked at Emmy. "I'd like to, if you'll have me, until after the funeral. But then, immediately it is over, I must go home."

177

15

ON THE MORNING OF THE FUNERAL I woke early. The idea formulated itself painfully, and this time the journey was downhill not up, no wild delight only a deadness of heart and spirit as though I were lost forever in a freezing cold desert. When I reached the cedar tree, I leaned against its trunk, conscious of the love and grief, the guilt and loss that had been encompassed between the then and now.

The pale shell of the Abbey, where the swallows were beginning to swoop and dive through the arches, spelled a timelessness that preached a stoicism beyond my reach. My eyes moved with deadening slowness towards the great balcony. Black tongues, like high tide marks, bore witness to the height to which the flames had leapt to ravage the walls. The windows that had been exploded by heat or spurting hoses were boarded up, the doors padlocked against vandals. The trellises of wistaria and roses had been burnt to ash; only the waterlilies gleamed in the dark waters of the moat. When I'd said my private goodbye, I walked uphill to the house that loomed over the little church without anyone suspecting I had left it.

I sat in the front pew with Adam on one side and Emmy on the other. Beyond Emmy were Ross, Trudy, Marcus, and Mr Brigstock. Aunt Louise was still in hospital, her hands and arms made poker-stiff by bandages. They'd chopped away her scorched hair and in clothes that had become a size too large she looked like a displaced person . . . as, in spirit, she would remain. Over and over again, as if speech would purge her of guilt, she cried: "I blame myself. If I hadn't given in to Dr Knox and taken one of his tranquilliser pills, I would have heard her bell."

"Louise, darling Louise," Emmy soothed. "She probably did not have time to ring it."

But she only shook her head in a sort of perpetual motion of grief, deaf to comfort. Every few minutes the tears would well over her eyelids, slide down her cheeks to soak into her collar. "I shall never go back," she said when we were leaving. "I could never go back to Saffron. Never."

Emmy kissed her damp cheek. "Of course you can't. No one expects you to. As soon as the doctor gives permission, Marcus is coming to take you to stay with them."

Head to toe in the aisle the identical coffins overlaid with cushions of roses rested on two biers. They'd opened the grave, taken away the granite slabs, but left the headstone. Reading my father's name I was struck by a blast of horror at what lay below the earth, but it would only be dust, I told myself, and bones purified until they were like ivory. This time there was no child to scream, only a massed assembly of bowed heads as the figure in the surplice intoned his psalm to the dead; no snow, instead the hot beat of a midsummer sun. Without moving my eyes tiny vignettes sprang into my vision. Nancy passing a handkerchief to Greville, and when he'd wiped his eyes, slotting her arm through his. Marcus, barely recognisable in a black suit with his hair trimmed, his eyes for once alert, missing nothing. And Ross, on the far side of the grave, between his mother and Sue, his glance down-bent until, as if thought communicated itself to thought, it rose to focus on me. I saw him through a haze overlaid by a boy's figure wearing a dense black coat.

During the last week Ross, Emmy, Sue, Mrs Martin, and I had existed in the vortex of grief that is the aftermath of sudden and tragic death. Friends stunned and shocked, had need to commit their feelings to paper, giving or asking for comfort. Others called. The mourning gap that between my mother's death and her funeral had been quiet, was filled with the perpetual sound of a telephone that the instant the receiver was replaced pealed again. The inquest, the funeral preparations and sessions with Mr Brigstock had eaten great holes in Ross's days. It was during that week that I discovered the trick of anaesthetising pain was to develop a tunnel vision, its scope strictly limited, the figure seen through the eye lens miniaturised. But the previous evening he had trapped me in a corner of the garden. Bafflement darkened the topaz eyes, and though there was no one within hearing distance he kept his voice low. "Mother tells me you've asked Adam to drive you to the airport straight from the churchyard? Is that so?"

"Yes. I've explained to her. She understands."

"What does she understand?"

"That I'm already a day late for a date in Paris I can't break. I promised to be there today."

"Yes, I know. The dress shop you're going to run with a friend."

He checked a rising impatience that was rare in him. "But do you have to run quite so fast, so soon?"

The tunnel vision wasn't working. I was haunted by a guilt I'd compounded by lying, by the knowledge of his devotion to Hermione. And a lie once told has to be repeated. I believed if I'd accepted a servitude of body and spirit my grandmother would still have been alive. I hated myself. And self-hate I'd discovered makes you cruel. Without looking at him, I could see his face. It hadn't changed except the week behind him had blanched it with fatigue. "I don't have any choice. I booked my flight two days ago. It's too late to change it now. If, after all your mother's kindness, it appears ungrateful, I'm sorry, but there isn't anything I can do about it."

"Or want to?" he suggested.

The silence hung between us and for a second my resolution weakened.

He said, his voice curt, but low-toned: "You want to turn your back on all of us and run for dear life?"

"Yes." It was such a little word, a single, half-audible syllable, and yet in the end, it was probably the last word we should exchange.

In a blur I realised that he had stood aside, leaving me room to pass. I went back to the house and began to list the names on the wreaths which Emmy had asked me to do.

When the service at the graveside was at an end, Adam touched my elbow. "You don't want to change your mind?"

"No. I've said my goodbyes. Everyone knows why I'm leaving. I have to go now or I'd miss the plane." Suddenly I sensed an unwillingness in him. "Is it inconvenient? Would you rather not."

"No, of course it isn't. It's just that I could use a drink. Okay, let's make for the car."

We had nearly reached it when Trudy called: "Hi!" She wore a black dress that came to her knees, a black veil sprinkled with plastic butterflies that was slightly askew on her head. "Well, you might at least say goodbye. Darting off. What a way to behave! Is that what they do in France, scarper once the earth is sprinkled over the coffin, instead of having a few civilised drinks while you wait for the will to be read?"

I turned to Adam in consternation, the reason behind his half heartedness plain. "I'd forgotten the will!"

"Obviously! Then as you won't figure in it, no reason why you should show any interest."

Trudy ran on: "I'm sorry you had such a rough time, and that I ran off like that. Crumple in a crisis, that's me. By the way what's happened to Carlo? In the middle of last night I started to worry about the little brute."

"He's with Nancy. She asked if she could have him."

"Goody, then I shan't worry any more. Sorry Marcus isn't around, but even though it isn't his house, Emmy asked him to help with the honours, you know handing round the baked meats." She giggled. "One thing, he'll make sure no one hangs on too long." She leaned forward, dabbed my cheek with a kiss, Adam she ignored. "If you send me a postcard from Paris, I'll send you one from Wimbledon Common."

When she'd scampered off, I said: "You could drop me off at the garage in the village. There's sure to be someone there who could drive me to the airport."

"Oh, what the hell! It's written on a piece of paper, duplicate copies tucked in Heron's and Brigstock's breast pockets. It'll keep. The last of all the wills and testimonies of Hermione Grace Delamain! Anyway, I doubt if they'll be able to throw out the last guest for an hour, so with all the preambles to wade through, I'll probably arrive in time to hear Brigstock read the final paragraphs that are the cherry on the icing. Wish me luck?"

"I always have, though you've never believed me. If you're not lucky, what will you do?"

"Not a clue. You have a star and you hitch yourself to it so hard, you're blind to alternatives. Anyway, Saffron will be mine. There was only you who might have upset the applecart." He grinned at me. "Saved by a whisker."

When he carried my bag into the departure lounge, there was still ten minutes before my flight would be called. "Don't wait," I said.

"In the circumstances I won't."

For a moment the brilliance of his ambition and greed—yes, I acknowledged the greed—melted from his eyes and, as nearly as possible for him to do so, he looked a little lost. "You're so damned small," he complained peevishly.

"I'm the same size as when I arrived."

"We never really got to know each other, did we?"

I knew him. He'd taught me that you could love someone you didn't respect.

He leaned forward, put his mouth lightly on my cheek.

"If you don't hurry," I said, "you'll miss the cherry on the icing."

Still he hesitated, and when he spoke it was without haste, spend-

181

ing precious seconds on me. "Any time you need a big brother. Well, remember you have one, me."

"How would I know where to find him?"

"Saffron," he shouted. "That's where I'll be," and he swung on his heel.

I watched him disappear through the same door that Ross and I, wrapped together in one coat, had left by. On my way to check in my luggage, I passed the counter where I had queued to change my traveller's cheques. Without a second's warning, he jumped out of the haze, the effect of which was that I took him with me, instead of, as I hoped, leaving him behind.

Jean-Baptiste gave me a baffled look. "But I do not understand. There are other empty shops in Paris. Because the owner became so impatient with the objections Lisette's father raised that she sold to a higher bidder, that doesn't mean you can't find another."

"Lisette was so angry with her father that they both lost their tempers and had a blazing row before she flew back to Rome. Oh, they'll probably make it up, but not for a while."

This was the second time we'd met since I'd been home, in a café of his choice on the outskirts of the town, where it was unlikely we'd be seen by his parents or their friends. His smile was sweet tempered, but his eyes were sad with frustration and reproach. Frustration because, encircled by his parents and Marie-Thérèse, he was outnumbered and beaten. Reproachful because I would not mount a rescue operation.

"So what will you do, where will you go when the day comes for you to leave the house?"

"I'm still undecided. There are various possibilities. One is that I may go to England."

Horror spread itself across his face. "Your grandmother and your uncle are dead, the house is burned down, what is there for you in England? Nothing but sadness and horrible memories."

"I wouldn't go anywhere near Meads Cross. Maybe to London which is fifty miles away."

"But with no friends, a stranger whom nobody knows, who will take care of you? What will you do?"

"Work or study. With a British passport I can do either. If I can't find a job, I'll take another course in dress design at an English art college."

"You have money?" His voice shook with agitation. "I don't want to imagine you in a cold garret, living on the sandwiches the English eat all day . . ."

"I have enough money. My mother left me some." F. 47,000 that I would never have the satisfaction of returning to Uncle Conwyn.

"London is a wicked city. Girls and boys no older than you inject themselves with heroin and then lie down and die in the gutters of Piccadilly Circus. That is what an Englishman told me."

"It's also a very big city, stretching for miles, bigger than Paris." That was my safety margin, its size. Jean-Baptiste wasn't to know there were prohibited areas into which I'd never put my foot, like Regent Street, Chelsea, and Pimlico. I tried hard to make him laugh. "You know me, one drop of blood and I faint. I'm the last person in the world to stick a hypodermic syringe into my arm."

He stared at me yearningly, his eyes misting over. "You do not love me. Although you do not say so, I feel it here." He pressed his hand against his heart in a gesture that in anyone else would have been comic, but in him was profoundly touching. "Maybe you learn that when you are in England!"

I had never said I loved him. My mistake was that occasionally I'd held out a faint promise that maybe one day I would.

I leant towards him. "You have to live and work with your parents. Your family and business are so interdependent, you can't separate them. They know, and they are right, that I wouldn't sit behind a cash desk, and I'd be hopeless at serving on Henri's night off. There'd be no peace; you'd spend your life defending me."

"If you loved me that would be my joy, my privilege. But you feel no love for me, do you?"

The word had to be spoken. "No."

He nodded ponderously, fingering the stem of his glass, while I watched a dream die in someone else. I had spared him a life that would have been soured by enmity. Marie-Thérèse would live in harmony with his parents, and in time, perhaps not too much of it, he would reach a stoical acceptance, perhaps even happiness when his first child was born. Only his dream was dead, and you could, if you worked at it, get by without dreams.

Mademoiselle Greux had not returned her door key. I had not asked her for it, but left it with her to be returned to the agent when I handed in mine. She came, either with some item of food she'd cooked for me, or to dust and vacuum the rooms, not because the rooms were dirty, or I was in need of feeding, but to prolong until the last possible hour the link with my mother.

Her glance when, very rarely, it connected with mine was one of black reproach. But except with my mother, she found communication so difficult, that she never quite drove herself to the point of speech. This time she had brought me some wild strawberry tartlets.

"Mademoiselle Greux, you really shouldn't! You're much too kind and generous . . ."

If my protest brushed her ears, it did not reach her consciousness. Speech like a flood that had gouged its way through a dam, gushed from her. "I sense it, all around me. The anger you feel against her. You misjudge her and heap a sin on your own soul. Why cannot you understand she wished only to make sure you never suffered as she did? That you should inherit what was rightfully yours when she was dead. When you were a little girl, hardly more than a baby, your father could have taken you with him to his rich home, been forgiven by his parents, if she had urged him to go. That was the great cross she bore, that, out of selfishness she had deprived you of your birthright. Her prayer was to redeem her sin, give you back what she had stolen from you." Her voice began to hiss through her teeth. "Do you not know she had a proud and independent spirit, that it crucified her to be dependent for charity on a man whose name was Delamain? But for you she'd have thrown his money back in his face. She even rejoiced when her life was coming to an end because she knew when she was dead your grandmother would take you into her home, make you her heir. If you do not understand her sacrifices for you, bless her spirit and let it rest, you are a wicked and ungrateful child."

The effort of sustained speech had left her on the point of collapse. I put my arm round her shoulders, kept it there though she shrank from my touch as though it were unclean. She had spoken words that needed to be said, words that I must take not only into my head but into my heart. The quiet ghost I glimpsed when I opened a door, looked over a shoulder, was a haunting of my own conscience, not of her spirit.

"I do understand." It was within touching distance of the truth. "And I don't blame her for what she did; only my uncle for what he did to her. Mademoiselle Greux, please believe me."

She grunted. "Now it is all for nothing, and you have been cheated out of your birthright. Who will inherit the fortune, the big house, and your grandmother's jewels?"

Because no one had told me, I could not tell her. "Maybe her grandsons. She had two."

Her voice rose to a paean of indignation. "One of the female line, the other born out of wedlock!"

It was a little after five when I opened the gate in the high fence, after visiting Gustave's mother to pay her his wages. He was sitting on the step, *The Times* propped against his bent knees. It had been raining earlier and he was wearing the highwayman raincoat. My heart raced in disbelief and then seemed to stop dead.

Alerted by the squeak of the gate, he tucked the newspaper under his arm, came to his feet as I walked with a slow dreamlike tread towards him. His smile was wryly enquiring. "Surely, I can't be all that much of a shock! You couldn't have persuaded yourself you'd seen the last of me when you bolted with Adam for the airport!"

"Yes, I did." No other idea had entered my head.

"Let you off that easy! Abject surrender!" His glance lay on me with a gravity that was at odds with the light, half-joking tone. "Are you going to ask me in?"

I opened the door, and when he paused in the hall, I took the raincoat and hung it up. His physical presence stole my wits, froze my tongue. I wanted to ask him why he had come, reopened a wound I believed, granted time, would close and heal. At that moment, when I'd never thought to see him again, his arrival took on a guise of cruelty.

I opened the salon door, and was absurdly caught in a triviality. "The only drink in the house is a bottle of white wine. I'm sorry, but I've been giving away everything I won't need. I took the Vermouth and a bottle of sherry to Gustave's mother half an hour ago."

"Who's Gustave?" he asked sharply.

"A boy who cuts the lawn."

"The wine would be fine. Or a late cup of tea, whichever is less effort for you, or nothing at all, except you look as if you could do with a drink."

When I returned with the salver he took it from me, poured out two glasses of wine. "How about drinking Mother's and Arthur's health? They were married at Caxton Hall last Saturday."

"To them both," I said gladly. "I can't imagine any man not being happy married to your mother."

I sat down in a low chair, and he took an upright one by the central table. "How's the boutique coming along?"

"It isn't. Lisette's father objected to certain clauses in the lease and the deal fell through. Lisette has gone back to Rome."

He looked startled, even vaguely shocked, I couldn't think why. "I'm sorry. You must be disappointed. What are your plans now?"

"A bit vague, with several alternatives to choose from."

"But you need premises, a partner, don't you?"

"No. Only room for an easel, a sewing machine. An attic with a good light would suit me fine."

"An attic! Where? Here in Paris?" When I didn't immediately answer, he said: "I'm sorry. You're thinking I should be answering your questions, not asking them. To be precise: why am I here? One of the reasons is these." He extracted from an inner pocket of his jacket two foolscap envelopes, laid them on the table. He stared at them for a moment, then his glance rose, questioned mine. "Women are supposed to be the curious sex. But you're not curious, which leads me to assume that Adam has written or telephoned you."

"No." I hadn't expected him to. With no evidence, I'd assumed he'd won: that will and ambition had triumphed. Now in a trice I became uncertain, poised on a knife edge of impatience to know.

He tapped the right envelope with his forefinger. "The will Hermione made in April, a month after Lorraine died. It was the fifth she'd had Brigstock draw up since the death of your grandfather, in which he made financial provision for his son and daughter and left the remainder of the estate to his wife." His finger moved to the second envelope. "And this is the draft will she dictated to me the Thursday before she died. It was never drawn up, so it has no validity except as an expression of her last wishes. I'll leave both copies with you. It isn't easy to skim through a will. Apart from being typewritten, the format and the language haven't changed appreciably since the days when it was inscribed on a roll of parchment. Would you like me to give you a summary of the main clauses?"

The cherry on top of the icing! I nodded because speech was difficult.

"In the April will, which is the valid one, after bequests to godchildren, employees in the house and on the estate, she left Saffron and the ten acres of gardens jointly to Uncle Conwyn and Aunt Louise for the tenure of their lives. The remainder of the estate, land, farms, cottages, she bequeathed to Adam. On the death of her two surviving children the house and gardens passed to him. There are substantial trust funds for Marcus and Marco. Her jewelry, with the exception of a few named items, such as a tiara to Trudy, she left to Aunt Louise. She made me an outright gift of five thousand pounds."

He'd won. His boast of survival was vindicated. I felt myself smiling. "So eventually Saffron, the whole of it, will be Adam's?"

"Yes. How soon depends on Aunt Louise. I doubt whether, even when she is recovered, she would wish to live at Saffron, or that it would be feasible for her to do so. It's possible she might be prepared to lease the house to Adam, but by no means certain. Meanwhile, when two people virtually die together, as it is assumed that the younger survived the elder, the estates will be faced with double death duties. That means months of confrontations with the Inland Revenue! They could insist that some of the land is sold."

"Adam would never agree, you know he wouldn't."

"The decision might not rest with him."

Even so, I would have been prepared to bet that, within a year, the blackened ruin of the balcony suite would be rebuilt exactly to its old pattern, with Alice Terson sitting in a replica of Grandmother's chair, though I doubted whether she would feed the turtle doves or recline like a queen in a *chaise-longue*.

He lifted the second envelope. "The draft of Hermione's last will. Provision for the inside and outside staff, gifts to godchildren are identical with the terms of the April will. The capital to set up the trust funds for Marcus and Marco is reduced to provide you with a legacy of one hundred thousand pounds. Again, she bequeathed all the land except the gardens, farms, etc. to Adam. The gardens, along with the house and its contents she left to you, with the same proviso that Uncle Conwyn should retain possession of his private wing as long as he wished to do so. With the exception of a few pieces she left to Trudy and Aunt Louise, she bequeathed you her jewelry. Until you reached the age of thirty, she appointed three trustees for you: Uncle Conwyn, Brigstock, and me. She also expressed the wish that when you married your husband should either change his name by deed poll to Delamain, or use it as a hyphenated prefix. Had she lived for this will to be drawn up and signed, you and Adam would have become joint owners of Saffron."

The terms of which had been known to him on the night of the party. I sat looking down at my hands, hearing the pleas that I'd refused to heed. And Uncle Conwyn? Grandmother had either deceived him or he had deceived himself, unless he had counted his private wing and his trusteeship over me amounted to ownership of Saffron.

Across the room I heard him say: "Invalid except as a testimony of her love and trust in you."

It broke from me, involuntarily, the compulsive shedding of a burden that I could no longer bear. My voice was an ugly harsh staccato. "She revoked it. It would never have been drawn up, never, even if she'd lived for years. I lied. The evening before she died, I did tell her I couldn't stay at Saffron, that I was returning to Paris." My flesh shivered, so that I capsulated that terrible scene. "She ordered me out of the house, forbade me ever to return." I closed my eyes as a protective shield against the repugnance or distress I might glimpse in his. "I see her waking in the night, remembering that I'd failed her, reaching for the cigarettes she'd hidden that I actually put into her hand instead of saying I couldn't find them. I see her . . ." My tongue dried in my mouth. There weren't words to describe the horror that lived inside me.

His hand gripped my shoulder, pressed so hard I was conscious of physical pain, his voice held under some tyranny of thought. "A night was an eternity to Hermione. She could have changed her mind in the morning. Grief, yes, but not guilt, I beg you."

I said, staring at that mask of naked, shameless hate: "That first day at Saffron, when she opened the safe, popped first one tiara on my head then another, she took it for granted I'd come to live with her. I knew she did, but I hadn't the courage to contradict her. That was a kind of lie, a lie of silence. She'd accused me of being greedy: I had been, greedy for her to love me."

He released my shoulder and when he spoke it was without passion, almost factually. "She went to sleep with a lighted cigarette in her fingers, set the bed alight. It could have happened any night since Lorraine died. For three years only a gossamer thread separated her from death. Any strain, a burst of temper, too much champagne, climbing a flight of stairs, could have killed her."

He was offering me false comfort like that you give to a weeping child. I laughed, and heard the bitter note. "Who implored me not to leave her? Who warned me she was old and vulnerable?"

"I did, but not wholly on Hermione's account. I had an interest of my own to protect. And a passion to possess human beings makes anyone vulnerable. The strong resist, try to escape. The weak become pitiable." He half frowned. "If you've known someone since childhood, you tend to accept unquestioningly their switches of mood and, in Hermione's case, her trick of keeping everyone guessing, which amounted to a form of despotism. I wasn't blind to her faults, but I wanted very much for her to be happy in the little while she had left."

I said, as though it provided a way out of the thoughts of betrayal that ran round and round the same circuit: "She wanted to buy me."

He answered on a laugh that confused me: "Who can blame her for trying!"

For a moment silence possessed the room, then he said: "Let me explain something. I didn't come here to summarise a couple of documents I could have posted to you. Not even to talk about Hermione." His hand reached out to lift my chin, then he bent forward and kissed me so lightly that, for a moment, I thought I might have dreamed it, but when he lifted his head, his face was as tense and strained as though he were holding his breath. "I came to talk about you and me . . . if you'll listen to me. Will you?"

"I'll listen," I said.

He put a space between us, and in the seconds before he began to speak, I looked at the face I'd loved on sight and knew that for once I had not cheated myself.

"Ever since you drove away with Adam, I've been making promises to myself, that I would be patient, give you time to recover from grief and shock. As nearly as I can describe it, it was as though I were making a ciné-film of the future, our future, continually perfecting it, adding a scene here, snipping out one there. Dropping in at the boutique in the rue Tronchet, taking you out to lunch . . . oh and dozens more." He stopped abruptly, and across the space that divided us, the bronze-green eyes took on an expression I'd never seen before: not fear but as though fear were only inches away, the calm that was at the centre of him shaken.

"But you won't be in the rue Tronchet for me to find. You'll have left this house. You could board a plane, fly to the other side of the world, be lost in one of a hundred cities. If you did not choose to find me, I would never see you again." He looked at me with such a passion of tenderness, my vision swam. "I love you very much. I don't want to lose you. And I'm not sure I can keep my promises."

The stillness in me was so profound it filled my whole being. I knew nothing except that in a handful of seconds my world had been made anew. "Then break them," I cried.

He pressed me so hard against him, I could feel the pulses of his heart keeping time with my own. "I love you . . ." For a little while the words that lovers the world over exchange were all we needed. But when our lips parted, I looked back for the last time. "Did you guess I lied?"

I watched a smile sketch itself over the passion written on his face. "One of the disadvantages of love is that it has a very deep-seeing eye. Does it worry you that you'll find it hard to keep any secrets from me?"

"I'm not a secret person, not any longer." The girl who'd been haunted by shadow images and ghost figures had ceased to exist.

"Neither am I, not with you." Radiance struck him. "As a wedding present, I'll give you the finest attic in London. If you hang out of the window, risk overbalancing, you can see the Thames and Battersea Power Station. All it needs is two new skylights. How's that for a bribe?"

"Irresistible."

Like a miracle I heard us laughing in a moment of life-giving irresponsibility. As he refilled our glasses, my glance touched the portrait of my mother. Fifteen years of her life had been devoured by a passion for retribution. She'd wanted to give me Saffron. Instead I'd received from her hands an infinitely richer gift. Tomorrow or the next day, or the one after, I would tell him the story of that fifteen years. But not tonight. Tonight was for loving, not remembering.